# bugger
# bucharest

# bugger bucharest

# maureen martella

BASEMENT PRESS

Dublin

First published in Ireland in 1995 by
Basement Press
an imprint of Attic Press Ltd
29 Upper Mount Street
Dublin 2

ISBN 1 85594 126 O

Cover design: Michael Dwyer
Typesetting: Jimmy Lundberg Desktop Publishing
Printing: The Guernsey Press Co. Ltd

Basement Press receives financial assistance from the
Arts Council/An Comhairle Ealaíon, Ireland.

Thanks to Lorelei Harris for having faith.
Thanks to Gay Byrne for helping me
to hang on to mine.

# PROLOGUE

JC CAME into the world at midnight, on the 23rd of June 1972. Everything had gone exactly as predicted. Except for one small detail.

'It's a boy!' the doctor announced triumphantly.

The newly delivered mother took one look at the blood-smeared grossly genitaled infant, and promptly threw up all over her sterile hospital gown.

She had been expecting a girl. The sex of the child had never been in question. Even the scan had verified it – twice.

'No, it's a mistake. My baby – my baby is a girl.'

Soothing murmurs floated above her head, muted whispers about new scanning machines, developmental stages ...

'I want *my* baby.' She could hear the frightened wail that was her own voice rising above the subdued buzzing in the delivery suite.

'Now, now, mother.' A rubber-encased hand patted hers; a huge glistening face loomed closer, its puffball cheeks bulging with importance. 'We must thank God for a safe delivery, and', he paused to smirk at the squirming baby, 'such a perfectly formed little man.' His voice began fading down a long tunnel: 'A gift from Gooood.'

'Good?' she echoed, puzzled.

'That's the girl.' Desensitised by power, he smugly swept the baby into her arms.

Nausea threatened to overwhelm her again. She was about to heave when the baby gave a plaintive little whimper. She darted a quick look at it.

Its blue eyes were wide open in terror, its tiny mouth agape with helplessness. Despite the stifling heat in the delivery room, the small naked body was shivering, the skin blue-tinged and unnaturally cold.

She touched its face apprehensively. The unwashed chin quivered as the mouth suddenly gave out the high-pitched cry of the newborn, its specially coded notes honed to perfection through the ages.

Her womb contracted and her nipples shot up like solid pink

1

thimbles as the forerunner of milk thundered through a labyrinth of ducts to reach its primordially designated outlets. She bared her swollen breast. The soft baby mouth latched on instinctively.

It contained shark's teeth.

# CHAPTER 1

THE INHABITANTS of the small town of Ballysheel slept undisturbed throughout the warm June night.

Nothing unusual in this, because in all the years of its existence nothing untoward had ever occurred in Ballysheel. At least, nothing that had ever threatened to disrupt the easy rhythm of its daily life.

'Peaceful' was a word frequently used by any outsider who happened on the place and consequently tried to describe it. 'Picturesque' was another, perhaps more apt, word, tucked away as the town was into the inverted elbow of a line of gently rolling hills.

Across the town's easterly approach a wide, meandering river flowed protectively, its water crystal-clear even at its lowest ebb. On the Ballysheel side of the river two massive oak trees of indeterminate, and often disputed age, stood proud and still, overshadowing the group of younger birches that trembled with every approaching gust of wind.

But on this June night nothing at all stirred. Even the river appeared motionless, clinging silently to the sandy banks that it normally rushed heedlessly past.

It was as if nature was holding its breath.

Suddenly a dog began to howl at the bright moon that turned night into day and cast shadows all over the town. The dog's owner impatiently locked his pet into a small windowless shed and hurried back to bed.

The dog whimpered unhappily to itself.

Ballysheel slept on.

A WEEK'S incarceration in Ballysheel Hospital's public ward didn't deter Ms Ryan from dressing her newly born son in the pale pink knits which she had toiled over for the previous nine months.

Ignoring the sensible hospital whites and the curious looks of her fellow inmates, she patiently directed flailing infant arms into lace-festooned sleeves and happily fastened row upon row of minute pink ribbons across the heaving infant chest. She carefully averted her eyes when nature dictated a nappy change.

'Jessie,' she clucked contentedly, nursing flesh of her flesh.

Despite his Cancerean birthright, JC was a grizzly baby. He cried loudly when he was hungry. But also when he wasn't. Wet nappies irritated him, dry ones made him uneasy. He cried loudly while being dressed, undressed, washed and even cooed over.

His mother sang obscure lullabies to him. He cried even louder. He managed to howl non-stop for the complete fifteen-minute journey home to their small red-bricked terraced house, a replica of the twenty-nine other red-bricked houses that clung to the outskirts of Ballysheel.

He cried as they crossed the threshold and continued for three long years.

On his third birthday, he fell in love. And he stopped crying.

The little girl from two doors down had playfully smeared pink cream from his birthday cake all over her little rosebud mouth. She then pouted provocatively at JC. Giggling, he flicked at the cream with his tongue and was immediately transported beyond bliss.

The two tots happily replayed their new-found game over and over until JC's playmate became even more adventurous and began smearing the luscious cream all over her protruding little tummy. Squealing with delight, JC dropped to his knees and was eagerly licking at the cream when he was suddenly felled by a sharp slap to the back of his head.

His playmate's mother stood over him her face contorted with fury. She threatened him with an agonising death and his mother with legal action, and disappeared out the door, dragging JC's cream-covered beloved with her.

JC howled.

His mother pacified him by breast-feeding him for twenty minutes. She then removed his soiled sailor suit and replaced it with a pink organza dress.

'Jessie,' she cooed.

JC sat sleepily on her lap and allowed her to feed him again.

IN THE unlikely event of her ever requiring a passport, Ms Ryan would have been obliged to claim 'Stargazer' as her occupation.

For that's how she earned her living. She drew up horoscopes. No frivolous occupation this, as she frequently pointed out to anyone who would listen. On the contrary, it required long hours of dedication and painstaking research -- long hours spent poring over maps of the heavens and charting planetary positions for any given time in the past, present, or future.

Human nature being as it is, most of her work consisted of drawing up maps of the future. Even in tiny Ballysheel there appeared to be a fulsome supply of people with a permanent hunger for information regarding the wonders that might await them around the next corner.

The fact that these wonders, or woes, would eventually be unveiled by time itself appeared not to be appreciated by these individuals. Nor was the fact that time gives freely of itself. Ms Ryan charged for hers.

She kept to a strict working routine. She began her appointments at ten o'clock sharp every morning and except for a two-hour break for lunch, she worked straight through until five every evening. Except on weekends. Work was taboo on weekends. Weekends were reserved for her friends. Her circle. And for JC, her one and only child.

When she was working, she took one appointment per hour, strictly on the hour. She allowed fifty minutes per client, not one second more or less. She was unyielding about this. Dogmatic.

'In everybody's best interests,' she insisted.

If the clients ever suspected that Ms Ryan held her own interests paramount, they never said so. Such was her popularity, or the popularity of her predictions, that her small tartan-covered diary was always choc-a-bloc with repeat appointments.

She was extremely fond of rituals. Every Sunday she attended Mass and benediction in Ballysheel parish church. And whenever she heard of the much longer, and far more elaborate, High Mass being celebrated, she made it her business to attend this also.

She would sit in a front pew, with the young JC on her lap, and listen intently as the priests sang the tuneless Latin chants over and over.

Tirelessly absorbing every feature of the Mass, from the wafting scent of the incense to each ritualised movement of the brightly robed celebrants, she would become so engrossed that she would hardly notice when JC invariably slid off her knee to gain a closer look at the proceedings.

She was always the very last person to leave the church on these occasions.

Except for one other, of course. When he spotted her leaving, little JC would leave his vantage point at the marble altar rails and toddle out of the church behind her.

Ms Ryan wasn't at all fond of sunlight. In the special room in her house where she received her clients, the window curtains were never opened. Ever. Even on the brightest, warmest day the heavy velvet drapes remained drawn. She used tall candles to light the room. Soft candlelight was conducive to relaxation, she often said, and she liked to make her clients relax.

The fact that the more relaxed they were, the fatter the envelopes they slipped into her extended hand was neither here nor there. She said.

She kept a small finger-bowl of water by the lighted candles. Nobody could quite remember its original purpose, not even Ms Ryan herself, but over the years people began to dip their fingers into the coolness of it and bless themselves on entering, and this now formed part of the ritual she employed.

She was known for her devotion to her clients.

Such was her devotion that she provided each and every one of them with a cup of tea and a thick slice of Battenberg cake before beginning their consultation.

This routine never varied. If the client wasn't partial to Battenberg, then they were limited to tea. Her devotion didn't extend to making concessions to individual taste.

She insisted on absolute punctuality. Each client must arrive precisely 'on the hour'. They ignored this rule at their peril.

'In everybody's best interests,' she repeated, 'to avoid embarrassing overlaps or any chance meetings between clients, either coming or going.'

After all, she did guarantee complete confidentiality to all her clients. It said so on her printed cards, directly under the proud boast: 'YOUR DETAILED PERSONAL HOROSCOPE COMPLETELY MAPPED OUT IN ONE FULL HOUR.'

SHE always refused point blank to read JC's horoscope. He was a mere five or six when he first began to broach the subject. But no matter how timidly he approached her, she would step back as if physically threatened, her face tightening defensively, her rouged lips clamped together as if in a determined effort to prevent unbidden words escaping them.

JC would then have to laugh off his request and pretend he was only joking, that the last thing he ever wanted was to have his horoscope read. He'd have to repeat this, over and over, until he convinced Mother and the tight frightened look left her face. Sometimes he even managed to convince himself.

She did, however, allow him to sit in the coveted client's chair. Sometimes.

If a client was late, even by one minute, Mother chose to ignore their existence for that day. At two minutes to the appointed hour she would have poured hot strong tea into the best china cups and cut two perfectly matching slices of Battenberg cake. The Battenberg was then carefully set out on delicate white doilies which all but covered the small plates which didn't match the fine cups. She would then carefully scrutinise her setting as she waited for the doorbell to ring, nervously brushing any wayward or sometimes imagined crumbs from the polished table.

The high-pitched peal of the doorbell would then echo loudly round the house, precisely on the hour. This was the signal for JC to head for the stairs and his room.

But sometimes, just sometimes, the bell didn't ring on the hour.

If it didn't, the moment was lost. For the client. For JC it meant being invited to join Mother in drinking the now cooling tea and eating the much-coveted Battenberg.

Nothing that he ever tasted for the rest of his life could compare with the Battenberg eaten in Mother's room.

Once past the appointed hour, the doorbell could ring to its heart's content. Mother would smile across the table at JC and continue calmly eating, or politely inquire if he'd like another cup of tea. Without either of them having to mention it, they both knew that they would now have a whole hour together before Mother had to answer the doorbell again.

Once, in religion class, his teacher had described heaven as a place of 'indescribable and permanent bliss'. This, then, must be heaven, except that it wasn't permanent. But to have Mother give him her undivided attention, to have her smile at him conspiratorially as they both ignored the tardily ringing doorbell – this was heaven enough for JC.

In summer he didn't mind so much when Mother was with her clients. He was allowed outdoors then. Into the garden.

Long, narrow and wildly overgrown, it provided a perfect backdrop for his favourite survival games. Alone amid the tall feathered grasses, stinging nettles and soothing dock leaves, he fought valiantly to protect his world against marauding hordes of savage invaders. He never tired of challenging them. No matter how terrifying they were. No matter how gigantic. Or gruesome. Or bloody.

In this place he was invincible. He was the master. He was king. He would hold the threatening creatures at bay with his sword, just long enough to size up their weakness, and then masterfully plunge cold steel into their evil hearts.

They didn't always die instantly; sometimes they sprawled on the ground, howling in agony, in which case he had to take a broadsword and slice off their heads quickly as an act of mercy. This usually stopped their howling.

But sometimes the severed heads turned into hissing, writhing snakes that turned on him, fangs dripping with milky-white venom. He knew that once this venom touched his flesh, he was doomed; he would be in their power for ever.

So he would leap for safety into the branches of the huge old oak that stood like a lone sentinel at the bottom of the garden. The sturdy trunk of the oak always felt warm, even on sunless days. It seemed to have a source of heat all its own. And its branches spread out like giant welcoming arms, always ready to comfort.

One day he thought he heard the tree whispering to him. 'JC, JC, come . . .'

But he couldn't be sure.

'Jessie! Jessie!' There was no mistaking that call. Mother stood in the kitchen doorway, her hand shielding her eyes against the evening sun.

JC dropped from the tree and ran towards her.

# CHAPTER 2

FROM HIS very first day there, JC liked school.

As each year passed he liked it more and more. There was always something new to learn and he found himself looking forward to every single class. Even the ones that other boys tried every ruse and trick to escape from. He even secretly enjoyed wearing the drab grey uniform that everyone had to claim to detest.

He never got into trouble. His teachers liked him. They mistook his acquiescent nature for obedience.

He didn't have any close friends, in school or out, but he didn't have any enemies either. Even the snakes in the garden were beginning to fade as he grew older.

Had he been given a choice, he wouldn't have chosen any other place to grow up in. He liked Ballysheel. 'Loved' would be too strong a word. But he did like it.

On his fifteenth birthday a group of Mother's circle of friends gave a small surprise party for him. The main instigator of this appeared to be Signora Goretti.

She was a petite, volatile Italian who had come to Ireland after finding herself, at the tender age of twenty-three, widowed and childless in Sicily. How she became widowed, or was childless, she never divulged, but a family connection had consequently arranged a job for her in faraway Dublin. She was to act as nanny to the nine children of the Italian ambassador there. And as helpmate to his semi-invalid wife.

She also never divulged how she coped with this situation, but when the ambassador and his family returned to their homeland, the Signora had remained alone and happy in Ireland.

Nobody had the faintest idea how she came to be living in Ballysheel, or, if they once had, they had forgotten. JC had a vague memory of Mother laughingly telling how the Signora had simply appeared one morning in the graveyard, carrying a small case and flirting outrageously with the local gravedigger.

But she had long since become a familiar fixture in Ballysheel. People hardly noticed her accent any more, or her flirting.

She now claimed to be forty-plus and in the right light could

9

pass for forty-minus. But Mother regularly proclaimed her to be as old as the Ballysheel hill.

Whatever her age, she always had a warm word, and an even warmer kiss, for JC whenever they met. This wasn't too often, because Mother tended to ration these meetings. She seemed to be under the impression that her friend the Signora had designs on him. JC was under the impression that the beautiful Signora had designs on every male that came within three feet of her.

'A Scorpio!' Mother said disdainfully.

The Signora's energy was almost palpable. She had only to cross the threshold to bring the house to life. The four other women from the circle had been content to raise a moderate glass of wine in honour of his birthday, then sit and reminisce with Mother. But the word 'moderate' had no place in the Signora's life.

She waltzed wildly down the hall and into Mother's room, pulling JC along with her. She put Mother's old records on the radiogram, playing them at a pitch they were never intended for, and then jived madly to them, twirling around until she was dizzy and her full skirt swung high enough to expose her slim thighs.

She then fed JC impossibly large wedges of birthday cake and giggled with delight when he ended up with soft sugar icing all over his chin. She petulantly refused to allow anyone else to wipe it off.

'Me. Me,' she claimed like a spoiled child.

Having cleaned his chin to her satisfaction, she pulled him around the room again in her version of a waltz.

Mother watched disapprovingly from the doorway, her wine glass held in a white-knuckled hand. Well used to the Signora's behaviour, the other women carried on drinking and chattering.

Becoming bored with waltzing, the Signora started yet another energetic dance. This one, she boasted, was a fertility dance much favoured by the young women in her home village in southern Italy.

'It guarantees satisfaction,' she said, winking flirtatiously at JC. 'Such a handsome boy.' The Signora, whom everybody, even JC, knew was renowned for her libido, began holding him far too closely.

Even in the throes of his own embarrassment, he was aware of Mother's face tightening.

'Such strong legs.' The irrepressible Signora poked at his thigh with a scarlet-tipped finger.

'That's enough.' Mother crossed the room in seconds and pulled the plug from the old radiogram. Violin music wailed to a strangulated stop.

There was an embarrassed silence, the chattering women halting mid-sentence to stare uneasily, first at the Signora and then at Mother.

She began noisily collecting their empty glasses.

'Jessie has some studying to do,' she offered, as if this justified her behaviour.

She was now sweeping even half-full glasses on to the ornate little tray.

'But it's his birthday,' the Signora protested, still clinging to JC.

'Please, Mother.' Embarrassing as the Signora's attentions might be, JC still preferred them to French verbs.

'Say goodnight to everybody, Jessie.' Mother wasn't listening.

'He didn't receive his birthday gift yet.' The Signora looked to the other women for support.

The group nodded, almost in unison.

'There!' The Signora clapped her hands victoriously. 'He must have his special birthday gift. Even you can't deny him that.' She arched her thin pencilled brows at Mother.

'He's only a boy,' Mother's voice quivered.

'He's a man!' The Signora moved towards the seated women.

One of them produced a parcel the size and shape of a small briefcase. It was wrapped in heavy brown paper which appeared almost grubby, greasy, as if it had long been overhandled.

It was held together by coloured twine which also looked as if it had seen better days.

It had to be a joke.

JC smiled hesitantly at Mother.

She pushed past the Signora and snatched the parcel as it was being handed over.

'No!' The Signora rounded on her furiously. 'I want to give it to him.'

'I'll see he gets it.' Mother's voice was strong and determined again.

'OK.'

To JC's surprise, the Signora shrugged her narrow shoulders in gracious defeat.

'Say goodbye, Jessie.' Mother's voice was still cool, but her eyes were shining with triumph as she hugged the parcel to her.

JC leaned dutifully towards the Signora's proferred cheek.

His lips were just brushing its scented warmth when she turned towards them, and kissed him fully on his pursed mouth. His startled lips dropped open and the Signora darted her hard little tongue between them. It happened so quickly that later he wondered if he had imagined it, conjured it up somehow.

But he hadn't imagined the swift rush of desire that flooded his groin. Shame-faced, he glanced at Mother.

She stood well apart from the other women, clutching the slim, grubby parcel, and JC saw to his amazement that her eyes were full of tears.

'*Strega*,' she whispered.

He knew what that word meant. He had heard it often enough in the bedtime stories the Signora had told him when she had baby-sat him.

It meant witch.


AS SOON as the women left. Mother put the parcel away and refused even to mention it again. Not that JC cared. What interest could he possibly have in a stupid, grubby old parcel that a pack of middle-aged women wanted him to have? He didn't care if he never saw it again. Besides, he was adept at blocking unwanted thoughts out of his mind. And he was getting better and better at this as time passed.

He could easily control his thoughts now. He deliberately put the parcel out of his head. He simply blocked it out of his mind ... for five full minutes. After that it became an obsession. He could think of nothing else.

His schoolwork began failing. He hardly opened a book. He didn't even notice, or care any more, about the girls who jogged around the school playing-fields. Even the ones who didn't wear bras.

He daydreamed during lessons and had nightmares during sleep. The daydreams were always the same: he would open the parcel to discover it contained some wondrous panacea for all the ills of the world, and a multitude of offers of unending sex for himself.

The nightmares were another story. They were filled with unmentionable horrors, things so dark and terrible that he woke up each time sweating, crying out in pure terror at the images that came tumbling out of the opened parcel.

Over the weeks the nightmares began taking over from the daydreams. They were torturing him, engulfing him nightly with a black foreboding that clung to him long after he woke. He began sleepwalking. Twice Mother found him wandering in the garden in the small hours, searching for something he couldn't name. He lost all interest in food. His slim body took on an emaciated look, his face became gaunt and pallid.

He knew that Mother was becoming concerned about him, but for the first time in his life he didn't care what she thought.

His only interest was in the small, grubby parcel that she had hidden away from him.

His rational mind accepted that its contents were bound to be dull, mundane everyday things, not in any way connected to the vivid horrors of his nightmares, no more than they would be to the wishful fantasies of his daydreams. He knew this. But the nightmares wouldn't go away.

He was almost sixteen years old when, for the first time since infancy, he began wetting his bed at night. At first out of sheer embarrassment, he tried to keep it a secret from Mother. He packed the wet night clothes and sheets away in a black plastic binbag and washed them in secret.

But as the bed-wetting became more frequent and the piles of laundry mounted, it became more and more difficult to hide them.

His mattress was also becoming a problem. He had turned it every way possible, but as the weeks went by there was hardly an area of it that didn't have a sodden tell-tale patch on it. And his room was beginning to stink.

When Mother finally confronted him with the evidence, it was almost a relief. He answered all her questions truthfully.

No, he wasn't drinking more than he used to.

No, he wasn't worried about school.

He wasn't being bullied.

His end-of-term tests didn't frighten him.

He had no idea why he had suddenly started bed-wetting.

A trip to their local doctor left neither of them any the wiser. In fact, it raised a few extra questions in JC's head.

Like . . . why would a fully grown educated man with a

medical degree suddenly begin nodding and winking like some word-shy neanderthal?

The GP leaned back in his swing chair, allowing his flabby five-pint belly to spill over his two-pint trousers.

'You do realise that', he winked grotesquely, 'bed-wetting might almost be considered a rite of passage by some people? In fact –'

But Mother had already slammed out the door, mumbling about the wrong people being locked up.

'Stone mad! Stone mad,' she kept repeating to herself.

JC assumed she was referring to the doctor.

He didn't know if the GP was mad or not, but one thing he did know was that, medical degree or not, grey hair or not, the obese man spilling out of the swing chair had more than a professional knowledge of bed-wetting.

Mother forbade him to consume any liquids after nine p.m.

The problem persisted.

She forbade cheese, or any class of dairy produce, after ten.

He still drenched the bed.

Then she came up with the idea of leaving his radio playing all night long, the theory being that this would prevent him sleeping too deeply so that, when the call of nature came, he would waken and head for the bathroom. JC obediently left his radio on.

Next morning his bed was bone dry. They celebrated over breakfast, a parched JC drinking enough orange juice to float four kidneys. The permanently switched-on radio was clearly the answer.

The following morning he woke up to Rachmaninov's piano concerto and a cloud of warm steam rising from beneath him.


MOTHER'S FRIEND Geraldine was a very sensitive medium. Everyone said so.

She held firmly to the belief that the spirit world was far better equipped to sort out corporeal problems than this world could ever be.

'We are all confined by our bodies,' she was fond of saying, and people seldom argued with this.

Mother had absolute faith in Geraldine's ability to contact the spirit world, so JC found himself sitting in a darkened living room, holding hands with both women.

Geraldine chanted a long chain of strange-sounding words

before repeatedly calling on a Red Indian called Manowaw to join them. They clasped hands even tighter and waited.

There was silence. Geraldine called once more. Manowaw didn't answer. Nobody did.

Minutes passed and JC was becoming restless when Geraldine suddenly announced that Manowaw was there.

JC didn't particularly want to see him, as Geraldine had told them earlier that Manowaw had lost both his scalp and lips to bloodthirsty fur traders in 1864. He kept his eyes firmly closed. But he expected to feel at least a change in the room temperature with the arrival of this long-dead Indian. An atmospheric variation, Mother's books called it. But there was nothing.

Everything remained exactly the same. Geraldine's hand was as clammy as ever. Mother's was cool as always.

He opened his eyes a fraction to squint at Geraldine.

'He's here!' she said.

Her face was radiant.

Then JC realised that the atmosphere had changed. The women on either side of him were both quite excited. Terrifyingly so. Their eyes focused on nothing that JC could see. They were both smiling, eagerly watching – nothing?

He looked around the gloomy room and willed himself to see . . . what? Anything. Anything different, out of place. Something . . .

The overstuffed print sofa sat there, as ugly and overstuffed as ever. The dried flowers, packed into every available vase and holder, were as dried and dead as if they had never encountered life-giving sap. The tribal masks that were Geraldine's pride and joy peered down from the walls, giving nothing away, their empty eye sockets staring blindly ahead.

It was a lifeless room, dead, fit only for –

Geraldine's long nails bit into his hand.

'Manowaw,' she breathed.

JC could feel her hand trembling.

On his other side Mother sat absolutely still.

*'Leave the boy to his destiny.'*

The voice came from Geraldine's tiny, lined mouth, but it wasn't her voice. Its harsh, grating tones were a million light years away from her sing-song soprano. There was no possible way that her narrow vocal chords could have made that sound. She might disguise or even distort her voice, but she couldn't possibly transform it into this deep throaty growl that sounded as if it emanated from a bottomless cavern in hell.

JC wanted to leave. He didn't want to sit here with these women, in this dead room. He didn't belong here. This wasn't his place.

Again Geraldine's lips moved and out came the rasping, terrifying sound. '*He has seen the dream world. Let him go.*'

JC tried to loosen his hand from her grasp but she held him effortlessly, her thin, fragile hand holding his in a vice-like grip. He couldn't get loose. He began to sweat. He thought he saw her face begin to change, her tiny lips disappearing altogether, leaving a wide gaping hole of torn flesh. Her frizzy grey-streaked hair began to darken. It was – it wasn't hair any more – it was red, sponge-like – seeping – dripping down her forehead and into her eyes – and her eyes – the red was filling up the empty sockets – empty – yet they were staring – watching him …

'*The boy knows. He has seen his destiny.*'

The grip on his hand loosened slightly.

JC ran. He didn't think about anything except getting away from the horror. He ran out of the house and down the darkened street. He ran until he was exhausted, not knowing or caring where he was heading; he ran until his breath came in loud wheezing gulps; then he doubled over, stumbling, gasping for air. He threw himself on the ground. His nightmare was with him again. He saw the images clearly. Heard the screams. It would never leave him.

He looked up directly into a lighted window. He was in front of the parish church and its colourful glass windows shone brightly through the night gloom. Above his head the image of the Virgin and Child stood out in coloured relief from the surrounding grey stone, the red-and-blue tinged figures lit from behind by strong lights within the church. The face of the Virgin was serene as she gazed down at her adored child.

JC walked towards the shrubbery near the church gate and searched in the dark until he found what he needed. He then retraced his steps, took his stance, and threw the rock with all might. He watched as it connected and shattered, first the serene face of the Madonna and then the child as the jagged lines ran down the broken window.

He rubbed his hand where Geraldine's nails had torn the flesh.

16

HE WAS almost asleep when Mother came into his room. She began nervously fidgeting, adjusting his books and tapes a fraction here and there, and then replacing them exactly as they had been.

She patted the pillows on either side of his head almost flat and then picked each one up and plumped it out again before carefully placing it underneath his exhausted head.

She checked his radiator for heat, frowning to herself as if its temperature displeased her. Then she turned down the volume on his radio until the rock music was almost inaudible, and immediately flicked nervous fingers at the dial again, sending the sound of a bass guitar reverberating loudly around the bedroom.

JC reached across and switched off the volume. Then he waited.

Mother didn't turn but stood staring at the radio as if she were trying to memorise the names of the stations that glowed red against its lighted front panel.

She traced out long, unfamiliar names with her fingernail, names that JC had never, ever tuned the radio to.

'Bucharest?' Her laugh sounded forced. 'I wonder if anyone actually listens to that station?'

'I suppose people in Bucharest do.' JC said the first thing that came into his head.

Then he made a mistake. He said the second thing that came into his head. 'Mother, if you don't want me to have the ... the birthday gift, it doesn't matter. I don't want it. I'm not even curious about it.' Once the lies started they came tumbling out. 'If it upsets you we'll get rid of it. It doesn't matter at all to me. I don't want it.'

Mother put her head down against the radio and wept. JC wanted more than anything to comfort her, to put his arms around her and hold her, but all he did was stare at the stupid red lettering beside her crumpled face.

Bucharest! Bucharest? He hated the fucking place. He hoped every radio presenter there dropped dead. He hoped the radio station collapsed around their ears. He hoped that nobody in the whole world would ever tune into that stupid fucking station, that the whole place would be blown to smithereens.

Bugger Bucharest!

Mother was crying.

She turned her tear-stained face towards him and held out her arms.

THEY OPENED the parcel together. At first JC thought it was simply full of tissue paper. What a joke that would be. On him. All those sleepless nights, the visits to the doctor, the horrible seance with Geraldine – all because of a box of tissue paper! Signora Goretti certainly knew how to play a joke, even if it was a cruel one. You had to admire her. He didn't know of anyone else who could play such a joke. And get away with it.

Mother removed layer after layer of the soft tissue and place each sheet carefully on the bed beside the twine and the grubby brown paper. From the moment the parcel was opened, there was the strangest smell. It wasn't exactly a stink, but it wasn't perfume either. It was revolting. Sickly sweet.

It reminded JC of some kind of medicine. The sort they might give to old people who were taking too long to die.

Mother was pulling out yet more paper. She had the strangest look on her face, a look even the funny smell couldn't account for. JC watched closely as she drew out a – a blouse? A shirt? – No. It was a kaftan. A bloody kaftan! Like the hippies used to wear, only fancier. It glittered in the light, every inch of it overstitched with fancy embroidery, all carefully worked in the same shiny gold and yellow thread, and set around the neck where the threads ended was a row of mirror-like buttons that seemed to wink at the joke as Mother lifted the thing carefully from yet more layers of tissue.

It had to be the sickest-looking garment JC had ever set eyes on. He would have preferred the tissue paper.

'Have you ever seen anything so beautiful?' Mother asked, with a completely straight face.

Totally oblivious to JC's horrified reaction, she stroked the folds of the kaftan as if it were ... She touched it as she might touch ... a lover.

When Mother went to bed, JC folded the kaftan up again.

He packed the tissue paper tightly around it, tied up the whole parcel as before, and pushed it as far back into his wardrobe as it would go.

It remained there untouched at the back of the wardrobe for three years. JC never wet the bed again and Mother never mentioned the kaftan. They lived as they always had. Companionably. They were almost happy.

# CHAPTER 3

JC was eighteen when the best-looking girl in the school asked him out. Well, not out exactly. She invited him to be her date at her seventeenth birthday party, which was to be held in her home. But she was the best-looking girl in the school. Except for her psoriasis. Even he had to admit that she probably had the worst case of psoriasis in the western hemisphere. But she also had the biggest brown eyes, the most perfect mouth and a body that hyper-activated his hormones every time he caught sight of her.

It was an undeniable fact that whenever she batted her long eyelashes, a hail of loose skin flakes floated about her, like a displaced snow blizzard. And her bee-stung lips were almost encircled by scar tissue, the rehabilitating shades of which varied from palest pink to angry bloodcurdling red.

And rumour had it that her long legs, tiny waist and gravity-defying breasts were also afflicted by this scourge. But to JC she remained the most desirable girl in the universe.

And she had invited him to partner her at her seventeenth birthday party.

JC HAD never been on a date. Mother never approved of him going out. She said he had everything he needed at home. And this had been true, up to recently. But ever since he had spotted Reena Scales in sixth-year Biology, his needs had changed.

The other sixth-year boys called her 'Fish Scales' behind her back, but JC stoutly and regularly sprang to her defence. After all, she was hardly to blame for her psoriasis. Was she? Or her name. That at least was her father's doing.

He knew the boys would give him a bad time when they found out he was about to date her. It didn't worry him.

Telling Mother was another story.

He lay awake at night planning different ways to broach the dating subject. None of them sounded right, no matter how often he repeated them to himself in the dark.

The actual morning of Reena's birthday arrived and he still hadn't told Mother. On his way to school he prayed hard for a miracle. He got it. Reena's father dropped dead of a heart attack while wishing her a happy birthday. In the circumstances, her mother thought it might be inadvisable to go ahead with a large celebration.

When he heard the news, JC was flooded with conflicting emotions. Relief for himself, sadness for Reena's father ... and pity for poor heartbroken Reena, whose psoriasis now knew no bounds.

Some weeks after her father's funeral, he saw her weeping piteously in the school library. He thought his heart would break at the sight.

No matter how hard he tried, she was inconsolable. The more sympathy he expressed, the harder she cried. When, in desperation, he said that death was inevitable, that it would come for them all, her wracking sobs almost brought down Jane Austen from the top shelf. He tried another tack.

He told her the story of the 'parcel'. How Mother and the other women had behaved as if it contained the Holy Grail, at least, he told her how he had fantasised about it, dreaming about what might be revealed when he finally tore away the grubby paper.

He didn't tell her about the nightmares, or the bed-wetting; he was, after all, trying to cheer her up.

When he acted out the opening of the parcel, the endless tissue paper, the awful stink and finally the sight of the embroidery-covered kaftan, Reena laughed fit to choke.

JC felt wonderful. The sad, weeping girl had disappeared, and in her place was this laughing, giggling woman, who was holding his hands as if she would never let them go. He was elated. At first.

Then he felt guilty. How could he have been so disloyal to Mother? He should never have told the story. Mother would feel humiliated, betrayed.

Reena asked to see the kaftan. She was smiling broadly.

He said that wasn't possible. But he also said that Mother attended a circle meeting every Wednesday night.

It was the second biggest mistake he had made in the eighteen years of his life.

WHEN the doorbell rang, he knew it was Reena.

But she didn't laugh when she saw the kaftan. Instead, she

stood open-mouthed, staring like a small child before a brightly lit Christmas tree.

'It's … awesome!' There was awe in her voice.

JC frowned in disbelief. Was she being sarcastic?

'It's … it's …' Reena, who was the brightest of all the bright stars in Honours English, was at a loss for words.

The psoriasis had obviously effected her brain. Didn't she notice the smell? The stink? Even after three years in the well-aired wardrobe, it still reeked like a billy-goat's arse. She had to be messing, sending him up.

He watched as she ran her hands along the folds of the kaftan. Jesus! She was caressing it.

If the psoriasis hadn't done her brain in, then grief over her father's death must have. He wanted her out.

'You'd better go, Mother will be back soon.'

She tore her attention away from the kaftan and turned reluctantly to face him. Her eyes were huge, staring, the pupils enormous.

A dart of fear hit him. There was a lump of ice forming in his stomach. He didn't know for sure what was happening here, but whatever it was, he didn't like it.

'I swear, she'll be back any minute.'

'Put it on.'

Jesus, she was nuts.

'Put it on!'

This wasn't gentle Reena. But it looked like her. The flaky face was unmistakable. The dry skin on the hands that were stroking the kaftan was Reena's all right. Jesus, she was repulsive. How had he ever thought he could fancy her?

Even her pouting mouth was a rasping, cracked grey thing, like rough-hewn granite instead of …

He realised that he had never really liked her. God only knew why he thought he had. No wonder they called her Fish Scales. Served her right that her father had dropped dead, old dead Scales …

He backed away towards the door.

She picked up the kaftan and moved after him. Her eyes still had that peculiar staring look. JC's arm went up defensively. She draped the kaftan over it.

'I'll give you two minutes.' She checked the birthday watch given to her by dead Scales.

21

What a smart man he was to die on the day of her party. What a great party trick. Happy Birthday, Reena Scaleface – *thud*! Top that for a show-stopper. JC wished he could drop dead.

'Two minutes,' she called after him as he headed for the bathroom.

In the small bathroom, the smell of the kaftan was overpowering. He felt nauseous. He didn't know which repulsed him more, the kaftan or Reena.

'One minute,' her voice called. She was laughing.

He'd show her! He pulled off every stitch of his clothes and drew the kaftan over his naked body. He'd show Fish Scales that he wasn't afraid of her. She couldn't just come here and boss him around. All right, he'd let her see the stupid kaftan on him, but then he'd tell her to go, to get lost. She couldn't just order him about in his own home. No way.

He swung around angrily and caught sight of his own startled reflection in the bathroom mirror. His reflection? In the tall, narrow mirror the image stood staring back at him. His image? The man in the mirror did resemble him, somewhat, but he had never actually looked like that. The brown curling hair reached almost to the wide shoulders. The eyes were a startling blue and skin – the skin, reflecting the gold and yellows of the kaftan, appeared to be glowing. It was almost iridescent.

In spite of himself JC felt his face begin to smile. The image smiled back. He touched his hair with a trembling hand and then smoothed the kaftan nervously. The shining image mirrored his every movement. His heart began to pound. The image watched him. His hand went, unbidden, down to touch himself, the image reflected him, watching ... He was unbelievably aroused ...

'OH MY GOD.' Reena got up from the bed, her eyes round with wonder.

He stood in the doorway. In spite of his six-foot height, the kaftan reached almost to his bare feet. He could see himself clearly reflected in the wardrobe mirror. He stood still, letting Reena look at him.

'JC. You look like – you look like a god!' Her voice was a whisper.

Afterwards, he couldn't recall crossing the room, or whose

mouth had hungrily kissed first, whose hands had torn at Reena's clothes until she was naked. All he could recall were flashing images of her full heavy breasts, glistening, arousing, satisfying – her soft mouth opening for him – her whole body opening for him, inviting him. Then he was entering her without awkwardness or hesitation, entering her with long easy movements, unhurried, rhythmic, each thrust creating ripples of exquisite pleasure, ebbing, flowing, spreading further and further until they came together and the world exploded in sensation – erupted – beyond the room – beyond everything he had ever known ...

Her voice called him back.

'Oh God!'

HE HEARD the girls giggling outside Higher Mathematics. They stood in a tight little circle with Reena in the centre. They were buzzing around her like honey bees around their queen. Reena was holding court.

He kept his head low and tried to sneak past, but they spotted him. Five pairs of knowing eyes were suddenly staring at him.

The owner of the sixth pair was too engrossed in her tale to notice him. 'Well, Janis Meehan did it, and she said it hurts like hell. She hated it, Janis did. She says it's all very well for boys but for girls it's –' Her babbling trailed off as she spotted JC.

He could feel the hot red flush rising from his neck and engulfing his whole face.

'Janis Meehan is a total and complete idiot.' Reena stood, legs apart, deliberately blocking JC's path. Her thick black hair was gleaming, her breasts were straining her school uniform to its limits, and even under the harsh fluorescent light her skin was dewy and absolutely clear, displaying not one single flake of the dreaded psoriasis that had always marred her perfection. Reena's psoriasis was nowhere to be seen.

JC ducked into Higher Mathematics. Behind him a new wave of giggling broke out.

He spent every free period that week huddled in the boys' toilets.

THE FOLLOWING Wednesday night he was watching a documentary on rebirthing when the doorbell rang.

He glanced at the clock, annoyed at the interruption. It wouldn't be one of Mother's clients at this hour and nobody ever called for him. He turned the sound up.

On the screen a wailing woman was crouched over in a foetal position. It looked agonising. She was contorting her face into unimaginable expressions in an effort to re-enact her entry into the world. Guiding her in this was a man whose square head and heavy jowls made him the dead spit of the perpetually snarling Rottweiler from next door. JC couldn't believe the similarities: the man even appear to drool slightly, from one side of his mouth only, exactly like the dog when he became over-excited.

The man was becoming excited now as he encouraged the woman on to greater efforts. JC watched, fascinated, as a thin dribble of saliva trickled down his mountainous chin. But his face suddenly disappeared from the screen, to be replaced by a close-up of the woman's mouth as she gave out a loud banshee wail.

The doorbell pealed again. The TV woman wailed louder. When the doorbell rang for the fourth time, he knew he'd have to answer it.

Janis Meehan stood under the porch light. She glanced nervously past JC to where the sound of the wailing woman was building to a crescendo.

'Is there somebody here with you?'

If only he had said yes. That's all it would have taken. One little word, and everything that followed might have been different. His whole life might have taken a different path. He'd have finished his exams, gotten at least six honours, then opted for a safe job in a bank and spent a contented life dealing with other people's money and greed. He'd have gotten old, fat and complacent ... and died a miserable but content old banker.

But it wasn't to be.

'No.' Two simple letters decided his fate. Mother might insist that people's destinies are written in the stars, but he knew better.

Two letters decided his.

'I heard screaming.' Again Janis tried to look past him.

'Oh! Yes, it's a – it's the TV. A documentary.' He gestured towards the flickering screen.

Did she take the gesture as an invitation, or had she always intended to barge in? She was suddenly behind him, standing quite relaxed, totally at ease, in his living room.

'Nice place.' She dropped her denim bag on a chair.

JC leaned against the still-open door for support. 'Did you want …? My mother is …' He watched in horror as her jacket joined the bag on the chair.

'Oh, don't worry about your mother. I passed her earlier tonight on her way to her circle meeting.'

She made it sound as if she was familiar with Mother's every move and as if this gave her the right to be standing here, jacketless.

'She doesn't like uninvited visitors,' he said accusingly.

'Oh, she'll be away for hours.' She began confidently picking up the small ornaments that cluttered the sideboard, examining each one carefully, as if assessing them for value.

JC was about to protest when a sudden screech from the TV made them both jump.

'Turn that rubbish off.' Janis's crisp tone was an uncanny replica of Mother's.

He was so taken aback by this that he reached out and unthinkingly switched off the rebirthing woman mid-screech.

'Well, aren't you going to show me?' The tone was still Mother's.

'What?' He was totally confused now.

She caught his hand and drew him towards the stairs.

She couldn't have forced him to go with her.

Physically he was twice her size. He could have brushed her aside, dismissed her like … So why then did he find himself walking with her, meek as a lamb, to where he kept the kaftan? And all the time he kept picturing the dribbling Rottweiler man ordering the woman to screech louder as she contorted herself into even more convoluted shapes. It wasn't as if he even fancied Janis. She was the nearest thing to a boy with her cropped hair and straight-up-and-down little body. Did she think she could possibly recreate the mystical experience he had shared with Reena? What a laugh. That had been a one-off, a once-in-a-lifetime job … Somehow all Reena's grief, and his pity for her, had triggered sensations and feelings that even now he couldn't explain. He'd never know for sure what had really happened, once he had put that kaftan on, but he was sure of one thing – it couldn't possibly happen again. Could it?

*

IT COULD. Janis's short little body gave him as much exquisite pleasure as Reena's spectacular one had. Her tight little breasts were just as sweet and welcoming to his tongue. If anything, he was aroused to an even more unbearable pitch, and their climax, when it came, rivalled in intensity the earth-shattering volcanic eruptions which they were both studying in Lower Geography.

But then he realised that Janis was weeping. He was instantly flooded with guilt. 'Please, Janis, don't cry. I'm so sorry ... I thought you ... I thought we both ... I'm sorry.'

She reached up and caught his hair in a scalp-wrenching grip, pulled his head down and rammed her tongue halfway down his throat.

HE HEARD the talk first among the fifth-year boys in the toilets.

'Hey has anyone noticed Janis Meehan lately?'

Cat-calls, whistles and loud sucking sounds rose in a lewd chorus of appreciation, the universal language of almost-men, its grunts, groans and whistles wordlessly communicating only to its own.

Although he was older and not part of the group, JC could interpret the sounds, having to his shame once passed this way himself. He knew that, translated into communicative English, they meant that the consensus was that Janis Meehan was now a much coveted, even highly desirable young woman. Yet the same Janis had hardly attracted the mildest ribald gesture from this group a few weeks back.

He watched her during Higher Mathematics. She did, somehow, appear more rounded. Her previously non-existent breasts were now raising her school blouse in a very interesting fashion. Her hair was no longer so sparse, or severely cropped, and it was awash with rich shining colour. She looked almost beautiful.

THE FOLLOWING Wednesday, JC showered after tea.

Mother raised her eyebrows but didn't comment.

Ten minutes after she left, the doorbell rang.

He had never liked Claire O'Reilly. Mainly because she didn't like him. But then she didn't really like anyone. Not even herself. Plus, she had a body like a North Sea herring, all bones and no flesh. And she had to be at least six feet tall. The girls in school all said she had bulimia. That apparently meant that she devoured boxes of sweets, tubs of ice cream, drank can after can of Coke and then stuck her head down the toilet and brought the whole mess straight back up again.

And here she was standing at his front door, smiling expectantly. JC took a step backwards. She walked past him without saying a word.

He stood uncertainly, his hand still on the door handle, and watched her walk to the stairs.

No way. This was not going to happen. He couldn't possibly touch her. She was a scarecrow. She spent her life vomiting, throwing up. He could picture all that food flowing out of her mouth, undigested ... whole bars of chocolate, cans of Coke, cream cakes, blocks of ripple ice cream – the colours still separate and distinct, not even intermingled – walnut whips with the walnut still intact ...

Her flat eyes looked at him expectantly. They had gigantic purple shadows underneath them. Unnatural. She looked sick. Or dead.

She yelled so loud when they climaxed that JC's heart almost stopped. Almost. Her eyes didn't look sick any more. Or dead.

They made love again. And again.

MOTHER DIDN'T have a circle meeting the following Wednesday. It was cancelled due to unforeseen circumstances. Their oldest tarot reader had passed on unexpectedly. A clot on the brain, they said. The whole circle was devastated, inconsolable.

Not because of the clot on the brain, although they did regret that, but because nobody in the whole group had managed to predict it.

This kind of thing didn't enhance their reputation at all.

JC spent the whole of that week comforting Mother. The kaftan and its effect on him were the last things on his mind.

By the time the next Wednesday came around and he was seeing Mother off to her meeting, he hardly cared if the doorbell never, ever rang again.

It had barely pealed out once when he wrenched the door open. The Gerber twins stood there, as alike as two peas in a pod.

# CHAPTER 4

BUSY PEOPLE tend not to gossip. They have neither the time nor the inclination for it. But Ballysheel was a slow-moving little town. Consequently, gossip spread there like wildfire.

The good people of Ballysheel couldn't fail to notice that a whole generation of their young girls had suddenly left all their ills behind them, and mysteriously blossomed.

This metamorphosis was far too sudden to be considered a natural phenomenon. The town people, who were mostly only one generation removed from their rural antecedents, were versed enough in its ways to be aware that nature, by its very nature, took its time. It wasn't usually given to quantum leaps. At least not in Ballysheel. So people looked elsewhere to find the explanation for such rapid changes in their young women.

When the nervous tics and frightening fits that had plagued both Gerber twins since birth, and that had been deemed incurable by medical experts, suddenly disappeared, Ballysheel took notice.

In school, JC was beginning to have a coterie of giggling girls dogging his footsteps and gazing moon-eyed at him in every class except mechanical drawing. And the old fallacy that teachers have eyes in the back of their heads may be just that, but that doesn't mean they are myopic. At least not all of them. In the staff room JC's name was frequently mentioned now, and not always with approval, as it once had been. Some of his teachers were becoming uneasy. Any class which contained the previously unobtrusive JC Ryan now tended to be more difficult to control. There was a strange energy abounding. Even the hard-line troublemakers were now treating JC Ryan with deference. The boy himself seemed unchanged, but there was no denying the unspoken fascination he now appeared to hold for his peers. And as most teachers jealously guard their position in the school pecking order, JC Ryan became a boy to be watched.

JC AND MOTHER were sitting together over supper when the doorbell rang. As it was Friday, they were having their favourite smoked fish. Mother had always taken a lot of trouble

29

over their meals. She was known to be a finicky shopper, taking her time choosing, and sometimes discarding, foodstuffs that to a less discerning eye might appear more than acceptable. But Mother could spot an about-to-wilt fruit or vegetable at twenty paces. Only the freshest of ingredients, the most aromatic of herbs, and the purest of oils were allowed into her kitchen. Even a simple fish supper could become a feast when Mother prepared it. All she asked in return was a hearty appetite, good table manners, and repeated and fulsome praise for her efforts. And an almost reverential attitude to the fish, fowl or flesh that was about to be eaten.

To be disturbed during a meal was, therefore, in her book, close to a cardinal sin.

The doorbell pealed loudly for the second time.

Not until it rang for the third time, a long continuous ring, did Mother abandon her now almost empty plate and reluctantly answer the door.

Mrs Ashe, a client of Mother's, stood with her hand firmly pressed on the doorbell. She was highly agitated. So much so that Mother's best chilling look, was totally wasted on her, intent as she was on her own purpose.

Her main purpose, however, stood beside her. Her name was Tish, and she was in every sense of the word, Mrs Ashe's purpose, for Tish was the only surviving child of the eight children that Mrs Ashe had dutifully brought into the world. She had then watched them succumb, one by one, to the disease that her blatantly faithful husband's genes had transmitted to them.

Yet, against all the odds, Tish had survived. She, alone of all her siblings, had escaped the Ashe family curse. But not before the treacherous genes had inflicted their cruel mark.

She stood now beside her Mother, a frail looking twelve year old, with a face that would make angels weep with envy and Botticelli beg for his palette.

If he didn't look past her eyebrows, that is, because perched just above them was the most revolting protuberance that had ever marred a human face. At least in Ballysheel.

The size of a small ostrich egg, it appeared uncannily like a second minor head trying to emerge from the child's pale forehead. The ugly sickly white growth, couldn't but draw all eyes, even the most unwilling, its vileness being all the more fascinating because of the sheer perfection of the features below it.

30

It gleamed whitely at JC.

Someone had made a brave effort to camouflage the horror by combing a long strand of Tish's brown hair over it, but instead of masking it , the draped hair only accentuated its ugliness, making a part of it closely resemble an obscene brown coconut.

It took the extremely nervous Mrs Ashe two cups of tea and a full slice of Battenberg before she could gather her wits enough to explain what had brought her here without an appointment.

Little Tish refused all offers of refreshment, preferring to stand unrefreshed and silent as if in grim penance for carrying such a distorted head.

Mrs Ashe was finally ready to speak. She clutched Tish's pale hand and drew in a deep breath.

'There is some talk.' At the sight of Mother's face, her voice faltered, but mother-love can make lions of lambs and she continued, '… that … that JC can …'

'Talk? What talk?' Mother was king of the jungle here.

'Talk of JC. They say he can –'

Mother drew herself up majestically. JC could almost spot her unsheathing claws. 'Out!' she bellowed, pointing towards the door.

'Oh no, please, you can't refuse.' Timid Mrs Ashe was bowed, but not bloodied.

'Out!' Mother began pushing her and the silent Tish towards the door.

Mrs Ashe bravely, if shakily, held her ground. She spoke directly to JC for the first time.

'They say you can cure people. You have the gift. It's known!'

Mother's face turned ashen. 'Jessie?' Her voice was a horrified whisper.

'He can! He can! Everybody says! He healed the Gerber twins and Janis Meehan, and Reena Scales.' The silent Tish had found her voice, and now couldn't be stopped. A torrent of names tumbled out in a verbal flash flood.

Mother's knees gave way and she dropped back hard into the wicker chair which stood fortuitously behind her. It creaked loudly in protest, threatening to topple over.

JC wanted to attend to her, or at least to hold her chair steady, but his feet were glued to the shag pile.

Mrs Ashe knelt in front of the wicker chair. She grasped at Mother's hands in desperation. 'Just let him try, Ms Ryan. Just let him try. She's all I've got.'

In her distress she had clearly forgotten all about Mr Ashe, the father of her one living child and her seven dead ones.

'I beg you with all my heart, as one loving mother to another.' Catching Mother's expression, she pressed her advantage. 'Only we know the true agony of seeing our child in pain ... please.' Tears ran down her plump face, leaving little white channels in her beige make-up.

JC wanted to run. But his legs refused to move. He wanted out! Out! Away from these people, the babbling little girl, the tear-streaked mother. But most of all he wanted to get away from the pain in Mother's face. He couldn't bear it.

Mother's pain was his pain; he felt every twinge, every ache, every stab as if they were physically connected, as if their nervous systems were one. When she clutched at her chest, his breathing became constricted. He wanted to tell her not to listen to this rubbish about him being a healer. He wasn't a healer! He had seen the changes in the girls he'd ... befriended. He'd have had to be blind not to notice them, but he had no notion of why they'd changed. It didn't necessarily have to do with him? Maybe they just ... And now this woman was begging him to ... to ... to ... with this child? He felt sick.

Mrs Ashe was now in a full pleading frenzy. She turned towards JC, her tears widening the white channels down her face. Suddenly she started walking towards him on her knees, leaving a trail of flattened shag behind her. JC watched in horror as she half sat up, like an overgrown, begging puppy, her plump arms raised in supplication.

'Please ... just lay your hands on her, try!'

The little girl gave a whimper of distress to see her mother humble herself like this.

Mother took a deep decisive breath. 'Jessie.' Calm now, she stood up.

Mrs Ashe's face came alive with hope. 'Just lay your hands on her.'

Mother moved determinedly towards her. She caught the overweight woman under her arms and pulled her to her feet as effortlessly if she were lifting a slender child.

Mrs Ashe sobbed quietly into her hands as Mother crossed

to her covered table where she kept her candles and holy water. Nobody spoke as she folded away the white cloth, lit the candles, and poured water into the small silver holder.

She beckoned to JC.

He felt his chest tightening. She placed her hands on his shoulders, and even through the cotton of his shirt, he could feel the icy coldness of her fingers. He began to shiver.

'Just lay your hands on her,' her voice was gentle but she refused to meet his eyes.

'Mother?' He tried to stop his voice quivering.

She didn't reply.

Behind him Tish said, 'You have to wear the Robe.'

He turned to see the child staring triumphantly at him.


HE CAME back down the stairs slowly. Mrs Ashe and Mother were standing together, watching silently.

Little Tish ran across to catch his hand. 'Isn't he beautiful? He's all shiny.' She looked up into his face. 'He's like God.'

Mother arranged the candles in a circle and placed the silver water holder in front of them. JC stood by the table and put one hand at the back of the girl's head. He drew a long breath before carefully placing the palm of his other hand against the growth.

He thought he felt it move under his hand. He definitely felt distinctly nauseous.

Both women watched anxiously, Mrs Ashe with her hands joined as if in prayer.

JC closed his eyes and concentrated all his energy on the horror beneath his hand. Sweat begin to trickle down his face and back. The candles were giving out far too much heat. And the kaftan was unbearably hot. He was naked underneath it, yet he was sweltering, his mouth drying out. He tried to concentrate on the growth. His breathing was becoming harsh, loud even to his own ears, his chest tightening. His hand was on fire.

The girl moved slightly and gave a weak sigh. Her mother began to pray out loud.

JC felt faint. His head began to swim. He removed his hand and looked at … *the thing*. It sat there, and stared back like a malevolent, grey-white unyielding eye.

'It's hot,' Tish complained. 'Burning.'

JC dipped his hand in the bowl of cool water and daubed it all over the growth.

'I'm sorry,' he said to nobody in particular.

The women and the girl stood in a disappointed little circle.

TWO DAYS later Mrs Ashe went into her daughter's bedroom to call her for school. The girl's bedclothes were stained with blood. She had begun to menstruate. And the ugly growth on her forehead had completely disappeared.

The town erupted with gossip.

# CHAPTER 5

FATHER DENNY was a parish priest who loved his flock. He would do anything for them. Except tolerate a bogus healer. Any parishioner in Ballysheel who was foolish enough even to refer to mysterious healing in the confessional left with a flea in his ear, and a penance as long as his arm.

'I'll give them mysteries,' he bellowed to his young curate, after stories of yet another healing reached their ears.

And he did. He gave them the Sorrowful mysteries, the Joyful mysteries, and the Glorious mysteries, all to be repeated one after the other until they learned their lesson.

Young Curate was of the opinion that Father Denny was being a bit harsh. This 'healer', after all, apparently made no claims for himself. He was, by all accounts, almost a reluctant healer. He was also, so they said, incredibly discreet. This aspect of his character greatly interested Young Curate. For Young Curate had a problem. It wasn't something that should unduly worry a professed celibate, but Young Curate was a man, and men by their nature tend to worry about such things.

Young Curate had only one testicle. This might have seemed sufficient unto his limited needs, but between man's needs and wants lies a great, dark, and relatively unexplored chasm.

The area in question was, however, anything but unexplored.

For Young Curate lay awake, night after night, probing and searching, hoping against hope, that the next finger check would discover the rightful number in his tidy little sac. He was doomed to disappointment, however, for no matter how hard or ruthlessly he searched, the highest number he could ever grasp was one. And now even his days were being taken over by this pursuit. At the most inopportune moments he found his hand wandering in hope to the afflicted area. Only two weeks back, during a long and tedious Confirmation ceremony, when in the throes of this occupation, he had caught the eye of a furious bishop.

Young Curate needed help, and he needed it quickly and discreetly. He made a careful note of the young healer's address.

*

JC AND MOTHER had listened patiently as Young Curate spoke non-stop for almost forty-five minutes. They had offered him tea, sherry, gin, platitudes and various opinions as to why the weather was so mild for this time of the year.

Young Curate had refused the alcohol, accepted everything else and then chattered on about the church roof, how exemplary a parish priest Father Denny was, falling moral standards in western Europe and how the USSR was finally about to collapse, thank God.

Not once did he mention undescended testicles.

Not at that meeting.

THE NEXT time he called, JC was alone. Young Curate drank half a bottle of gin, pronounced Father Denny a born-again fascist, and told JC that he had only one ball.

Then he wept.

JC PULLED on the kaftan nervously. He hoped it would work. Nobody could help but feel pity for the distressed Young Curate as he wept and drank the remainder of the gin. But JC had never 'healed' a man before. He wasn't even sure how to … go about it. The laying-on of hands was obviously a pre-re-quisite to healing. JC didn't know why. In fact, he didn't know anything about healing … he just did it. The problem here was where he would be required to lay his hands.

Young Curate finally relinquished his hold on the gin bottle and lay down naked on JC's bed. He was almost comatose with the drink, which relieved JC of some of his embarrassment. But unfortunately not all, he realised, as he gazed down at the young curate's almost infantile genitals. The whole area surrounding them had a vague pastel-hue; it was pinky white, virginal in its almost hairless purity. Even the few brave pioneering hairs that grew there were an inoffensive baby blond.

JC pressed a tentative finger where he supposed the undescended testicle might be hovering. The skin felt surprisingly rough. He prodded a little harder. Young Curate grunted drunkenly, but didn't move. Heat radiated from his body. JC tried to visualise the maverick testicle moving down into its rightful place. He tried not to stare at the woebegone little penis, furtively hanging its head in humiliation at its imperfectly arranged grouping. He concentrated hard on willing the missing piece into its rightful place, thinking of it boldly filling out the lopsided pink sac until it rounded it out with the symmetrical perfection that nature had always intended for it.

Then for no reason other than it had now become part of the ritual, he flicked holy water over the young curate's groin. It splashed all over his dejected-looking genitals, and clung glistening in forlorn hope to the lonely pubic hairs.

JC watched as it ran in tiny rivulets down the crevices between the plump pink thighs and hummocked groin.

Young Curate snored on.

JC shook him awake and helped him dress.

HALF AN HOUR later Young Curate was violently sick all over the church vestry. The house of God began to reek of vomit and sour gin. Despite a raging headache, Young Curate collected a bucketful of soapy water and a mop and scrupulously washed every inch of the tiled floor until it shone like an unblemished soul. He then knelt and begged forgiveness from his maker for both his vomiting and his ego.

He was soaking in a steaming hot bath when he tried to recall what had happened with JC. To his shame he couldn't remember a thing after the first few drinks. He hoped that he hadn't embarrassed the boy too much. He would pray for him.

He fingered his rosary beads and lay back, wallowing in the relaxing heat as he recited the familiar Hail Marys, over and over to himself.

Almost unconsciously his right hand reached down.

'Jesus!'

The yell echoed around the tiled room.

He leaped to his feet, which was a drastic mistake as the soapy water had made the bath extra slippery. Without a solid foothold, his feet slid along unobstructed, the motion of which sent him crashing back down again cracking his already throbbing head against the side of the solid bath tub. Blood began seeping from the broken flesh.

He didn't even notice. Not the blood, nor the pain, nor the sharp metal cross on the discarded Rosary that was cutting into his bare buttocks.

'Please God, let it not be my imagination.'

He reached down again, his heart pounding. He had imagined it once before, in a dream.

'Please God, not this time. This time let it be real.'
He moved his fingers carefully, counting out loud.
'One ... two. Two! Two! Oh sweet Jesus, thank you.'
He had two balls!

# CHAPTER 6

JC HAD TO be persuaded to go to the hospital. Mother did the persuading. She had gone from being totally opposed to his healing to being obsessed by it. Her obsession took the form of referring constantly to it, neglecting her own clients in order to facilitate those who wanted to see JC, and arranging group meetings for what she called 'healing sessions'. She lost all interest in her astrological charts, drawing one up now only in order to forecast the most favourable times for holding these 'healing sessions'.

The turning point for her had come about one Friday morning when a huge sackload of mail had been delivered for JC.

This mail had apparently been accumulating for some time in a post-office sorting room. The reason for the delay in its delivery, was its lack of a proper directive address.

Some of the envelopes were addressed to 'The Healer, Ballysheel'. Others said, 'The Ballysheel Healer', and one large pink envelope with a New York postmark read simply 'Holy Healer, Ireland'.

Except for the exotic American one, all of the envelopes and cards carried an Irish postmark. Even so, JC was stunned; he'd had no idea that anyone beyond the town limits even knew of his existence, let alone his healing.

The American envelope was the biggest surprise. All the more so when JC opened it to discover it contained an unsigned card, with the message 'Pray for me' carefully inscribed in exquisite copperplate handwriting. Sitting close beside him Mother also appeared shocked, but for a completely different reason. She was grasping three one-hundred-dollar bills that had fallen out when he had torn open the envelope.

She scrutinised them carefully, one by one, and declared them kosher, a word JC had never heard her use before. She then quickly divided the mail into two separate mounds. Pushing aside the postcards, she began to open the letters carefully.

They contained requests for pictures of JC, for pieces of his clothing, items he had touched, and for souvenir holy pictures. And for appointments for private healing sessions.

They also contained cash, cheques, and postal orders that altogether totalled five hundred pounds.

MOTHER SOUNDED faintly breathless as she hurried ahead of him through the hospital gates. His strides were three times the length of hers, yet he kept falling behind.

'Come on Jessie, don't dawdle.' Her pace barely slowed as she turned to reprimand him.

For a second he considered throwing himself down on the hospital lawn like a rebellious kid. 'No, no, Mother, not another inch ... not one inch!'

But watching her small, determined little back rushing towards the brightly lit hospital, he knew he couldn't disappoint her. He drew his long rain mac carefully around the bright kaftan in a futile attempt at covering it. He had never actually worn the thing in the street before. He felt stupid, conspicuous. As if every eye in the town was focused on him. For the first time in weeks the kaftan made him uncomfortable. Out of place.

Even the woollen scarf and the heavy waterproof didn't disguise it much. He felt like a sap. But Mother had insisted that he wear it; she wouldn't take no for an answer. But then she didn't have to stride through the cold wet streets of Ballysheel looking as if she were dressed for a wild night out in the Kasbah.

Like most other towns, Ballysheel had its fair quota of 'hard men'. Men who sincerely believed that anything remotely feminine was fit only to be sneered at, seeing as it represented a flaw in nature, something that existed only by default, when the weary Creator ran out of testosterone.

The last thing any sane person needed was to draw the attention of these men. Or their wrath. He didn't even want to imagine what they might make of a six-foot-tall, long haired youth wearing what they'd surely term a dress. He pulled the mac tighter around him.

Mother meant well, as usual, by insisting that he visit Sister Vera. The Sister was an honourary title, bestowed on her by Mother's circle group. Until her hospitalisation, Sister Vera had been the backbone of the group. Her phenomenal energy had been the envy of all. It never flagged. Ever. Others might experience bursts of energy which lasted days, weeks, months even, but inevitably everyone came to those times when life became too much, when it was necessary simply to sit back and let the thermals of life carry one along, a hapless victim of destiny. But not Sister Vera. She was one of life's indomitable movers.

'Take control,' she was fond of saying. 'The stars merely provide guidelines, they map out possible pathways, but the route you eventually take must be of your own choosing.'

A favourite occupation of the other circle members was trying to guess her true age, which she guarded as if her life depended on it. Perhaps in a way it did. Her face looked fifty, but her hands were the gnarled, withered hands of an eighty-year-old. Yet when confronted with such awesome vitality, few people stopped to notice her hands.

That was, of course, before her stroke.

She lay now, her head supported by the stiff, starched pillows that are to be found in every well-regimented hospital ward.

It was as if every available ounce of energy had been sapped from her small robust frame, leaving behind an arid, empty shell. Her well-toned skin that had been her pride and joy was now a dull muted parchment, lifeless against the vivid hospital whites. It was visibly lined for the first time since JC had known her.

One side of her mouth was pulled downwards towards her chin, as if permanently snagged on an invisible nail. Her eyes were full of pain, whether at her predicament, or caused by some terrible discomfort, JC couldn't tell. Someone had brushed her thin black hair back from her face, cruelly exposing the grey roots that she had always painstakingly covered. Sister Vera had no control here. She didn't even have dignity.

JC could hardly bear to look at her. He wanted to remember the smiling, energetic woman, who had once whispered to him that he would change the world, that he would reshape it beyond recognition. He had been fourteen then, going through a nervous, anxious stage, and her words had been sweet music to his ears. They filled him with self-confidence.

He had found out much later that she said exactly the same thing to everyone under sixteen. But none the less, he remained grateful to her.

She tried to smile at him now but succeeded only in making

a pathetic grimace with her poor snagged mouth. He wanted to cry out in protest at the injustice of it all, but he was too aware of the small groups of people who were gathered around the other beds in the ward. He could hear them all speaking in the false hushed tones that relatives use around those they suspect will soon be making their final journey. He wanted to yell, to make some noise – anything to affirm life – and drown out the awful whispers of death.

Mother gestured to him to take off his mac. He frowned at her – puzzled, then looked down again at Sister Vera. She looked back with her pain filled eyes. He knew what he had to do. It didn't matter that he might attract curious glances – the scorn of the whisperers – that didn't matter, nothing did, except breaking this awful whispering acceptance.

He threw off his mac and scarf. He wasn't uncomfortable any more. The kaftan felt good on him, it brushed against his skin like warm encouraging fingers.

Mother took two heavy wax candles from her bag and placed them upright on Sister Vera's locker. She filled a small wooden bowl with holy water, lit the candles and carefully positioned the water bowl to form a triangle with them.

The low murmuring around the other beds died down, then fizzled out altogether. Ignoring the curious stares, Mother nodded to JC.

He bent low over Sister Vera with his arms outstretched. She tried to raise her hand to touch him, but succeeded only in moving it a few feeble inches. JC clasped the frail hand and willed his strength into it. Her pain glazed eyes watched him as he pulled back the hospital bedding and moved both his hands slowly along her body. Her right foot was twisted awkwardly inwards, in a cruel imitation of her curved right arm. JC touched the twisted foot gently, then allowed his fingers to rest on it for a second. He tried to visualise it straightening itself, aligning itself with the thin leg and ankle above it.

He then caught the locked curved arm between both his hands, and began to raise it, slowly, gently. Before he had drawn it even halfway up between waist and shoulder, it was almost straight, the newly freed hand and fingers beginning to flex as if waving in celebration.

His body was drenched with sweat, but the energy coursing through him was exhilarating. He was invincible now.

He placed his hands on either side of Sister Vera's face and concentrated. The hospital ward faded, the curious faces disappeared, there was nothing now except this all consuming energy. He was on fire.

He couldn't have said how much time passed before he heard Mother's voice calling.

'Jessie.'

His eyelids were heavy. He had difficulty opening them.

Lying back against the pillows, Sister Vera was smiling up at him, her mouth no longer cruelly distorted but smiling in almost perfect symmetry. And the pain had left her eyes.

Mother held out the container of holy water.

He sprinkled tiny drops of water all over Sister Vera, stopping only when she caught his hand and kissed it.

Then he noticed the crowd that had gathered around the bed.

Out of nowhere there was a sudden bright flash.

'Who?'

It hurt his eyes.

'It's all right, Jessie. It's all right.' Mother's voice was calm; she was totally unperturbed by the sudden appearance of the photographer.

'What are you doing?' JC yelled at him.

There was another bright flash.

JC tried to pull the camera from him, but the photographer was too quick on his feet; and he leaped back, still brazenly clicking away.

The curious crowd was getting bigger; they pushed forward to get a closer look at JC. Separated now from Mother, he called to her across the heads of the crowd.

As he did so, he saw her nod in recognition to the red-headed photographer.

He grabbed his mac from where it lay on the bed, elbowed his way through the crowd and ran.

JC'S SUDDEN departure only fuelled the excitement in the ward. Everybody wanted to know what was happening. What had happened.

The photographer was almost hyper-ventilating with excitement. He was everywhere at once, flashing, snapping, clicking from all angles. He appeared to want photos of everything, from the dripping candles to the now well-rumpled bed of Sister

Vera. He took several shots of JC's abandoned scarf.

Even the more reserved hospital visitors now gave up all pretence of dignity and scrambled to reach Sister Vera, displaying all the decorum of flesh-hungry piranhas.

They stared, prodded, touched and fought to stay as close to her as possible, risking life and limb to do so as a stream of newcomers fought their way in from the side wards.

And in the middle of all the chaos, Sister Vera sat laughing. As if it were all a huge joke. The woman who, not ten minutes before, had been knocking on the doors of eternity was laughing fit to burst. Long, loud belly laughs, which became even louder as more people pressed towards her. Tears of laughter ran down her face as she doubled over in uncontrollable mirth.

Panicking medical personnel came running, calling out for people not to panic. Then they themselves ran faster, not knowing what they were running for, or towards.

The on-duty ward nurses pleaded for people to 'Please vacate the ward ... please.'

The patient in the bed next to Sister Vera's, suddenly swung her feet on to the tiled floor, and reached out to touch her, forgetting about her dangling IV tube which momentarily snagged on to someone's handbag, before breaking free of its restraint to spray the crowd with its pain-masking drug.

Sister Vera laughed harder. The excited voices around her rose higher.

'Silence!' the inappropriately named nurse, Serena, bellowed at the top of her voice.

She was completely ignored.

People were now arriving from other floors. Word of a miracle in ward six had spread like a bush fire, and nothing draws people more than the hope of witnessing a great miracle.

Except perhaps the hope of witnessing a great tragedy.

At the far end of the long ward an old man was calling out weakly.

Matron arrived to restore order. She marched into the ward, flanked by two sisters.

'What in God's name is going on here?' she thundered. She couldn't be heard above the din. Drawing in a massive breath, she raised her voice a full octave. 'Shut up!'

Her powerful voice resounded around the ward.

The old man at the far end of the ward obligingly stopped

calling, as his soul went to meet its maker.

Matron pushed her way towards Sister Vera's bed. The hushed crowd automatically parted for her. The sight which greeted her stopped her dead in her tracks.

MISS VERA HARTIGAN, a terminally ill patient of undetermined years, who had been practically immobile for two full weeks, was now standing by her bed unaided, laughing uproariously.

'Look, Matron.' She held out her hands and wriggled her fingers like a boastful concert pianist about to perform. The crowd applauded. Sister Vera reacted like an old trooper.

'Watch this!' She raised her right leg in a rhythmic kick, higher and higher, until it appeared that she might tear herself in two if someone didn't call a halt.

The onlookers cheered, encouragingly.

Then there was a sudden gasp of horror as the crowd watched the startled woman collapse heavily on to the floor.

Matron had fainted for the first time in her life.

The photographer snapped away busily.

# CHAPTER 7

FATHER DENNY threw down the paper in disgust.

Young Curate knew what was coming. He had already seen the photos and read the article. And this was in a local paper. God only knew what the nationals would make of the story.

'Miraculous healing!' Father Denny all but spat the words.

'"Medical world astounded",' he quoted.

'Medical world?' His voice was dripping with sarcasm. 'What medical world? Ward six in the local hospital? Hardly the Mayo Clinic, is it?'

'Perhaps, er, we should –' Young Curate attempted.

'The woman was obviously an hysteric. Not a blessed thing wrong with her that a bit of fuss and attention couldn't cure.'

'Well, she's certainly getting that.' Young Curate nervously picked up the discarded paper.

'Just look at it, did you ever see the like?' Father Denny grabbed the paper from him and tut-tutted disapprovingly at the offending photos. Young Curate peered over his superior's shoulder. The biggest photo, and the most eye-catching, was one of a laughing Sister Vera doing a high kick for the camera. Her thin leg was clearly exposed up to her bony thigh. It was not a beauteous sight.

'Titillation, that's all they're interested in!'

Young Curate would have liked to point out that the sight of this particular leg was unlikely to titillate even the most depraved individual. But he remained quiet.

There were other smaller pictures surrounding the large one.

The most compelling to Young Curate was one of a clearly distressed JC reaching out towards the photographer. He seemed to be pleading with him. Every line of JC's body was that of a betrayed child.

Young Curate felt a sudden stab of pity for him.

'Look at him,' Father Denny cried, pointing, 'what sort of get-up has he got on him? It's like something a girl might wear to a dance. And look at the state of that hair. God Almighty how could anyone take him seriously with a head like that? A healer is right! He looks like he's in need of a bit of healing himself. Or at least a good barber. Have people gone stone mad? Have their lives become so impoverished that they need to turn to this kind of fallacious mumbo jumbo?'

'They – they say he's a – a man of God – that he – '

'Man of God?' Father Denny laughed. 'Man of the circus more like. That's where he belongs, with the clowns and the bearded lady, and the performing seals. He's no more than that. A performer. Look at him. Playing to the crowd!'

'I – I don't think he was –' Young Curate swallowed.

'Playing to the crowd?' Father Denny finished impatiently for him. 'Then what was that photographer doing there? And the reporter, and all those people. Where did they come from? "I WITNESSED A MIRACLE!"' he quoted from the paper. 'Well, wasn't that a grand bit of luck now, having all those witnesses present? Funny how you never get any of these healers performing miracles on the quiet. The urge to perform a miracle only seems to strike them when they have a good receptive audience. Not to mention a camera handy. Wouldn't you call that a bit suspicious now?'

Young Curate said nothing. Not even when his brand-new testicle began throbbing.

'And what about the collection?'

'Pardon?'

'The collection, man, don't you ever listen?'

'I'm sorry?' Young Curate hadn't the faintest idea what Father Denny was talking about. But then, that appeared to be his cross in life, as he was condemned to work with men who spoke a completely different language to him. Men who served the same master, yet daily forced him to plough through a morass of language and meaning which he could never hope to interpret.

'Surely you noticed that the church collection is down by twenty per cent?'

Young Curate had to admit that he hadn't.

'Well it is, so what are we going to do about all this?' He indicated the paper.

Try as he might, Young Curate couldn't make the connection between the drop in church funds and the healings.

'I don't understand, Father?'

'The meet-ings! The meet-ings!' Father Denny enunciated the words as if speaking to someone deaf. 'He's beginning to hold meetings on Sunday mornings. In – our – parish. On our very doorstep!' He pounded the table in front of him. 'We've had enough to contend with lately. Emigration, pub quizzes, aerobics, they all take their toll, and now this. This! Of all the scourges for a parish to be afflicted with, a spiritual healer must be the worst.'

Young Curate's new testicle throbbed with guilt.

His superior poured himself a lone tot of whiskey and drank it quickly. 'You know what they're like.'

Young Curate was astounded at this inference that he might actually know something. That he might have acquired some knowledge during his four years in university, five years in the seminary, and twenty-eight long months in this Godforsaken parish. Maybe Father Denny wasn't as implacable as he pretended to be. Maybe they could ...

'Father, perhaps I should have told you ...'

'Adolescents! Even in middle age! Always needing to be entertained. Always on the look-out for something new ...' he sighed. 'It's the television of course. That's what whetted their appetites. Television and titillation – that's all they want – everything in short bursts. They all have a shorter attention span nowadays – entertain them and move on – that's what they want. If a sermon goes over ten minutes nowadays, they're all checking their watches. Coughing. Blowing their noses. Clearing their throats. Low on attention and high on phlegm. That's the scourge of the television age.'

'Maybe we could try to –'

Father Denny's glare stopped Young Curate in his tracks. 'We're not here to pander to the whims of modern life. We're here to nurture their immortal souls. For two thousand years that's been our job. Guardians of their souls, that's what we are, not servants of Mammon.' He sighed again. 'But you can't run a parish without funds. Empty pews mean empty collection boxes. Something will have to be done.'

Young Curate sat silently.

THE RINGING of the Angelus bell woke JC. It was midday, yet he was still exhausted. He hadn't gotten to bed until the small hours and even then he had found it impossible to sleep. The phone had rung incessantly, until he had finally taken it off the hook. Unfortunately he hadn't thought to disconnect the doorbell.

Ever since Sister Vera's cure, the house had been under siege. Pressmen in hooded anoraks, and photographers with leather jackets and faces to match, camped outside their front door twenty-four hours a day, totally disrupting the smooth flow of everyday life along their small terrace.

At first the neighbours had quite enjoyed being in the spotlight, delighted to catch glimpses of their own homes, and sometimes their own faces on the TV news. Some of them even went so far as to give press interviews, happily chattering on about JC and his 'gift'. They were always at great pains to add that they, of course, had recognised his special talents from day one.

One man solemnly recounted the story of his unhappy Rottweiler which had barked constantly, day and night, until a very young JC placed his healing hands on it. From that day to this, the man explained to his spellbound audience, his dog had never again barked at night.

He omitted to mention the part played in the saga by four other neighbours. They had in fact taken out a court injunction against the noisy dog and its owner. The storyteller also omitted the part played by the District Court judge, who had judiciously ordered that the dog be kept tightly muzzled between dusk and dawn to enable people to get some sleep, and perhaps even prevent bloodshed.

But popular storytellers seldom allow themselves to be weighed down by anything as burdensome as the truth.

After weeks of being assailed by the media, however, the novelty of reflected fame was beginning to wear thin. When JC's next-door neighbour opened his blinds one sunny morning to reveal a French newsman urinating into his window box, battle lines were drawn. The now-elderly Rottweiler was brought out and his muzzle removed, and the press were threatened with extinction. An English tabloid journalist, famed for his affinity with animals, threw the dog an egg sandwich. The Rottweiler pounced immediately. On the journalist. No one was badly hurt in the ensuing melée, but the Gardaí had to intervene.

In defence of his dog, JC's neighbour pointed to his wilting hardy annuals as clear evidence of the foul French deed perpetrated on his property.

He vehemently denied that he had ever called the newsman 'a fucking Frog'.

The contrite newsman, with his eye still on the main story, offered his profound apologies, a gallic shrug and a bottle of vintage Chardonnay as a recompense.

JC's neighbour ignored the shrug, told him to stuff his apologies, but accepted the offer of the Chardonnay. As soon as he was in receipt of the bottle, he drank half its contents, declared it to be superb, then rammed the broken cork back into its neck and told the astounded Frenchman that he would keep the rest for his birthday which was fortuitously a mere two months away.

# CHAPTER 8

IN DIRECT contrast to the rising neighbourhood anger, and JC's weariness with the leech-like press corps, Mother appeared to be invigorated by the whole business.

As JC's energy lagged, hers soared. She was constantly rushing about. Talking to pressmen, arranging bigger and better healing sessions. And now she was beginning to interview prospective managers. She had decided that this was what JC needed most. A manager.

'A manager?' JC stared in disbelief.

Mother stroked his cheek. 'You're tired, you need someone to organise your life.'

He looked at her, searching her face for some sign that she was teasing. There was none.

She placed her hand across his protesting mouth. 'I know, I know, you think I can continue to organise everything for you, but I can't be everywhere at once.' She sat back in her wicker peacock chair, and closed her eyes to signal the end of the conversation.

'No! No more, Mother! It's over. No more sessions. No more healings. No more publicity. I'm going to stop all this right now ... ' He paused nervously as she opened her eyes.

'I'll tell the truth! I'm no healer – I don't know what I am – I just – I just –'

She lunged out of the chair at him. 'What do you mean, you're not a healer? What do you think you've been doing all these months? All those cures? All those people? Sickness, wiped away? What was all that about?'

'I don't know! That's the truth. I don't know, Mother!'

The anger drained from her face. She sighed wearily, her right hand reaching out for the nearest support which happened to be the heavy window drapes. They swung open, flooding the room with bright sunlight. She reeled back blinking in protest.

'Mother?'

There was a sudden flurry outside. Faces were pressed against the glass, bodies jostled for position as the crowd of reporters tried to peer in. A flash bulb popped.

She dropped the curtain cord in alarm.

JC rushed to close the drapes, 'You see! We can't live like this. Nobody could without going crazy.'

'It wasn't my choice,' she snapped, her swoon forgotten.

'Do you think I'd have chosen this … zoo?'

'Then let's put an end to it. We can live like we used to. We were happy then, weren't we? We managed well enough. And if we can't, well, I – I can get a job.'

She threw him a scathing look.

'There are some jobs out there, Mother. I can try. Anything would be better than living like this.'

She turned away and began unstacking a new batch of folding chairs that had been delivered earlier that morning.

'Mother?'

She carefully opened out chair after chair, arranging them in a neat row, one next to the other. But her hands were slightly unsteady, and she didn't move with anything like her normal brisk determination. He realised for the first time that she was tired. More than that: she looked as if she was on the brink of exhaustion.

He should have spoken up before. He could see that now. Mother would work herself to death if someone didn't stop her. If he didn't stop her. She had always looked out for him. Now it was his turn to look after her.

He had never wanted for anything, thanks to her. She had provided for all his needs. All his life. She was much more than a mother. She was everything to him. That's why he had never, ever felt the need for a father.

Hardly ever.

When he was very small, he thought that mothers were all that anybody had. It wasn't until he went to school that he realised that some children had an extra parent that they called a father.

He asked what they were for. And everybody laughed.

After that he didn't ask again for a long time. When he finally brought up the subject again none of his classmates were of much help to him.

Some said fathers were for reading you stories. But Mother did this. Others thought they were for teaching you football or hurling, or fishing. But he wasn't interested in any of these activities.

Tim Murphy was the oldest boy in the class. He was six, two whole weeks older than JC. He knew everything. When the teacher was in good humour, she called him a prodigy. When she was in bad humour, she called him a know-all.

Tim said, 'Fathers are for giving babies to mothers.'

JC couldn't wait to get home and ask Mother when his father had given him to her.

For a second Mother's face had taken on a tight funny look, then she picked him up and sat him on her knee. 'Everybody doesn't have to have a father,' she said very slowly. 'Some people are lucky enough to have mothers who love them so much that they never have need of a father. From that first magic instant when they began developing inside their mother's womb, they received all the love and nurturing they could ever possibly need from her, and her alone.'

JC was so astounded by this revelation that he blurted it out to his friends before school even began next morning.

'Babies grow inside their mothers!' he informed the wide-eyed group of five-year-olds.

This stunning piece of information completely eclipsed any budding interest in fathers and their purpose.

JC became the hero of the day, if not the month, for extracting this information from an adult. Tim Murphy's nose was knocked right out of joint. He had said that God gives a seed to the father, who then gives it to the mother, when he loves her, which showed how little Tim Murphy knew, even if he was six.

JC was ten before he mentioned fathers again at home. In the intervening years he had somehow learned without quite knowing how that it was a subject to be avoided. It might upset Mother. And the one thing he could never bear to do was to upset Mother.

He waited until he was alone in the house with Signora Goretti before asking the question which was again puzzling him.

'Where is my father?'

She had stared at him for a long time with her huge dark eyes.

'If I tell you, can you keep it a secret?'

JC nodded his ten-year-old head vehemently, treble-crossing his heart at the same time.

The Signora looked intently into his eyes. 'You are a child

of the moon, the stars, the universe.' She moved back to gesture widely with her arms. 'Your creation had no place in it for puny earthly sperm, tiny blind creatures that swim in the darkness, seeking to impregnate that which they wish to conquer. Struggling to achieve their mindless place in the great ocean of life.' Her voice rose melodramatically. 'You didn't come from those beginnings, *caro*! You are a child of the great Mother Universe!'

JC didn't understand one word she said. But when she asked if it was all becoming clear to him now, he nodded, wanting her lilting voice to continue rising and falling like the soft notes of a lullaby.

She had caught him against her, pressed him against the soft warm breasts that smelled as exotic and foreign as the Signora herself.

'You were born of a cosmic eruption, in the womb of the universe. A universe that needs no impregnating, for she is complete. Whole! Not for her the needs of weak earthly flesh.'

Above his head she sighed sadly, but JC was now lost in his own fantasy. The soft breasts were having the strangest effect on him. He began to imagine that he could see the outline of the pink nipples that must be lurking beneath the smooth fabric of her blouse. He raised a tentative exploring finger and was just about to feel for them when the front door slammed and Mother's voice was calling.

Next day he solemnly repeated all he could remember to his classmates. Not about almost touching the protruding nipples, but what the Signora had told him about his origins.

The boys fell about the schoolyard laughing. 'Your mother's friends are all crazy, everybody knows that,' one convulsed boy said.

'Yeah, like calls to like,' another started chanting.

JC had never known such rage. It was the one and only time in his whole life that he consciously hurt another human being. He pounded at the boy's face with his fist until the others pulled him off. They held him as he stood panting over the prone boy, shocked at what he had done, sickened by the sight of the thin trickle of blood wending its way slowly from the battered nose.

Tim Murphy, always the peacemaker of the group, took over. 'Let it be now, lads. Fighting solves nothing.' He placed himself squarely between the two antagonists. 'Anyway, my dad says nobody can choose their parents. He says if we could, then half of us would have different surnames. So if JC says he didn't have a father then that's his business. Now shake hands and make up.'

JC's sullen opponent held out his hand. They shook.

The peacemaker stepped back, satisfied.

That day the school broke up for the summer holidays. One week later, while visiting his maternal grandmother in Belfast, Tim and his unemployed father were blown to pieces by a car bomb. The people who set the bomb apologised. They said it was a case of mistaken identity. People were outraged. All summer long, they took to the streets in protest. There was hardly a town or village in the country that didn't march. Then the bitter autumn winds came and drove people back indoors again. Before the clocks had gone back, Tim's image had faded from the posters and everybody's mind.

But not JC's … He merely locked it away in that special compartment, he had labelled 'forbidden thoughts'. The same place that he kept the word 'father' in.


THERE WAS a loud resounding crash as Mother stumbled against the pile of folding chairs. They flipped over one by one like collapsing dominos before she could catch them.

She put a hand to her forehead and began to tremble. JC watched in horror as her eyes shot back in her head, and her teeth began chattering. Her whole body then stiffened before appearing to crumple lifelessly.

'Mother?' JC caught her as she fell. She was a dead weight in his arms. He couldn't detect any sign of breathing. Her face was ashen. She was dying. He knew it with absolute certainty. He didn't need to feel for a pulse or check her heartbeat. Mother was dying.

'No..o.o..o...ooo.' He heard his own voice howling like a trapped animals.

The doorbell, which hadn't sounded for a full five minutes, began to peal non-stop.

There was a loud pounding.

'No..o..o..oo.' He rocked Mother in his arms.

The pounding on the door became louder. He could hear voices calling. Somebody was kicking at the heavy door. They were shouting his name.

'Mother?' He carefully arranged her lifeless body on the sofa before going to the door.

The red-haired photographer from the hospital frowned into his face.

'What's going on?'

'It's Mother ... she ...' He couldn't say it.

The redhead slammed the door shut in the faces of the other clamouring journalists. Ignoring their yells of anger and loud curses, he ran across to Mother and picked up her limp wrist. His freckled face paled.

JC slumped down on to the floor. 'Mother?'

The redhead caught him roughly by the shoulders. 'Get up!'

JC slumped down lower.

'You can help her.' The redhead was pulling him to his feet, dragging him towards Mother. 'Help her!'

JC stood uncomprehending.

'Jesus.' The redhead impatiently propped Mother's head back at an angle, and blocked her nostrils with one massive hand. He placed his mouth over her open lips and began forcing air into her lungs.

JC ran as he never had before. He took the stairs three at a time. The kaftan was lying on his bed.

He had taken over from the redhead and was pressing his hands on Mother's waxen flesh when she suddenly drew a long shuddering breath. He continued the pressure until her skin regained its healthy pink look. By then the ambulance had arrived, and the room was full of people and lights and noise.

Yet another flash bulb went off, close to his face. He wanted to tell them to stop, to get out, but he couldn't form words. He couldn't even stand without support.

The ambulance men were strapping Mother on to a stretcher. They insisted that she was in no danger. 'We'll take good care of her,' they reassured JC.

The redhead guided him to a chair, before turning to his colleagues. 'He brought her back from the dead,' JC heard him say excitedly to a cynical-looking reporter, 'He did! I'm telling you! She had no pulse. She was dead. I know a corpse when I see one, I've seen enough of them to –'

'Get out ... out.' JC finally found his voice.

The reluctant pressmen began moving half-heartedly towards the door. JC looked appealingly at the redhead.

58

'OK now, lads, let's clear out. Let's give the boy a chance.' He began pushing the others.

He was the last of the journalists to leave. At the door he paused to hitch both his heavy cameras on to his shoulders and make a half-hearted attempted at straightening his crumpled jacket.

Before slamming the door shut, he turned and winked at JC.

THE HOSPITAL insisted on keeping Mother in for observation, despite her own GP proclaiming her to be fit as a fiddle.

'Mind you, I'll still be very interested to see the results of some of these tests,' he grinned slyly.

In one single afternoon, she'd had a brain scan, several x-rays, blood tests, and her patience sorely tested by an array of curious people who constantly tried to peer in at her through the glass panel at the top of her room door.

The hospital had put her in a private room to protect her privacy. It didn't. Medical people are as plagued with curiosity as everybody else, and this was the very hospital where Sister Vera had experienced her miraculous cure.

The eminent cardiologist who was called in to consult on Mother's heart asked if he might have a private word with her. The staff quickly scattered. Mother's blood pressure soared.

The eminent man sat on her bed and nervously cleared his throat. He kept his eyes fixed on the immaculate bed cover. Mother's pulse rate trebled. He caught her hand and explained that his perfectly healthy and well-tested wife was childless for no known medical reason. She had so far spent a king's ransom on her search for maternal fulfilment. All to no avail. They were prepared to try any avenue in their quest for parenthood. Any avenue. He looked up from the bed cover for the first time. His eyes were deep-ringed with anxiety.

Mother promised to arrange an appointment with JC.

IT WAS well after dark when JC got home, yet a small cluster of reporters still hung around the front door. He turned back quickly before they spotted him, and retraced his steps along the short terrace of houses. The narrow laneway running along the back of them was unlit and spooky at night. The big old trees that grew at the end of the gardens overhung the dark laneway, creaking and groaning in protest at their age. They blocked out what little light came from the houses at this hour. As a child JC had distrusted this place even in daylight, never wanting to venture beyond the safety of Mother's call. Walking through it now as an adult, he liked it even less. But it was either this, or face the reporters at his front door.

He had almost reached his own garden when he heard it. It started as a soft shuffling sound behind him in the dark laneway. It could have been footsteps, but if it were, it was unlike any footsteps that he had ever previously heard. And above the shuffling, even above the noisy creaking of the trees, there was an unearthly guttural rasping, an eerie snorting sound that owed nothing to anything either human or animal. Certainly to nothing of this world.

All of JC's childhood terrors returned to assail him. He started running, but the horror kept pace with him, it's breathing becoming more insistent every second.

Sheer terror enabled him to vault his back gate with ease. He stumbled momentarily, but quickly steadied himself and made a lightning-fast dash for the back door.

But it wasn't fast enough. He had almost reached safety when the beast was on him, spinning him around, pinning him to the wet grass.

His loud scream came out as a whimper. 'Please, please, I beg you, please.'

Two vicious malevolent eyes stared at him from behind a terrifying black mask.

'Oh Jesus – please – please – don't.'

He had barely gotten the words out, when he recognised his assailant. 'Jesus Christ!'

It was Satan! The hound from hell! Well, next door.

The huge Rottweiler snorted and snuffled behind its restraining muzzle. Then it whined piteously before settling down heavily on his chest.

It took two full minutes for JC to regain his equilibrium. Then he punched the animal off his chest and staggered towards the house. Satan followed him, whining continuously.

'Shut up, you stupid mutt.' He kept his voice low, still conscious of the other terrifying predators at the front door.

The dog whined louder, and raised a massive paw to tear at the restricting muzzle. The watery eyes pleaded with JC.

'No way. You've got to wear it.'

The dog whined again. Louder.

A light went on two doors down.

The dog raised its head again. JC quickly reached behind its ears and began to unbuckle the muzzle. With one quick shake, the dog flung the offending leather halfway across the garden. He then stretched his huge neck and gave a blood curdling wolf-like howl before following JC into the darkened house.

JC fumbled around in the dark until he found a candle. The reporters would be watching for any sign of life. He wasn't going to give it to them.

The huge Rottweiler padded around the house as surefooted as if it were broad daylight.

JC found some cold chicken and half an apple tart in the fridge. He shared both of them with the grateful dog.

He then followed the animal up the unlit stairway.

They both slept soundly through the night.

# CHAPTER 9

FATHER DENNY'S Sunday sermon was on false prophets. His normally quiet tones, reverberated loudly around the vaulted ceilings, before echoing back to assault the ears of startled Mass-goers. Father Denny was extremely angry.

He pointed an accusing finger at his congregation. 'What profit it a man if he gains the whole world yet loses his immortal soul?'

The church was silent.

'Speak out!' he commanded. 'Speak out against false prophets. Those who do not, are as ... idolators.' He thumped the ornate pulpit rail.

Ten feet below him, in the third pew, a startled infant gave a loud wail. Its embarrassed mother, a visitor to the town, hushed it as best she could, but the baby wouldn't be comforted and continued to sob quietly to itself.

Directly behind Father Denny, a huge stone Christ, its flaming red heart exposed to the world, stood silent witness, its stone tears petrified in misery.

'First I am the Lord thy God ...' Father Denny thundered, causing the baby to wail loudly again.

The stone Christ wept on silently.

'Thou shalt not have strange gods before me.' He drew a deep breath. 'False prophets are the spawn of the devil!'

The congregation shifted uneasily. There was a wave of throat-clearing. A sudden burst of communal coughing.

Father Denny knew he had struck a nerve. He glared furiously at the coughers, daring them to continue. They were silent.

'Allow them to touch you and you will surely be tainted with the evil which gave rise to them in the first place!'

Young Curate, who was sitting at the side of the altar, blanched visibly.

'That taint of evil will not wash away easily. It clings to the soul of men, burning its evil stain, so when the day of judgement finally comes, the mark will be visible for all to see.'

Father Denny had been prepared to forgive JC for not being

a churchgoer. He was prepared to forgive his mother for her ungodly fortune telling; the woman did have to earn a living after all. He might even turn a blind eye to the odd laying-on of hands, but from the moment he heard that the boy claimed to 'bring back the dead', the line had been crossed. This was blasphemy. Father Denny had no choice but to denounce him from the pulpit.

'Those who turn to false prophets will burn in the flames of hell for all eternity! And', he paused, 'they will not be welcome in this church.'

There was a stunned silence in the church. Even the unhappy baby held its breath.

Father Denny could smell victory. It was working. The old missionaries had been right. The threat of hellfire and damn-ation was still the best way to bring them to their senses. Why hadn't he thought of this before? Like a too-lenient parent you could lose respect by being too tolerant, too liberal. The old ways had a lot to recommended them after all.

There was a sudden commotion in the front pew. Mrs Ashe noisily gathered her prayer book and rosary beads and stood up. Her flame-red hair glowing like a beacon under the church lights, she busily shepherded the now womanly looking Tish into the centre aisle. They stood together as Mrs Ashe beck-oned to her husband, who was in the second pew. As he was a rather rotund man and had been sitting at the enclosed end, at least nine other people had to shuffle to their feet to allow him to pass. Father, mother and daughter then genuflected low towards the high altar before marching single file down the long church aisle, their best Sunday shoes tapping a hollow beat with each step.

A low murmur rippled around the congregation. Heads nodded, and necks strained as the curious watched the self-conscious little parade depart.

'Brethren,' Father Denny reprimanded.

Before he could continue, the Gerber twins and their four siblings were led out of their pew by their widowed mother. The two girls and their lookalike sisters walked, heads respect-fully lowered, down the aisle and out the door. Their mother, still wearing her two-year-old black mourning coat, walked with her head held defiantly high. The heavy church doors slammed behind them.

From the sacristy, behind the altar, the elderly church warden, whose pain-wracked stoop had been a feature of the parish for years, stepped out, and walked proudly down the church, displaying his now ramrod-straight posture for all to see and wonder at.

'My dear brethren,' Father Denny was visibly shaken now and his voice had lost its authoritative ring, 'we must – we must be forever vigilant.' He paused, almost forgetting his text, then quickly recovered, 'against the forces of evil.'

One complete pew emptied as its occupants, all women and children, walked noisily out of the church.

Father Denny stood, his sermon now totally forgotten, gazing in horror as his congregation dwindled before his eyes.

FATHER DENNY was beginning to drink. Not just the odd glass of sherry before a meal. Nor the remnants of the altar wine that had been his usual fare for most of his priestly life. Nor the usual hot toddy before bedtime to encourage restful sleep. Or even the small brandy after dinner, to facilitate digestion. He was beginning to drink seriously. And frequently. And openly.

Empty whiskey bottles began to litter the parish house.

They turned up in the swing bin in the kitchen. In the coal scuttle by the fireplace. Under the cushions of his favourite chair. They stood brazenly on the kitchen dresser and came rolling out from under his bed when a long-flexed vacuum nozzle was sent in to search out hidden dust.

His housekeeper carefully collected them, soaked them in hot water to speed up the removal of their labels and then deposited them in the green bottle bank outside the new supermarket.

She had no intention of allowing nosy bin men to chortle over the evidence of Father Denny's little aberration; nor of allowing them to gloat over his human frailties in the local pubs. She had never encouraged gossip about her employer. It was a mark of honour with her. She might confide her worries about him to her neighbours over a cup of tea. She might voice her concerns about his wellbeing to her bingo-playing friends. But she never gossiped. She prided herself on that.

The nuns who lovingly dressed the church altar, and dutifully tended to Father Denny's vestments, began to notice an unpleasant odour clinging to both. But being wise virgins of long tradition, they kept their own counsel, meantime remaining downwind of the good Father whenever possible.

His once immaculate cassock now began to reek slightly in spite of the diligent efforts of the saintly nuns. It was fast becoming shabby and stained, and carried a sad aura of neglect. As did Father Denny himself.

Young Curate, on the other hand was blossoming. The once shy and self-effacing young man was becoming robust in every sense of the word. He strode purposefully about the parish, shoulders back, handsome head held high.

'He walks like a mitred bishop,' the gravedigger was heard to remark.

His new air of self-confidence drew people to him. The regular Saturday confession-goers, whose numbers had dwindled as drastically as the Mass-goers', began to rise discernably. The startling thing was that the queues all formed outside Young Curate's box. He had difficulty getting through them, while Father Denny sat in his box in lonely solitude.

But Father Denny wasn't exactly unhappy. Of course he wasn't exactly sober either. But ever since the Sunday of his 'big sermon' he was resigned to his fate. If the people wanted a young showman and miraculous cures, for now, then so be it. Father Denny had seen other fads come and go, and at sixty-one he could afford to wait out this one. And if the parishioners preferred to confess to a handsome, virile young priest, well, nothing new there. It had long been noted in church circles that the more physically attractive a priest might be, the more he tended to attract penitents. That was the way of it.

If one must confess one's frailties to one's Creator, on bended knee, then let it be before a pleasing specimen of His handiwork. If one must accuse oneself of all kinds of misdemeanours, and speak of forbidden forays into the delights of the flesh, then let it be within the sight of a pair of eyes that looked as if they too could know temptation.

Father Denny drank from the small bottle which he kept in the corner of the confessional box. He read contentedly from his office while further down the church a continuous stream of people stepped in and out of Young Curate's box, busily plying him with their sins and their problems.

No, Father Denny wasn't exactly unhappy.

*

APART FROM his popularity in the confessional, Young Curate was also in great demand at parish meetings. Mass-going figures might be down, but the same stalwart ladies who were known to be the hardest workers at every parish function kept up their attendance at parish meetings.

Young Curate knew that without these unpaid volunteers, the whole parish infrastructure might well weaken to the point of collapse. He felt, therefore, that it behoved every man of the cloth to show kindness and consideration, if not actual familiarity, to these exemplary figures. There was also no denying the fact that all this new-found attention was extremely flattering.

Blushing committee ladies vied with each other to offer him their latest titbit, straight from their hot ovens.

Forceful matrons changed and shifted the position of their folding chairs in order to place themselves in his clear line of vision. Especially when wearing their real imitation-silk suits, or their newest, almost flesh-coloured tights.

Bold looks were thrown, and sometimes a feminine hand lingered just a little too long on his black suited shoulder, or hesitated a fraction before relinquishing his firm handshake.

Boyfriends, fiancés, and husbands, even when in close attendance, appeared quite oblivious to these subtle manoeuvres. But Young Curate himself was only too painfully aware of them.

Was this the price he had to pay for his cure? This discomfort when in the company of attractive women? Was he being punished for his vanity in wanting to be a whole man?

When one young wife leaned across him to hand out fresh jellied doughnuts, and her soft young breasts pressed into his back, he wondered if he should have remained as God made him. Lopsided and imperfect. And impervious to temptation.

For Young Curate was absolutely devoted to his celibacy. It was central to his being. To what he was. What he wished to be. He had no desire to be anything but a celibate for the Lord.

That night he checked his new testicle. It was intact and firm. But was it his imagination, or had it grown bigger? He fell asleep holding on to it, checking and re-checking it for size and structure. And durability.

In his sleep he became a referee in a ball game. But this was no ordinary ball game. In this one, JC and God were the only two players, each one competing with the other to gain possession of his new testicle. They were grabbing and pulling at it, cruelly ignoring the fact that it was still attached to his body. JC was wearing his beautiful kaftan and God was even more pre-possessing in a long white robe embroidered with golden stars.

They danced around each other like TV wrestlers, flinging wild insults, and abuse, not one word of which Young Curate could make out because the audience of crazed women was yelling so loudly.

The women all wore identical hats and sensible tweed suits. Their faces tended to blur and shift, becoming interchangeable, difficult to separate one from the other, yet he recognised at least two of them from the parish committee.

They were shouting obscenities, but whether at God or JC he couldn't tell. They all had plain country faces. None of them could remotely compare in beauty with either God or JC, who were both ethereal and earthy, all at once. They were fire and water and …

God and JC both grabbed at his scrotum, and began pulling. Young Curate screamed in agony, trying to escape their grasping hands. Suddenly there was another hand in the game. But this one was on his forehead. He screamed again, louder this time.

'What is it son? What is it?'

He was in his own bed and Father Denny was standing over him, his big countryman's hand smoothing his forehead.

'Is it a nightmare you had?'

Young Curate looked up into the tired lined face, and wished he could tell him. But that could never be. Father Denny would never understand. Sexuality was a foreign country to him. All he knew about was running a parish. And that was fast slipping away from him.

EVEN IN his waking hours Young Curate was haunted by JC.

Stories of his healing were everywhere. Not a single night passed but there was some mention of him on one news programme or another. Weeping mothers, wailing children, pubescent girls: they all had their stories to tell. Encouraged by carefully coiffured interviewers with heavily made-up, bland faces, the plain people of Ireland laid bare their souls in an outpouring of televised passion. With little or no prompting they told tales of lives that had been blighted by some terrible physical failing, and that were now happily spent in celebration and joy, thanks to the intervention of 'The Healer'.

68

Old men appeared on camera, displaying strong supple limbs that a healthy eighteen-year-old might envy. Yet these same limbs had once been withered and deformed by crippling arthritis, their owners proudly boasted. The interviewers nodded busily, barely stopping to check their profiles on the studio monitors.

After watching scores of such interviews, Young Curate couldn't help but notice that there appeared to be a predominance of young and beautiful girls giving testament to JC's gift. Of course TV's insatiable appetite, for the young and beautiful could account for this. But on the other hand, perhaps JC's healing warranted closer scrutiny.

Young Curate became so caught up with this idea that he fell asleep for the first time in weeks without thinking about how young Mrs Finnegan's breasts heaved when she led the church choir in the Hallelluia chorus. Or how the muscular thighs of the girls on the hockey team seemed immune to the cold. Even when the girls wore the shortest of gym skirts.

In his dream that night, God won the ball game. He trounced JC a glorious two-nil.

# CHAPTER 10

SATAN THE ROTTWEILER took up permanent residence with JC. Uninvited. He simply refused to leave. His owner tried everything, short of dynamite, to shift him. Nothing worked. He refused to budge.

He followed JC around the house all day, watching his every move with adoring eyes. The rest of humankind, at least those he came into contact with, he appeared to view with barely concealed hatred.

Most of all, he hated Mother.

She had finally arrived home from the hospital to the welcoming arms of a delighted JC and the bared teeth of a salivating Satan. No words could convince her that he meant her no harm. And no amount of pleading could make the sullen Satan offer her the paw of friendship. She wanted him out. As in all things, JC gave way to her wishes, the only stipulation being that Mother would have to get rid of the dog herself. And that's how Satan came to live with them.

They kept out of each others way as much as possible, Satan and Mother. The Rottweiler found it politic to spend his time in JC's room when he wasn't busily patrolling the garden. The reporters had by now discovered the back entrance to the house, yet they all wisely gave it a wide berth. Especially the English one who had previously boasted long and loud about his natural rapport with animals. Satan, for his part, was scrupulously fair to all the pressmen; he threatened them all with equal ferocity.

Only to JC did the dog ever show his soft underbelly.

Literally so. He would lie on his back, huge paws threading the air in a canine invitation to play.

JC didn't need much persuading. He would dart towards the massive dog, feigning pretend slaps to the dribbling jowls. The dog would then leap to his feet, and bound around him barking excitedly, until JC threw his full weight across him and they both fell over in a threshing heap on the carpet.

Mother hated these games. She watched them with her lips pursed tightly, wringing her hands till the knuckles showed

71

white. She would frequently remark on the dog's great age, and then wonder aloud just how long these large dogs tended to live, on average.

JC locked Satan in the house when they went to conduct healing sessions. The days of holding them in Mother's room were long past. The huge numbers attending now couldn't possibly be facilitated in a private house.

He would have liked to take the dog with him to the sessions. But with crowds of over-excited people scrambling for places and attention, it was hardly a place for a dog. Satan always howled when being left. But only until JC was out of earshot. Or so the next-door neighbour said. He reported that once the car disappeared around the corner, the dog snoozed the evening away. JC wanted to believe him.

One freezing winter night he felt particularly bad about leaving Satan. The dog had been uneasy all day. Grizzly. He didn't look any unhappier than usual. But that would have been difficult, given that his usual expression was one of total misery. Even when he was well fed and content.

After tea, he had tried his usual trick of staring pitifully into JC's eyes, his own soft brown doggy ones brimming with what looked uncannily like tears. Then he flopped down on the ground, giving little pathetic whimpers. And finally when JC was leaving, he skulked behind the sofa howling like a bereaved banshee.

THEY WERE sitting in the car before Mother passed any remark about the dog's behaviour. 'You'll have to get rid of him, he's a bad-tempered beast.'

'He was upset tonight for some reason.'

'Upset? That dog is a born actor. He should be up in the Abbey Theatre.'

But JC was uneasy. There was something different about Satan's howling tonight.

'Better take that scowl off your face. People expect you to look happy. They depend on you to lift their spirits.'

JC looked out of the car window. The brightly lit hall they were approaching would hold at least two thousand souls, yet the crowds waiting outside must have numbered almost twice that. They stood patiently in a long winding queue, their breath billowing like exhaled smoke on the frosty air.

He could see lines of young people, their faces reddened by the bitterly cold wind, their feet tapping a warming staccato against the freezing pavement. And huddled against what shelter they could find were groups of elderly people, some obviously sick or in discomfort, others appearing healthy enough. Yet each and every one of them carried the same expression on their face. It was one of hope and expectation. All of them were, without exception, hoping for a miracle of some sort, and most of them, he knew, were here against the advise of their doctors, and in some cases, their priests.

He felt a surge of pity for them. All of them.

'Stop the car!'

The driver turned to look inquiringly, not at him, but at Mother.

'I said, stop the car.'

'Are you sure ...?' the driver began nervously.

'Don't be ridiculous.' Mother's tone was scathing.

'Do as I say.'

'Jessie, if we stop here they'll trample you. Look at the size of that crowd!'

JC reached for the door handle.

'Stop ... stop.' Mother grabbed at his hand.

The car screeched to a stop.

JC was out of the car before the bewildered driver could turn round.


A YOUNG GIRL of about fifteen was the first to spot him.

'It's him! Look! It's him!'

She ran towards him, her long pale hair streaming out on the wind.

'It is you?' Gazing up into his face, she began calling, 'It's him, over here, it's him.'

Muffled figures broke away from the queue. They moved slowly at first, hesitantly. Then they began hurrying, the more able-bodied of them running, rushing to be the first to reach him.


HE THREW off his coat and began touching heads, faces, bodies. He tried particularly to reach the elderly, the ones he had seen from the car. But it was difficult, impossible; there were just too many people. And there were more and more arriving by the second, crying out for him to touch them, to bless their children, their loved ones. He was being engulfed by a swarm of pleading humanity.

'Don't push,' he cried, 'don't push.'

But his cry went unheeded. Perhaps the people at the back misunderstood, because they pushed even harder, forcing the front of the crowd closer and closer to him.

There was no escape. Behind him towered the remains of what had once been a thriving flour mill. It was derelict now, its windows and doors solidly blocked up against any would-be trespassers. In front of him the compacting crowd was making any forward movement impossible.

He could feel the rough-edged granite blocks of the mill wall pressing hard into his back, tearing at the fabric of the kaftan as the crowd swept him backwards.

His breath was being forced from his body. Yet the crowd kept on coming. Even when there was no more space, they kept on coming. The young girl who had first seen him was being sucked into the throng. Her face was turning purple. She was gasping for air, struggling, there was another great surge forward and she was lifted by it until her face was on a level with his.

That's when he knew she was dead. Her cold bloated face was pushed against his, her ice-blue eyes stared, unseeing, straight into his.

And still the crowd surged forward.

'For God's sake, move back!'

Then it happened. He couldn't tell exactly how – one minute he was fighting for breath – on the ground – feeling the life being crushed out of his body – and the next he was rising into the air. Without any thought or effort on his part he was levitating, his feet leaving the ground, his whole body rising upwards – above the pleading faces – up over their heads, up, up – until he could see out across the huge crowd – see the startled upturned faces – all staring – wide-eyed – all looking towards him.

Hands grabbed at his feet, at the hem of the kaftan. They were pulling at him, tearing. He felt a shoe being dragged from his foot. He looked for the girl, but he couldn't see her anymore – just hundreds of blurred faces – and pale hands – all reaching out to him.

Someone was screaming – voices were calling his name – repeating it. They were chanting. The noise was unbearable – agonising, his eardrums – were about to explode.

Then suddenly it was all fading. The crowd was disappearing. He was leaving them behind – being drawn into a white, whirling vortex where the light was brighter than anything he had ever known, and he was falling into it …

THE LIGHT was hurting his eyes. It was blinding him.

'No!' He raised a hand to block it.

'JC?'

'It hurts!'

'Open your eyes, JC.'

'No!' Whatever this was, he wasn't ready.

He hadn't wanted to die – not like that poor girl – dead eyes staring – vacant – unseeing. He wasn't ready for that. 'I can't die. I …'

'You're not dead! Open your eyes.' The voice sounded impatient. 'You're here in the hospital!'

He opened his eyes slowly, carefully squinting into the light.

Two tall white figures stood over him. One was definitely an angel. The other one had a stethoscope hanging around his neck!

'I'm not dead?'

The angel smiled and shook her head. Her eyes were the exact aquamarine of the tropical oceans that sometimes washed his dreams.

He gave a long sigh, and passed out again.

# CHAPTER 11

MOTHER WAS keeping something from him.

She re-arranged the already perfectly arranged flowers. She then attempted to straightened the ramrod-straight sheets, and care-fully brushed invisible specks from his pyjama-clad shoulders. She offered him cool drinks from the selection of bottles standing on the hospital locker.

The only thing she didn't do was meet his eyes.

'I knew it,' she was mumbling, 'we should never have started this. Never. I knew it would end badly. I knew!'

He asked about the girl, but Mother was adept at changing the subject. 'I could have lost you. Another couple of minutes, they said, and ...' One large solitary tear bounced down her cheek. She wiped it away brusquely, and then kissed him over and over. Then she straightened the sheets again.

He asked the nurses about the girl. They said they would ask the doctors.

He wasn't allowed any visitors, except for Mother. For his own safety, they said. Safety? In a hospital bed? How could he be unsafe in a hospital bed? Surely a hospital bed was the safest place in the whole world? In the universe? And what was he being kept safe from?

Mother kept forgetting to bring him a newspaper.

The staff told him that the TV set in his room didn't work.

He had to know if the girl was really dead. He had to know if he was to blame. He had a right to know if he was a murderer.

On his second night in the hospital the angel appeared at his bedside again. He knew she would tell him the truth. She did.

The girl who was crushed by the crowd wasn't dead. Her name was Ann O'Neill and she was alive. She was fifteen years old.

He hugged the angel in gratitude and happiness.

She then told him that Ann O'Neill was in this very hospital, in a deep coma. She was being kept alive by life-sustaining machines that were the pride and joy of Ballysheel hospital. Without this wondrous technology it was doubtful that she'd have survived. But the angel didn't hold out much hope for her recovery. 'Her EEG lines don't look promising,' she remarked. 'It might have been better if she had died outright, like the old man.'

'What old man?'

'The old man who died during the riot outside the hall. Now come on JC, just two more pills.' She held out a small plastic tray. 'No, he wasn't crushed. He wasn't even in any danger of being crushed. But the excitement of it all was too much for him. And of course, he did have a dicky heart. Now will you swallow your pills?'

His teeth chattered against the glass that she held to his mouth.

'Of course he was very old. But then again the doctors said that, barring excitement, he could have lasted another ten years. Maybe even longer!'

The angel picked up her drugs tray, smiled at him and left.

His head was spinning. He felt sick. He couldn't properly digest either the pills or the information the angel had just given him.

The girl, the girl was alive, only just, but some old man that he had never even heard of had died – because of him – because of the 'riot' outside the hall.

So he was a murderer.

Mother had tried to prevent him getting out of the car. She had known what would happen, but he wouldn't listen – even the driver had – Jesus Christ, even Satan had a premonition that something terrible was about to happen, but he wouldn't listen, not to anyone. If he had really wanted to help those people he should have waited until they were all safely inside the hall. Mother knew that, that's why she had tried to stop him, but he wouldn't listen, and now he had a death on his conscience.

The pills the angel had given him were making him drowsy, soft fuzzy clouds were taking over his head, but he fought against them. He had to think clearly; find some way to make things right, but his eyelids were lead weights forcing him into ...

He sat up rigid in the bed.

He could save the girl! The doctors mightn't hold out much hope, but he could save her – of course he could – he had brought Mother back to life, hadn't he? He would save the girl, heal her. His eyelids closed.

\*

NEXT MORNING everyone remarked on how much better he looked.

Even Mother had to agree.

'Dangerously healthy,' was her comment when she caught him pacing excitedly up and down the room.

And no, she hadn't forgotten to bring in the kaftan. His early-morning phone call had taken her by surprise, but here it was.

She almost threw the large plastic bag across the bed, giving a little shiver of distaste as she did so.

Yet when he removed the kaftan from the bag, JC saw that all the tiny tears at the back had been stitched over so painstakingly that they were practically invisible. Only a dedicated or a very loving hand could have completed such work.

He hooked the heavily padded hanger on to a protruding nail that jutted out just above the tall hospital window, and stood back to admire the kaftan.

Its long shimmering folds appeared to cascade down the window like a rich golden waterfall. And with the morning sun shining behind it, outlining its full length, the whole effect was magical.

He reached out with an exploring finger.

Behind him Mother gave a loud cough.

After she left, he lay gazing at it for a long time.

He hardly noticed the pain of his bruised ribs. He hardly noticed the comings and goings of the nursing staff. His whole attention was taken up with the kaftan.

'It looks ... holy!' The little blonde nurse stood, hands clasped, in front of it.

JC concentrated on the kaftan and ignored her.

She had barely left the room when a porter arrived, holding a young probationer by the arm.

'Go on. Ask him.' The porter nudged her towards JC.

The girl nervously produced a photo which she pushed into JC's hand.

He continued to stare at the kaftan.

'It's my mother, she has cancer.'

He looked down at the picture. A hugely overweight woman smiled cheerfully from the photograph, proudly displaying a wide gap left by two missing front teeth. Her mischievous eyes seemed to say, 'So what? ... Life is good.'

JC turned to the nurse.

'That was taken six months ago, she doesn't look like that any more.' The girl was on the verge of tears.

He closed his eyes. He held the photo, and tried to visualise the woman, laughing, dismissing her illness. It wasn't difficult. The face in the photo wasn't the face of someone who gave in easily.

'Tell her,' he opened his eyes, 'she'll get better. Tell her to do as her doctor says.' He handed the photo back to the trembling girl.

She caught his hand and kissed it. 'Thank you. Thank you. They said you'd help. I love you!' She ran out of the room crying.

Her forgotten companion stood watching JC for a few seconds. His narrowed eyes were brimming over with pure unadulterated hatred.

THE HOSPITAL wasn't yet ready to discharge him. This suited JC perfectly. He needed a place to think.

Mother didn't mention, but he could imagine, the swarms of newsmen that must be camping on his doorstep. If he was news fodder before, he must be headline material now there was a death on his hands. Nothing excited newsmen more than a sudden mysterious death. And someone to point an accusing finger at.

But he was safe from them here. On the private floor of the hospital, visitors were rigorously vetted by the nursing staff. And newsmen were definitely not welcomed.

He demanded a working television set, and, lo and behold, it turned out that all the set in his room needed was a slight adjustment. The porter plugged it in.

His own face greeted him on the one o'clock news.

Apparently he was comfortable. And being kept in for further tests. The newsreader didn't elaborate on the nature of the tests.

JC tried another channel.

Depending on which channel he tuned into, he heard himself variously described as 'a man of God', 'a conman', 'the new Messiah'. Or, most disturbing of all, 'a schizophrenic'.

He was still reeling from the last opinion when the parents of the comatose girl appeared on screen. They were tearful but restrained, clutching each other for support.

Speaking with quiet dignity, they both agreed that they didn't hold anybody responsible for their daughter's 'accident'.

'People were simply carried away by ... by the moment,' the mother said. She disclosed that she herself had been the one seeking a cure that night. She had gone to the hall early hoping to secure a place at the top of the queue. Her daughter was to follow on later. She had wanted to study for her French orals first.

'She's aiming for six honours in her Junior Cert,' the girl's father added proudly. 'She's very ambitious. Her dream is to work for the Common Market.'

They never had met up that night.

'Maybe, if I had waited for her?' The mother's voice trailed off.

Her husband placed a comforting arm around her shoulders.

The reporter swung away from the suffering parents, to confide in hushed tones to the camera, that there was to be an inquiry into these 'healing sessions'.

'People are demanding answers!' he solemnly announced. 'Answers as to how a so-called "healing session" could lead to a riot that left one old man dead, and a beautiful young girl with her life hanging by a mere thread.' He paused for half a second, then continued. 'The families of Thomas Nolan and Ann O'Neill deserve answers to these questions! This is Seán Murphy, reporting from Ballysheel.'

Onto the screen flashed a likeness of a smiling Ann O'Neill, reclining on a sun-baked strand. Her tiny bikini was a garish greeny yellow. Her long hair was pinned up on top of her head making her appear older than her years. She was looking directly into the camera, holding her smile patiently.

JC waited, but no likeness of Thomas Nolan appeared.

He changed the channel. Here, Ann O'Neill was smiling again, but this time she was gap-toothed, and holding a small puppy in her arms. She was about ten years old.

Ann's picture made way for an unseasonably tanned presenter, who was nodding emphatically towards a serious-looking man in a dark suit.

'In your experience, doctor, what type of person is likely to ...' he waved a slim hand, 'seek out a', his hand waved, disdainfully this time, 'healer?'

The serious-looking man frowned seriously, then drew in a long thoughtful breath. 'Well ...'

The presenter leaned towards him. 'I mean are they likely to be the less well educated?' His tone implied that this might well place them on the intellectual level of endangered baboons.

'Well ...' The interviewee frowned, giving the question serious consideration.

The presenter's slim finger rose nervously towards his ear. 'In other words ...' he prompted.

'Well ... that might be one interpretation ... but in fact ... statistics show us that ... the likelihood of any one of us approaching ... or indeed turning to ... or being directed ... you see we must be careful not to assume ...'

JC switched the set off.

HE COULDN'T just walk into intensive care to get to the girl. He knew that.

There were strong feelings about him in this hospital. Not all good. Some of the medical staff had made that patently clear.

But it wasn't the ones who regarded him as a phoney that worried him. Their concern appeared to be primarily for the welfare of their patients.

It was the others that he had to be wary of. The ones who saw healing as their sole domain. And woe betide anyone who dared infringe on their territory. Their beloved market forces didn't apply here. They would brook no opposition. He knew that. And they gave no quarter.

But not all the staff were against him. The heart specialist whose wife was expecting their first child was on his side. For not only had his wife conceived after one healing session with JC, but she had also stopped decimating their shared bank balance.

To a frugal man, this was the biggest miracle of all. He told JC that he would be forever in his debt. Which position he much preferred than to being in the bank's.

Mother finally brought in the Sunday papers. Every single edition carried a feature on him. Details of his life were splashed across double-page spreads. Stories about his childhood that were heart-wrenching, touching and mostly untrue.

People who had been queuing outside the hall that night

vied with each other in print to tell the most colourful story.

Eye-witnesses told of seeing him cure people with a mere touch of his hand. Others said he held back a crowd of thousands with one finger. He was seen to levitate until he rose twenty feet above the flour mill.

One woman insisted that he had transmogrified into the Virgin Mary before her very eyes.

Others swore that they had clearly seen his heart beating outside his body. Surrounded by glowing red flames.

A young hospital doctor interviewed at length said that JC was a normal young man with, good muscle tone, a strong heart, healthy lungs and a normal pulse rate, and as far as the medical profession could tell, he was as mortal as the rest of them. He had blacked out from a simple lack of oxygen, caused by the pressure from a mass of human bodies pushing against what was after all, simply another fallible human body. He had sustained a couple of bruised ribs, and what was all the fuss about?

If people had seen him rising into the air that wasn't surprising. Given the situation, and the heightened emotional atmosphere of the occasion, the young doctor said he was surprised, that people hadn't seen the Holy Ghost fly past.

Then he added, quietly, according to the paper, 'We shouldn't forget that an old man died that night, and a young girl is still in intensive care.'

When pressed for further medical insight, the doctor said that, in his humble opinion, JC was neither an oracle nor a saint. Nor was he a medicine man, a messiah, or even, as far as he could tell, a Freemason. He was, however, a young man who was in need of some medical attention. And fortunately, he was now in the best place to receive it.

The doctor gave his medical and personal opinion freely, and fully, withholding only his own name which he didn't want published as his mother read this particular paper.

JC felt a lot better after reading that interview. It renewed his faith in the human race. Here was somebody who nailed his colours to the mast. Here was somebody who was prepared to call a spade a spade. So he declined to give his name! Nobody was perfect.

He slept easier that night, than any other since being in the hospital.

Next morning Mother rang to say that Satan had disappeared. He had simply leaped over the back gate and legged it.

'Did you report it?'

'Who to?'

'The gardaí, Mother.'

'They have better things to do than look for a dog who doesn't know when he's well off.'

'It's their job.'

'Don't be ridiculous!'

That night JC dreamed about Satan.

He was drowning in a sea of human faces when Satan swam alongside and rescued him. The young doctor from the newspaper interview was standing on the shore, calling out to a huge crowd: 'His body is perishable. It's mortal! But his heart isn't human. His blood pressure is non-existent, and he doesn't have a soul. Throw him back in.'

But Satan wouldn't allow the gathering crowd anywhere near him. He stood by JC snarling, fending off all comers.

He was abruptly woken by the angel asking if he needed a sleeping pill. She said there was a vicious-looking dog roaming the hospital grounds. His barking was disturbing the patients, keeping them awake. The gardaí had been called.

At first he thought this was all part of his dream, then he heard Satan howl.

He leaped out of bed and pushed the window open. In the garden below, the dog howled out a greeting.

The angel called off the gardaí. Then she rang Mother.

'A man answered the phone,' she reported back to JC. 'He said he would collect Satan, and you're not to worry.'

So JC lay awake worrying for most of the night. He regretted not taking a sleeping pill.

# CHAPTER 12

IT WAS the angel who got him into intensive care.

'The small hours of the morning, that's the best time,' she said. 'Everybody's guard is at its lowest then.'

They crept silently along the quiet corridor. The hospital tiles felt cold and hostile to his bare feet, in contrast to the warmth of the kaftan against his skin.

The nurse on duty was expecting them, but even so, she stared curiously at him when he walked into the narrow room, and her plump face flushed bright red when he squeezed past her to get to the girl.

The figure on the bed looked smaller than he remembered. Thinner. She resembled more the child in the TV photograph, than the young woman who had smiled flirtatiously at the camera as she posed in the brief bikini.

Of the vibrant girl who had confronted him outside the hall there wasn't a trace.

Her eyes were half open. Or half closed. They were a peculiar blank white, with no discernible colour showing at all. Not even a trace of iris or pupil peered from beneath the half-drawn lids.

It gave her a strange eerie look. The plethora of tubes and wires, attached to her at all angles, didn't help. This was a rejected little puppet, cruelly discarded by a giant hand.

JC bent over her. He touched her face.

He was calling her name when he saw her chest move slightly. He looked hopefully at the angel. She shook her head.

He called the girl's name again. Louder this time.

'Ann? Ann O'Neill? Can you hear me, Ann?'

The only answer was the constant rhythmic beep from a machine that resembled nothing that he had ever seen or heard before, yet he knew that its electronic beat was carefully imitating a living pulse.

It sounded almost human.

But he had no sense of anything human inhabiting the room. He touched the girl's pale forehead. It was warm. She was alive. But he felt no sense of life, no connection, no energy.

Nothing.

The nurses watched him, nervously, the shift nurse glancing uneasily towards the door every now and again.

JC closed his eyes and willed the girl to respond. But he knew it wouldn't happen. He picked up her hand. It wasn't cold, as he half-expected, but it was dead. He held the childish hand between both of his, and once more willed his energy into it. It remained flaccid and lifeless between his palms. He placed it gently back on the bed.

He could do nothing here.

He turned abruptly, and left the room.

The angel called softly after him.


HE REFUSED breakfast the next morning. He didn't touch his lunch. When Mother arrived he asked to be left alone.

At four o'clock, the news was all over the hospital

The girl had died. Or rather, the doctors had switched the machine off.

At four-ten, JC discharged himself.

Ballysheel's one and only taxi driver sucked noisily on his teeth and stared belligerently at him in the rear-view mirror. JC paid no heed.

There was a small group of newsmen pacing up and down outside his house, swinging their arms and stamping their feet in vain efforts at keeping warm. They surrounded the taxi, voices calling out in a rough male chorus.

He paid what he knew was a ridiculously inflated fare for such a short journey. The taxi driver sat defiantly still sucking at his teeth, while JC held his painful ribs with one hand, and dragged his large case from the cab with the other.

The newsmen buzzed around unhelpfully, aiming cameras at him from every angle.

He pushed his way silently through them, ignoring the non-stop questions that were fired at him. At the door he dropped his case, then turned to face them.

'Ann O'Neill died a few minutes ago.'

The buzzing stopped for a second. Was it his imagination, or did he see pity flit across the hardened faces around him?


MOTHER HUGGED him so tightly, she made him wince. Then she apologised repeatedly until his head ached.

Satan, unable to cope with such a joyous reunion, tore hysterically around the kitchen, howling his welcome.

The red-haired photographer, who was actually standing drinking tea in the kitchen ordered Satan to sit. To JC's amazement the dog obeyed him instantly.

It was a strange homecoming.

The redhead moved about the kitchen with an easy familiarity. He rinsed out his tea cup and set it to drain on the sink. JC watched in disbelief as he lit up a cigarette without a word of protest from Mother.

'Hugh ...' she indicated the redhead, 'Hugh thinks you would be better off to give a proper press release to the journalists. They have my heart broken,' she said in explanation.

'It would get them off your back. At least some of them.' Hugh blew out a trail of cigarette smoke. 'I know how their minds work.'

He winked at Mother and laughed. Mother almost smiled at him. Even Satan looked marginally less miserable.

The strangest thing of all was that Hugh hadn't lifted a camera since JC walked in. Yet both his cameras were within reach. They were lying on the dresser, side by side, their straps hanging down in perfect unison, almost intertwined.

The other journalists had practically clambered over each other to get a shot of him entering the house. And here was the hungriest of them all, on the inside, seeming more intent on blowing smoke rings at Satan than on capturing him on film.

This was the strangest homecoming.

Mother produced thick slices of Battenberg and offered one to JC. She poured him tea, in one of the best china cups.

Hugh blew smoke rings.

Satan slept.

SOMETIME DURING the night JC woke up screaming. Yet try as he might, he couldn't recall what had frightened him so much.

Mother gave him two of his prescribed pain-killers and a mug of hot milk.

The next morning he couldn't move his legs. He was about to call out when Satan raised his huge head and shifted his weight lazily from across his ankles.

He stayed in bed all that day. And the next. Mother tried tempting him down to the kitchen with all sorts of fancies. Nothing worked.

She told him that there was great sympathy for him in the town. She said that hardly anyone blamed him for what had happened. She said that nobody blamed him for what had happened – well, only a few stupid, ignorant people, those with their own axe to grind. She pursed her lips and looked off into the middle distance.

It was a look that JC was becoming familiar with.

She said that if he didn't believe her, he had only to watch the news. Even the newscasters wore a sad sympathetic look whenever his name was mentioned. Which was a lot. An awful lot.

JC had made up his mind to stay in bed for the rest of his life when Mother announced that the gardaí were downstairs looking for him.

He pulled the sheets up over his head. Satan curled up protectively at his feet.

HE WAS almost asleep when the dog leaped up snarling.

Two heavy-set men stood at his open bedroom door. They were two of the shiftiest-looking characters that JC had ever set eyes on. One wore the collar of his grubby mac turned up around his beefy face. He squinted furtively over it, as if expecting to be pounced on at any second.

The other one might have been his twin. Except that his pale mac was immaculate and left jauntily swinging open to display a pristine white shirt, the collar of which was so tight it was threatening to cut off the blood supply to his head. Above the garroting collar his face was, not surprisingly, a mottled brick red, a perfect colour match for the small red notebook carried by his companion.

'This is Detective Murtha and, and, er.' Mother clearly couldn't remember Dirty Mac's name.

'Sergeant Littlewilly.' The little squinting eyes watched Satan, who stood not four feet away, teeth bared to the gums.

'Order that monster out,' Mother said.

Satan gave a final departing growl before obediently padding heavily down the stairs.

Both gardaí visibly relaxed. Murtha smiled at JC. 'How are

88

you feeling, son?'

The friendliness of the tone took JC by surprise.

'I'm ... I'm fine.'

'Good. You'll be back on your feet in no time, then?'

JC didn't answer.

'His ribs are still very painful,' Mother offered.

'Oh yes.' The detective nodded as if he had just recalled JC's crushed ribs. 'But then you were lucky,' he added slyly, 'others didn't get off quite so lightly.'

'That wasn't JC's fault.'

'No, no of course not.' He shook his square head and smiled a wide friendly smile.

JC knew instinctively that if he could, this man would fit him up for everything, from the Flight of the Earls to the Potato Famine.

'Could I sit here?' Detective Murtha indicated the bed.

JC reluctantly moved his feet aside. He should have kept the dog with him.

Sergeant Littlewilly turned down his collar, took a pencil from his pocket, and opened his notebook.

A pencil? Pencil can be rubbed out. Surely straight policemen used pens?

As if he had read JC's mind, Detective Murtha handed a biro to the still fumbling Littlewilly.

'Now son, in your own words, tell us what happened last Wednesday night.'

'We were in the car together ...' Mother began.

'Mrs Ryan, I could murder ... a cup of hot tea,' Detective Murtha smiled again.

Mother stared deafly into the distance, carefully pursing her lips.

The detective smiled again. 'Please?'

JC was now convinced that tea was not the only thing that this smiling man could murder.

Mother made as if to leave but she cannily remained hovering around the doorway.

Detective Murtha sighed in defeat. 'Go ahead, son, tell us what happened.'

WITHOUT ONCE taking his eyes off Mother's face, JC recited the story he had already told over and over again to the doctors, to the angel, and even to Hugh.

Mother nodded encouragingly at every second word.

JC spoke so fast that Sergeant Littlewilly had trouble keeping up. Every few seconds he pleaded, 'If you could just say that again ...'

This was the signal for Mother impatiently to repeat JC's last spoken sentence.

By the time they were halfway through the story, the veins in Detective Murtha's neck were threatening to explode.

JC could feel mad insane giggles beginning to rise in his throat as Mother slowly repeated yet another sentence for the benefit of Sergeant Littlewilly's slow-moving pen.

Unaware of the effect she was having on the senior detective, Mother inquired of the sergeant, 'Got that?'

Still writing, he nodded his massive head, and said carefully. 'I ... was ... being ... crushed ... betwixt ... the ... wall and ...'

It was too much for JC. He doubled over on the bed, almost hysterical with giggles. The harder he tried to contain them, the worse they got.

Mother and Sergeant Littlewilly stared at him in bewilderment.

But Detective Murtha's face was a study in anger. Its brick-red tones turned a furious puce, and the large yellow teeth were bared in a snarl that rivalled anything Satan could produce. This was a pit-bull out for blood.

'Two people are dead because of you, laddie, and you think it's funny?' The last word sent a furious spray of spittle in JC's direction.

Sergeant Littlewilly coughed, raised his pen, and reiterated nervously, 'Betwixt the walls and ...'

JC dived under the bedcovers, choking.

THE GARDAÍ finally left, Sergeant Littlewilly happily clutching his now well-filled little red book.

Detective Murtha was anything but happy. Even his mac had taken on a rumpled aggressive look. He brushed at it impatiently, as if this might wipe away any contamination it could possibly have contracted from JC's bed.

Detective Murtha's dislike of young men was well known. The only people he disliked more than young men were women and girls. Everyone else he could tolerate.

JC watched from his window as the gardaí got into their car. Before it drove away, Detective Murtha glanced back at the house. He was smiling broadly. It was a terrifying sight.

# CHAPTER 13

HUGH LAUGHED till the tears ran down his face. 'God, where do they get them from?'

JC patted Satan's shining coat. 'He definitely didn't like me.'

'No! It wasn't you! That's just the way they speak to all young lads – and journos.' Hugh laughed again. 'I could tell you some stories.'

'You keep your stories to yourself.'

JC hadn't heard Mother use that tone with Hugh before.

But Hugh just laughed. He was a man of permanent good humour.

Maybe the wine helped. They had just finished two bottles between them, Hugh drinking as much as JC and Mother put together. In fact, the time Hugh had begun to spend in the house could well be measured by the lowering stock of wine in the wooden rack above the fridge. Mother had always kept a supply of wine in the house. Even when funds were at their lowest, there was always a glass of wine for her friends. They liked nothing better than to drink chilled wine as they gathered around the kitchen table. JC had always loved the sounds they made. The clinking of their wine glasses. The tinkle of ice as they swished it around in the glass to prevent the wine warming up in the heat of the cosy kitchen. And their voices ... always their voices – rising and falling, soft and secretive sometimes, like the women themselves. They were women who whispered a lot, as if they were wary of being overheard by someone who mustn't be privy to their secrets, someone who might possibly intrude – yet their faces always lit up at the sight of the small boy peering around the kitchen door. Sometimes they would have mock quarrels as to who would hold him next, who would be the next to kiss his soft baby mouth, to caress his fragrant cheek, to brush his silken hair. Even the words they used to describe him were tender, gentle-sounding words. As gentle as the women themselves. Sometimes it was almost like having a whole group of doting mothers. But at the end of the day, he always knew whose child he was. Nobody could ever make him feel as special as Mother did.

He watched her now across the table, as she sat smiling at

Hugh. She looked exactly as she always had. She didn't appear to grow older at all, the way other people did. In fact, sometimes she didn't look much older than the girls he ... the girls. Mother had no idea of what had occurred between him and the girls. It was the one secret he had to keep from her.

He suddenly realised that, except for the young curate, they had never had a man visit them before. Oh, men had come to the house as clients, but that was different. That was Mother's livelihood. That was how they lived. She was well paid for the time she spent with clients. That was business.

But she never spared them one second over their allotted time. Not one second.

It was different with her friends. Nothing was too good for them. They were given all the time in the world. Freely.

But they were all women. Every single one of them.

He had never thought it strange, because that's how their life was. Mother's world, and therefore his, was a world of women. A gentle world filled with love and tenderness and soft whispering sounds.

But now Hugh was here. At Mother's behest. Big, bulky, and loud, his presence was somehow incongruous in Mother's kitchen. It disrupted the pattern. Changed things.

His bellowing laugh rang out loudly now at some remark that Mother had made. Did he really find her remark so funny, or was he just sharing his seemingly endless good humour with whatever company he found himself in?

JC watched him closely. He drank glass after glass of wine with gusto, and to no effect. He was as good-natured on his sober arrival as he was after he had consumed a whole bottle of wine. And he showed no preference for one wine over another, nor did he care which temperature it was served at. He simply opened the bottle and drank.

And he smiled as he drank, making it appear as if his small white teeth were straining the wine before allowing it to pass down his throat.

But unlike Detective Murtha's, Hugh's whole face joined in when he smiled. His blue eyes crinkled up almost to slits, and his sandy eyebrows rose up and down energetically, as if eager to emphasise their solidarity with the whole happy business.

It was hard not to smile back at such a man.

*

HUGH WAS helping JC to draw up the press statement. They were having problems with it. Whenever JC felt that he had it just right, Hugh thought the opposite. And vice versa.

They had been working on it for hours. What to JC had seemed a simple matter of saying how sorry he was for what had happened that night now appeared to be much more complex.

'You can't just say that you apologise for what happened. That's tantamount to admitting that you're to blame for the two deaths.'

'But I am.'

Hugh turned to Mother in exasperation. 'Talk to your son. If he gives out a statement like this, he's accepting culpability. Some smart barrister could massacre him in court.'

'Who is talking about court?'

'JC, you're a babe in arms, son. You don't know the half of it.'

'Half of what? I saw those parents on TV. They said they don't hold anyone responsible for their daughter's "accident", they called it.'

'Wait 'til the dust settles, then see if they don't start yelling for compensation. And if they don't, there's sure to be someone who'll tell them that they owe it to their dead daughter, if not to themselves, to find someone to hold responsible.' Hugh poured himself another drink. 'That's how things are, son. You may find yourselves fighting lawsuits for the rest of your lives.'

Mother said nothing.

'Look, I know how you feel, JC. But you didn't cause those deaths. OK, people were there to see you, but you got out of the car when you did because you felt sorry for them. Right? You couldn't be expected to foretell what would happen. Could you?'

JC glanced nervously at Mother.

'Oh no!' Hugh's face was crinkling up with laughter again. 'Don't try to sell me that one.' He wagged a reproachful finger.

'But I want people to know how sorry I am, and the truth is I do feel responsible. I do!' JC insisted when Mother shook her head in protest.

Hugh threw a comforting arm across his shoulders. 'Listen, son, the crowd lost control that night. You're not responsible for their behaviour.' For once he looked serious. 'If you issue that statement,' he said pointing to the notepad on the table, 'they'll hang you.'

Mother gasped.

'Well, as good as,' he grinned.

IT WAS Mother who suggested the compromise.

JC could give an interview to Hugh. An exclusive interview. He could talk about his gift of healing, how precious it was. How much he valued it. And how he was prepared to abandon it because of what had occurred that night. Through no fault of his! Hugh could see to it that the interview was properly written up, make certain that JC didn't incriminate himself.

'Mother …'

'He'll make sure you're portrayed in a sympathetic light.'

'That's what you think I need, Mother? To be portrayed sympathetically?'

'It's not only your needs that have to be considered,' Hugh said quietly.

JC looked at Mother's worried face and knew he was beaten.

Talking to Hugh about the healing was much easier than he'd expected. Whenever he was at a loss for a word, Hugh quickly filled one in for him.

Hugh had already told Mother that he must be alone with JC if the interview was to work. Mother seemed quite happy with this arrangement. She clearly trusted Hugh. JC felt he had no option but to do the same.

He went right back to the very first 'healing' with Reena.

He described her psoriasis. How ugly it had been. How bad it had made her feel in school. Unwanted and left out. Marked. How the boys had all jeered her about it, calling her Fish Scales.

He also described how beautiful she really was under the psoriasis. How she moved with an easy long-limbed gait through the dingy school corridors, making everyone else appear clumsy and ungainly by comparison.

He told Hugh about her father's sudden death, how badly she had taken it. How he had come across her in the library, weeping as if her heart would break.

He recalled how she had come to the house while Mother was at her circle meeting. He described showing her the kaftan, the effect it had on her. He said that after putting it on he had touched her.

'Touched her?' Hugh sat, pen poised above the writing pad.

'You know, like in a healing session.'

Hugh's eyes crinkled up. He grinned slyly at JC. 'You ... touched her? Like in a healing session?' His shrewd eyes were alive with merriment.

In spite of himself, JC laughed. 'Yes, exactly like in a healing session.'

'You wouldn't kid old Hugh now, would you?' Hugh picked up his brimming wine glass, and stared into it as if he had just discovered something fascinating floating on the top.

'What do you want me to say?' JC could feel his own face breaking into a wide smile.

Without drinking, Hugh put the glass back on the table.

'Just tell me the truth. It's always the easiest, I find.' His pale blue eyes were guileless as they looked into JC's.

'I need to go to the bathroom.' JC stood up.

In the bathroom he stared at himself in the mirror. He felt a sudden longing for the comfort of the kaftan. It always made him feel better, stronger. But he had to go back downstairs. He had to talk to Hugh. Hugh was a clever man. He had interviewed a lot of people. Maybe it was a mistake to have agreed to do the interview.

Satan was sitting outside the bathroom door, waiting for him. He gave a worried little whine and rubbed his strong body against JC's legs.

JC made up his mind.

'WHERE WERE we?' he smiled at Hugh.

'You were about to tell me the whole truth, and nothing but,' Hugh grinned back.

'Right!' He took a deep breath. 'Well, next time I saw Reena her skin had cleared up ... completely.'

'Hey! Hold on now, aren't we missing out on something here?'

'No. That's it. Her skin was perfect, absolutely clear.'

Hugh tapped his empty wine glass with his pen. *Ping!*

'Did you light any candles in the room?' *Ping!*

'No.'

'Use holy water?' *Ping!*

'No. All that came later.'

'So you just put on the kaftan? And you touched her?'
*Ping! Ping!*

'Where did you touch her?'

JC didn't answer.

'Her face?'

Relieved, JC nodded.

Hugh laughed as if an idea had just struck him. 'Why did you take her to your bedroom to touch her face?'

'The kaftan was in the bedroom. I took her upstairs to show her the kaftan.'

'I thought you didn't like the kaftan?'

'I didn't in the beginning. But I had told Reena about it, and she wanted to see it.'

'So you told her about a kaftan that you didn't like, and she wanted to see it?'

JC sighed. 'I was trying to cheer her up.' Hugh was beginning to irritate him. Why was he so interested in what had happened in the bedroom? The important thing was that Reena had been cured. Surely that's all that mattered. What happened between Reena and him was their business. Hugh was worse than Mother. He thought he had a right to pry into everybody's private life. But private meant private. It didn't mean something that was to be shared with the whole world. In that case it would hardly be private any more, would it? JC smiled to himself.

'What?' Hugh was grinning again.

Now that JC really looked at Hugh's grin, it was pretty inane. Did the man never look serious? And why had Mother suddenly befriended him? Who was he anyway? And how could anybody trust a man who smiled all the time? There had to be something strange about a grown man who had a perpetual grin on his face. And why did Satan trust him? Did he cast some peculiar spell over women and dogs? Was that it? Was it a spell that only men were immune to? Well someone would have to remain in control here. Someone would have to outsmart smiling Hugh. Smiling Hugh the Poo!

*Ping!*

'What's the joke?'

That's for me to know and you to find out, Hugh the Poo!

Can't cast your spell on me, Hugh the Poo!

'I'm tired, can we finish this tomorrow?'

'Sure, no problem,' Hugh smiled, but his eyes didn't crinkle up quite as much as before.

Satan followed JC up the stairs.

They rolled around on the bed in mock battle.

JC won.

\*

HUGH DIDN'T arrive at his usual time next morning. Mother said he had arranged to meet some newspaper people.

'Plenty of them just outside the door. He could have had his pick.'

She frowned at him. 'He'll be here at two on the dot. He said to tell you to have your story straight.'

'What?'

'I think it was a joke. Wasn't it, Satan?'

Christ, Mother was actually patting the dog. Hugh must have cast a spell on her.

# CHAPTER 14

FATHER DENNY looked around the packed church before sending up a silent prayer of thanks to his maker. He had never really doubted that this would eventually happen, of course, but none the less, it was still a miracle of sorts.

Row upon row of pious, prayerful faces filled the pews.

For months he had been forced to gaze down at half-empty pews. Now there wasn't enough spare space in any of them to swing a rosary.

Earlier on he had watched cars battling for places in the car park. So many, in fact, that he had had to call on the younger altar boys to form a human chain across the gateway in order to dissuade the more determined drivers from forcing their way into the already jammed yard.

Even the flower-laden hearse had trouble gaining access. And it wasn't until a spray-painted Ford Fiesta had been pushed aside that the legitimate mourners could alight from the shiny black Mercedes that had ferried them the twelve hundred yards from their house to the church.

Never before in all his eighty-two years had Thomas Nolan caused a traffic jam. Nor such determination in so many souls to enter a church.

God did move in mysterious ways, reflected Father Denny.

THE SONS and daughters of Thomas Nolan wept copiously, right through the moving service. Especially the ones who had emigrated years before and who had never once forgotten to send him a card at Christmas. The only dry-eyed relative was the daughter who had nursed him through several bouts of bronchitis, a severe heart attack and a dose of painful shingles, which he had contracted through having to share a bed with his youngest grandson, who was then suffering from a particularly virulent case of chicken pox.

She sat now, looking relaxed and at ease, as her expensively dressed relatives cried loudly over the flower-draped coffin. Her simple bunch of early daffodils was totally overshadowed by the huge colourful wreaths which her siblings had commissioned to express their undying love for the father they hadn't seen for twenty years.

FATHER DENNY reminded his captive audience that Thomas Nolan had led a irreproachable life. He reminded them that Thomas Nolan had never once turned his back on his Church. The same church that he had been baptised into when he was barely three hours old.

'Three hours old, when the holy water of life washed him free from the stain of original sin.' Father Denny's voice cracked with emotion, as if he were recalling a moment he had personally witnessed, instead of one which he had had great trouble tracing through the parish records, on account of Thomas Nolan being a foundling whose parents had never been traced. Thomas Nolan had, in fact, first graced the steps of Ballysheel parish church clad only in a blood-stained newspaper, his umbilical cord trailing dangerously long and jaggedly cut.

He had been baptised within the hour.

'What is the true measure of a man?' Father Denny asked the silent congregation.

'Is it the wealth he accumulates, during his lifetime?

'Is it the esteem he is held in by his fellow man?

'Is it the power he wields in this temporal world?

'Or is it,' he paused, 'a lifetime of devotion and respect which he shows to his Church and his God. For never forget – the Church and God are one. The Church is the incarnation of His will upon earth. Discard it and you discard our Lord Jesus Christ. When Thomas Nolan knocked on the doors of Heaven, did the Lord call out, "Who's there?" *He did not!*' Father Denny pounded the pulpit to emphasise each word. 'He said, "Welcome, Thomas, I know you, for your face was never turned from me."'

Father Denny nodded his head sadly. 'How many of you will the Lord recognise when your time comes?'

The part-time undertaker, standing discreetly behind a marble pillar, coughed and checked his watch.

'Pray, dear brethren, for the soul of Thomas Nolan, but pray also that his devotion to this Church will be taken as an example by all of us, young and old. For by their deeds shall you know them! And by your loyalty shall He know you. Let us pray.'

The congregation knelt as one.

*

JC TOLD Hugh everything he could remember about the healings. But no matter how hard Hugh pushed, he refused to divulge any intimate details about the girls. Or himself.

Hugh had taken to using a tape recorder during their talks.

To his surprise, JC found its low whirring sound a great help when discussing past events. It didn't help with the actual recall, but it did keep him on his guard, and that way prevented him from disclosing things he preferred to keep secret.

Mother left them alone, for most of the time. But JC could still hear her moving about the house. She supplied him with regular cups of tea and sandwiches, and Hugh with endless glasses of wine.

Their days together became quite pleasant. Even enjoyable.

And if Hugh appeared to want far more information than anybody could possibly use in one newspaper article, then JC had to remind himself that he was, after all, a professional, as Mother frequently pointed out.

IMMEDIATELY AFTER the funerals of Ann O'Neill and Thomas Nolan, there was another flurry of attention from the media. Then it eased off. The number of disruptive phone calls dwindled and some days the reporters didn't turn up at all at the house. Finally, they stopped coming altogether.

On Hugh's advice JC hadn't shown himself in public for well over a month. Both Mother and Hugh now supplied him with whatever he needed. Hugh even took Satan for his daily walk. In between the talks with Hugh, JC watched TV. And videos, which Hugh selected. Hugh also brought him books from his own collection. Mother frowned at some of the more lurid covers among them, but JC hardly glanced at them, preferring to watch the flickering shadows on the box.

He spoke into Hugh's tape machine almost every day for two full weeks, with Hugh displaying as much interest in the minute trivia of his everyday life as he did in the outcome of the large healing sessions that had gained him so much attention from the media. After two weeks of constant listening, Hugh decided it was time to adjourn to his own place to begin writing up the article.

'You can ring me if you think of anything world-shattering that we might have overlooked,' he grinned as he packed up his writing materials and tapes.

JC was surprised at how empty the house felt without him. Even Satan appeared to mope. Mother was the only one who seemed unaffected by his absence.

She was still handling the trickle of mail that arrived for 'The Healer', promising daily to re-route it back to the senders. It was a job someone had to do. And she began to talk more and more about taking up her horoscope readings again.

JC said, 'Good idea,' and continued watching TV.

Satan ate and slept.


HUGH'S VOICE on the phone was an excited babble. His publisher friend said the article should be extended into a book. JC wasn't hot news any more, so a newspaper article about him wasn't likely to set the world on fire. But a book now, that was another story! His familiar laugh bellowed down the line.

'In fact, kiddo, the sky might be the limit, money-wise. We could all make ourselves a packet.'

He laughed again but this time it was more of an ironic chuckle. JC could picture his eyes crinkling up, almost closing in wry amusement at this turn of events.

'Well, how do you feel about that?'

JC didn't know how he felt, so he didn't answer.

'JC, I asked how you felt?'

'I ... I don't know.'

'Well, better make up your mind, kiddo, the offer won't stay open for ever.' Hugh wasn't laughing any more.

JC listened for the giveaway *ping!* against a wine glass. It didn't come.

'Well, it's up to you, kiddo. I'll get back to you.' The phone clicked. He had hung up.

# CHAPTER 15

MOTHER AND Hugh were in a deep discussion about the book when JC had his first dizzy spell.

Hugh had been babbling on and on about editors, and graphic artists, and layouts until JC's head began to reel with the unfamiliarity of it all. The whole book business was acquiring a momentum of its own.

There was talk about contracts, and meetings with solicitors to sign the necessary papers. Hugh had already brought a perfect stranger into their home one morning and expected JC to speak freely to him.

They were the exact words he used. 'You can speak freely to John, he's going to be our agent.'

Their agent?

JC had excused himself, and gone to the bathroom. He stayed there until John and the embarrassed Hugh finally left.

Now Mother was happily discussing the whole business with Hugh. She sat wide-eyed as he went on and on about sales and percentages and distribution. She seemed enthralled by it all. JC did the only thing it was in his power to do. He refused flat out to meet any more of the people involved.

No, he wouldn't agree to meet them if they came all the way to Ballysheel. And he wouldn't talk to them on the phone.

Hugh appealed to Mother. She disappeared into the kitchen to make tea. Hugh told JC that he had no choice but to meet people if they were to go ahead with the book.

JC didn't answer. He sat on the floor smoothing Satan's coat. Hugh called Mother in from the kitchen. That's when JC had the dizzy spell.

First the room began to tilt slightly, then it swam before his eyes, everything in it beginning to appear as if they were underwater. He was six years old again ... a small frightened boy strapped into a carnival chair-o-plane ... being whirled high above the noisy carnival crowds – he could even hear the hurdy-gurdy music, the calls of the fairground barkers, and the delighted screams of people all around him as they revelled in their self-inflicted terror. He was convinced that he was about to die as his breath caught in his throat before he was promptly sick, all over his new clothes, the chair-o-plane, and anyone unfortunate enough to be walking below.

Mother had loudly berated her friend Geraldine, for daring to hand him into the care of the the burly chair-o-plane attendant. Timid Geraldine, who had been busily occupied telling fortunes in the small bell-shaped tent that day, had pleaded that she had felt sure that the six-year-old JC would be far happier swinging high above the massed heads in the fairground than sitting bored behind her velvet-covered table.

She was wrong.

JC had adored being close to her, listening to her soft assuring voice telling people of the happy times that were ahead of them. He loved hearing her tell about the 'tall dark strangers', 'the pleasant surprises', 'the heartfelt wishes' that were about to come true. He loved the familiar jangling of her gold wrist bracelets, the sounds they made when she swept her hand rhythmically back and forth, back and forth, over the crystal ball that sat enthroned in regal splendour on a stand in the centre of the table. He loved hearing the gasps of surprise and the tiny nervous giggles that sometimes came from the young girls whenever Geraldine disclosed yet another secret about their lives.

He had hated being scooped up into the arms of the young roustabouts. He hated the sweaty man-smell of them, the rough black chest hairs that escaped from beneath their brief singlet tops. He hated their big rough hands tickling him, trying to make him laugh. He pleaded to be left where he was, in the cool musty darkness of the fortune-teller's tent.

Nobody listened. Not even Geraldine.

'You need some fun, and fresh air,' she insisted.

The roustabouts plied him with warm fizzy drinks, and huge suffocating whorls of cotton candy that clung like a sweet pink cloud to a long thin stick. They insisted that he taste it, and laughed uproariously when he choked and spat out its cloying pink mess.

They strapped him into the chair-o-plane ride, assuring him that he would love it.

All his protests went unheeded, so he clamped his mouth shut and didn't open it again until he vomited all over the heads of the crowd below.

Everybody paid attention then.

Mother took him home. She bathed him and wrapped him snugly in a fluffy white dressing gown that smelled of talcum powder and her skin.

Then she sang him to sleep.

WHEN THE room finally stopped spinning he found himself sitting on the sofa, with Mother on one side and Hugh on the other. One of them was frantically calling his name, begging him to speak, while the other was forcing sips of warm brandy past his lips.

Neither of them ever again mentioned him having to be involved in anything to do with the book.

But even without any further input from JC, the book managed to be completed. In weeks. Hugh was euphoric when he finished the final draft. In a wild burst of imaginative creativity, he had decided on the title: *My Story*, by JC Ryan.

To the publisher he insisted that it was the most fascinating true story of the times. When he was alone with JC he laughed, and called it the greatest work of fiction since the Bible.

After attempting to read it, twice, JC gave up in disgust.

'How could you say such things about me?' he asked the grinning Hugh.

Hugh shrugged and drained his fourth glass of celebratory wine. He laughingly put on a strong American accent, 'Hell, it's all just rock and roll, baby, the truth don't hardly sell no more. An' we all gonna be rich as Croesus.'

Mother loved every word of it. She wept as she read out heart-rending passages describing how the tiny JC had healed small suffering animals when he was barely two years old. How wild savage dogs had turned meek as lambs at his approach.

'It didn't happen, Mother, you know that!' JC protested.

'But it could have, you always adored animals, and you see the effect you have on them.' She pointed to Satan who was snoring happily at his feet.

'I feed him, Mother, that's why he likes me.'

'Nonsense. I feed him sometimes, and he hates me.'

As if to give weight to this statement Satan growled, right on cue, in Mother's direction.

'Mother, I never ever healed an animal.'

'But you could have, if you had been asked.'

107

'It's all lies, lies.' JC took the manuscript from her hand and threw it in disgust towards the fireplace. It landed in the cold ashes, sending up a billowing cloud of grey-brown ash, which hovered above it for a second, then gently settled back, almost obliterating his name from the front page.

Mother rushed to retrieve it. She brushed at it almost tenderly with her skirt. Two big tears slid down her cheeks. 'I never imagined you could be so cruel. So heartless.'

'What?'

'Turning your back on all those people who believe in you.'

'What people?'

'All those people who have faith in you. Who know that you are special. That you have special gifts. They are all waiting patiently to read your story.'

JC couldn't believe his ears. 'Nobody's waiting to read my story, Mother. That's all just hype being put about by Hugh and his friends. Do you really think there are thousands of people out there waiting to hear all about the life of a nobody from Ballysheel? I haven't done a healing for months. I doubt that anyone out there even remembers my name. By now they'll all have moved on to something new.'

'No ... you're wrong! People are waiting! Waiting for you! They are! I'll show you.'

She pulled him along with her, up the stairs and into her bedroom. From underneath the base of her bedside lamp, she retrieved a small key and carefully unlocked her double-sided wardrobe. She reached in and began pulling out large black refuse sacks. Six in all. Her hands trembling with excitement, she turned one sack upside down.

Letters, cards and small boxes of every shape and size tumbled out. She tipped out another bag, allowing a small avalanche of letters to fall across the carpet. She was reaching for a third when he stopped her.

'What are they?' His mouth hung open in dread.

'You know well what they are.'

'But I –' He couldn't believe it. He didn't want to believe it. She couldn't possibly have kept all this from him. All these hundreds of letters – thousands – they were open ... She had opened them, kept them, after they had agreed ... They had agreed, for God's sake not to accept ...

'What have you done, Mother?'

'I answered as many as possible. I couldn't just ignore them. I couldn't. Ask Hugh. He understood. It wasn't easy. All these requests for help. I sent on pieces of fabric from your old shirts and things. It didn't really cost anything, only time and postage. And there have been other cures,' she had the grace to look embarrassed, 'since you gave up.'

She took a pile of letters from the wardrobe drawer and held them out to him. 'Look, Jessie, every single one is a verified cure,' she peered into his stony face, 'verified! By doctors, some by priests. Don't look at me like that, Jessie.' She held up the letters, letting some of them fall at his feet. 'Verified cures.' She began crying, weeping silently into the bunch of letters.

He held her against him, trying to contain his anger. His fury. Poor Mother. She wasn't to blame, she only wanted to help. This was Hugh's fault. He should have known better. He was a man of the world. He knew the lie of the land. And he had allowed Mother to accept all this mail behind his back. Hugh knew that he had sworn off healing since the death of the young girl.

He had agreed to the article only because Hugh had said he should tell his side of the story. He had said it would put an end to speculation, to any chance of him being sued for compensation.

'Give them what they want and you'll be left in peace,' he had said.

He knew that was what JC wanted more than anything in the whole world. To be left in peace.

And all the time he'd been encouraging Mother to keep answering the mail, keeping interest alive.

Now poor Mother was feeling guilty, sobbing like a baby.

Well, her kind heart may have gotten her into this predicament. But her son would get her out of it.

He'd burn this bloody manuscript and any other copies that were in existence. No way were they going back to the nightmare of reporters camped on their doorstep and TV cameras poking in their windows. Poor Mother, he'd protect her from that, at least.

Against his chest she gave a long shuddering sigh. JC gently walked her to her bed.

'Don't worry, Mother. I'll take care of everything.' He kicked the pile of letters out of his way.

She gave a final little sob. 'Careful, Jessie, there might be some cheques left inside some of those.'

HE WAITED until she was asleep before creeping quietly downstairs, carefully avoiding the last step with the built-in creak. Satan padded silently behind him.

In the unlit kitchen he groped around until he found the heavy choke chain. Hushing the dog's yelp of delight at the sound of the chain being lifted, he fastened the collar quickly around its neck. Satan's whole body began to tremble with anticipation at the prospect of an unscheduled late-night walk with his master until, unable to contain himself, he began to howl with impatience.

Terrified that the noise might have woken Mother, JC opened the back door to allow the impatie t dog to run ahead of him. There was no sound from upstairs. He grabbed a rain mac from its hook behind the door and followed the dog.

But fast as he ran, Satan was impossible to catch.

The clanking of the loose choke chain became fainter and fainter in the darkness ahead of him as Satan increased the distance between them.

THE DOG made straight for his favourite stomping ground, the river walk. He knew there was always an abundance of timid ducks to terrify on the waterway. Not only that, but the river bank was a favourite hideaway for scurrying brown rats, which were a delight for any dog whose hunting genes were frustrated daily by the constraints of town dwelling. Here at night, in the dark, Satan could play pretend games of hide-and-seek, kill-or-be-killed, excitedly sniffing out and forcing his prey to break cover, then making a lightning-fast dash after them in an attempt to sink his teeth into their panting flesh.

Of course he never actually caught anything, as his quarry either dived into the water, or made for undergrowth far too dense for his great bulk to penetrate. But even dogs dream. And Satan's dreams mostly consisted of fresh, still-pulsating meat being ripped bloodily asunder by his sharp fangs. Dripping dismembered bodies were the stuff of his nightly forays into his dark underworld. Steaming offal torn into bite-sized chunks and swallowed still warm and tasting of bitter salt and sweet, sweet blood. He raised his huge head and howled with delight.

*

'GOOD BOY.' JC ran up and caught the trailing chain before patting Satan's soft smooth coat.

The old adage was true he thought, petting a gentle animal was soothing, calming. He could feel the tension of the past hours evaporating. The anger he'd felt at Hugh's betrayal was fading.

He sat on the river bank and hugged the huge dog close to him. Resting his head against the massive chest he could hear the big strong heart within pounding its life-sustaining rhythm. His eyes began to fill with hot tears.

A cold dripping tongue swept his wet cheeks. JC cried even harder. If only people were as loyal as animals. If only they were half as easy to understand. Why couldn't they be as uncomplicated and as straightforward as this great beast?

He looked questioningly into the big black eyes.

Satan stared back at him.

# CHAPTER 16

AFTERWARDS HE could never remember if he had been lying awake, or if it had been Mother's scream which had woken him.

Time became all jumbled up in his head. He remembered the sun shining in the window, so it must have been past ten o'clock, because the sun didn't reach this side of the house until ten. He knew he must have been up earlier, or perhaps he had gone to bed very late, because his blinds were open. Mother never touched his blinds. This room was his domain. His sanctum.

The only clear facts that stood out from that whole terrible day were that his blinds had been open. And the sun was shining.

Everything else was a jumble. Even though the young garda had explained patiently exactly what had happened. Even though he had repeated it, over and over, to a disbelieving Mother. Even though JC had listened, had heard, it was still all jumbled up in his head. Convoluted. He couldn't make sense of it.

Hugh was dead. Dead. They would never see him again. He wouldn't sit drinking wine in their kitchen ever again. He would never look up with that funny grin on his face when JC walked in the door. His great bulk would never again make the chair creak when he shook with irrepressible laughter. His eyebrows would never jig up and down again in that peculiar way when he didn't quite believe something JC told him.

After that first bloodcurdling scream, Mother had gone unnaturally quiet. She sat sipping the brandy that JC had poured for her, holding on to the glass with both hands, as if it were supporting her and not the other way round. She appeared not to listen as the embarrassed young garda finished the story.

It was JC who asked, 'Are you sure? There couldn't be a mistake, could there?'

'No mistake, sir, even though the body', he lowered his voice respectfully, but he needn't have bothered, Mother wasn't hearing anything, 'it was very badly burned ... but still identifiable. His landlord ...' he glanced at Mother, 'did the necessary. The flat was his property, after all.' The garda was on surer ground here. 'Burned to near rubble it was. The whole building will have to come down. Terrible thing.'

The destruction of property was clearly something the young garda deplored.

'How did the fire start?' Mother suddenly spoke.

'We're not sure, ma'am. Investigations are continuing.'

'You must have some idea. Was it ... malicious?'

'Investigations are continuing, ma'am.'

'Did he ... was he badly burned?'

'He didn't suffer, ma'am.'

Her withering look made him blush. He shifted uneasily, securing his garda cap even tighter under his restraining arm. 'The doctor thinks he may have had a heart attack,' he blurted out in an attempt at reassurance.

'A heart attack?' Mother and JC spoke in unison.

'I ... I shouldn't be telling you this, but that's what the doctor said when he saw the ... when he examined him. So he wouldn't have suffered ... well, not from the fire.' He nodded in relief. 'He would have been de ... gone before the fire got to him.'

Mother put her head down on the table and wept, great long shuddering sobs which rocked her narrow shoulders, and brought a curious Satan running in from the hallway.

JC put his arms around her.

'No! Leave me alone!' She stood up and walked towards the stairs, moving as if each step were a colossal effort.

JC and the garda stood watching until she disappeared up the stairway.

'They'll need to speak to both of you,' the garda said.

'They?'

'The detectives doing the investigating.' He drew himself up importantly. 'This may well be a murder case. Arson and murder! This won't pass lightly.'

'I thought you said ... ?'

'Didn't want to upset your mother.' He placed his cap squarely on his head. 'Women don't have our constitutions.'

THE GARDA had barely left when all hell broke loose. As if at a given signal, the phone and doorbell began ringing together. Cars squealed to a stop outside, disgorging noisy, camera-wielding newsmen. When JC refused to answer the door they tapped and then hammered insistently on the front window.

Satan sat in the hallway, growling threateningly at the raised voices outside.

114

JC turned on the radio to drown out the din. He fiddled at the dials until he found a station playing heavy-metal music, then turned the volume up full. He crossed into Mother's room, lit the candles and curled up in her big chair. He tried not to think about Hugh. Instead he filled his mind with pictures of the happy times he had spent in this room with Mother. After a time he could almost hear her voice asking if he wanted more tea, more cake. He rocked himself in the chair.

The voices outside were beginning to fade now. Maybe they were giving up. Going away. There was nothing he could tell them about Hugh's death. They didn't care about Hugh anyway ... they might claim that he was one of theirs, but since he began writing the book they had ostracised him, treated him like a leper. He had told Mother that in Ballysheel's tiny hotel where the visiting journalists stayed, they wouldn't even get him an after-hours drink. All the years he had spent in the business and they wouldn't even ... so much for the camaraderie of the press. Well, at least they needn't be jealous about the book any more. Everything in Hugh's flat had been burned, so the garda said. To ashes. That meant all his photographs, his notes, tapes. Even the final draft of the book. The final draft! But there was a copy here, the one he had angrily thrown into the firegrate. The one Mother had so lovingly rescued – it was here in this house!

He got up and began searching frantically. It was nowhere in Mother's room.

But it had to be here. Mother had kept it. She hadn't appeared to notice its blatant sexual innuendoes, its jibes about 'hands-on healing'. She had seen it as a book about the power of faith. About a belief in the spirit above all else. It was something she had always put her trust in, despite having to survive in a materialistic world, she said.

Hugh had laughed when she said that, and opened another bottle of wine. He had topped up all three glasses and raised his. 'Here's to the power of the spirit, may it make us all rich.' Catching sight of Mother's expression, he had added quickly, 'In wisdom and fortitude.'

Both Mother and JC had sipped at their wine without enthusiasm.

He had to find the manuscript.

He knew all of Mother's hiding places. He pulled out the wooden bread bin from against the kitchen wall. Behind it were two opened letters, both addressed to him. Both asking for prayers. And both claiming that the supplicant was enclosing money.

There was no money in the envelopes, and there was no manuscript behind the bin. He put the letters back and pushed the bin tightly against them. He searched carefully under the tiered vegetable rack. Underneath the bottom tier he found an old astrology magazine covered with dust. Pressed between its yellowing pages were twenty ten-pound notes. They reeked of musk and damp.

For as long as he could remember, Mother had never moved or really cleaned the tall mahogany wine rack. The most she ever did to it was flick a damp duster at it. And even that not too enthusiastically. She maintained that a layer of dust could prevent light from spoiling good wine.

He reached in behind the rack, forcing his arm along as far as he could into the narrow confined space. At first all he encountered were fine cobwebs. They clung to his hand and shirt cuff as he clumsily tried to brush them off before reaching back in again. This time a small black spider ran along his arm. Startled he jerked his hand back, and felt his knuckles catch against something stiff and unyielding. The spider disappeared behind a bottle of Bordeaux as JC tugged at the manuscript until he pulled it free.

It still showed traces of its encounter with the sooty fire grate, and it was further embellished with dust from behind the wine rack, but his name still stood out clearly on the cover.

Not for long, he determined.

He dropped it into the kitchen stove, then threw a lighted match in on top of it.

He watched as it burned. It curled up slowly, almost leisurely, at the edges, smooth white page after page turning black and wrinkled before collapsing in on itself like a burned-out wave and disintegrating into a charred heap of ashes.

When it looked as if the close-packed paper next to the spine might refuse to burn, he poked at it with an ash retractor until it burst into flames, leaving only the heavy clips that had held it together intact. He slammed the stove closed and went back to sit in Mother's chair.

Satan came to lie at his feet. JC fell asleep with the sound of the doorbell ringing in his ears.

When he woke an hour or so later, his face was wet with tears. The doorbell and phone had stopped ringing, and a voice on the radio was talking excitedly about stone statues that were moving of their own volition before hundreds of mesmerised people.

He turned the radio off.

There wasn't a sound from upstairs.


HUGH'S FUNERAL was quiet and dignified. Hugh had been a Protestant.

JC spotted a couple of newsmen. But neither of them approached him. They appeared to be there strictly as mourners. Hugh had no family and no wife, so there was only a handful of people present. The publisher had sent a wreath. Business commitments had prevented him attending. The card on the wreath said 'Always loyal'. JC took this to refer to a character trait of Hugh's, rather than a declaration of intent from the publisher.

Mother was supported by her friend Geraldine and three large glasses of brandy. The other members of her circle had offered to come, but Mother had dismissed their offer. She had a strange air of acceptance about her. Resignation almost. This was so unlike Mother that JC knew it had to be an indication of how deeply she was affected by Hugh's death.

After the funeral she packed a small bag, and said she was going to spend some time with Geraldine. She didn't look at JC as she spoke.

'If you need anything, you'll know where I am.'

He wanted to tell her that what he needed most was her, but he decided against it. She looked as if any demand on her, no matter how minuscule, might push her over the edge. When he embraced her, he could feel her bones through the thin fabric of her dress.

'Take care of yourself, Mother.' He was determined not to cry.

'And you, son. You take care.' For the first time since Hugh's death, she hugged him warmly.

They both wept.

Geraldine bustled her out the door.

There wasn't a reporter in sight. More statues had begun to move in villages further west.

*

IT WAS eleven thirty that night when the doorbell woke him. Jesus Christ, they were back. He curved his pillow up around both his ears and held it there. It didn't help. The ringing persisted. He lay still for a couple of minutes and let the sound wash over him. It didn't stop.

He felt the anger erupt from somewhere deep inside him. He ran to the window, pushed it wide open and screamed down at the top of his voice, 'Fuck off, you bastards! You can go and screw yourselves if you think I'm going to let any of you into this house ever again. You're nothing but a pile of shit. Shit! Shit! Shit!'

Down below him, one solitary figure in white stood looking up. It took a couple of seconds before it registered with him just who it was standing there. It was the angel from the hospital.

Once inside the house she inquired about his long-healed ribs. Then she insisted on checking them out for herself, despite his protests. She proclaimed them to be well healed, which didn't exactly surprise him. Then she told him not to worry about Mother, which did surprise him. She said everything was going to be fine, that he had nothing at all to worry about.

She sounded exactly like Geraldine in the fortune-telling tent, all those years ago. She carefully buttoned up his pyjama top, smiled into his face, and brushed a hand gently across his cheek.

Then she picked up her bag and left.

HE SETTLED into a routine. He played music, cooked for himself and Satan, and watched TV. And waited for Mother's return.

The angel paid him two more visits. She seemed to know instinctively when he most needed reassurance. That's when she appeared. He always felt a lot happier after a visit from her.

Mother phoned to ask if he was keeping body and soul together. He said he was. She believed him and rang off.

He tried not to think about Hugh. Tried not to think about the fire consuming his body. Burning him, turning his flesh black, burning it beyond recognition. Maybe he had had a heart attack in his sleep. And the fire didn't come until later. Much later.

He didn't leave the house, not even to buy a newspaper, so if they were showing any further interest in Hugh's death, he didn't know about it. But he doubted they were. On TV now, the big story was moving statues. Newscasters and visiting journalists were in an almost orgasmic frenzy about this new phenomenon.

Foreign professors with unpronounceable names, and local county councillors with crooked toupées, were invited to debate the likelihood of stone statues becoming mobile in areas where even the state bus company failed to run. Frizzy-haired sociologists of all sexes wondered hesitantly on camera if more workshops on developing interpersonal relationships, or counselling the unemployed on life skills, could be the answer and what was the question again?

A renowned artist and poet, who had painted the sun spinning in the heavens above a statue, denied the allegation that he had spent some of his Arts Council grant on mind-altering drugs.

A priest in whose parish a statue was said to weep real tears during daylight hours vehemently denied that he had pronounced it a miracle.

And the bishops denied nothing. Except requests to be interviewed.

Meantime, according to the TV, half of the plain people of Ireland were flocking to the sites of these wonders, eager to be part of something that purported to be bigger than the humdrum fare of daily life.

The other half of the plain people were too busy trying to put food on the table to have time to wonder if there was more to life than surviving.

'Moving statues won't butter the parsnips,' was the quote from one desperate woman queuing for assistance to buy shoes for her children.

# CHAPTER 17

HE WAS in the back garden brushing Satan when he heard the car pull up out front. He knew it wasn't Mother because she never did anything without announcing it first.

He ran into the house and turned off the TV. After giving a dutiful warning bark, Satan lay at his feet, watching uneasily as JC nervously chewed at his fingernails.

They both waited for the doorbell to ring. It remained silent.

JC ordered Satan to stay, and tiptoed quietly across the room to the front window. He pulled the heavy drapes a fraction to one side and peered out cautiously from behind them.

Staring directly back at him was a huge bloodshot eye which promptly disappeared from view as Detective Murtha gave a startled leap backwards. Satan bounded across the room and it took all of JC's strength to prevent the dog smashing through the glass in an attempt to savage the intruder.

Detective Murtha was in no mood to accept JC's apologies for the banished Satan. He did ask twice if the kitchen door was securely locked. As if in reply, Satan howled in frustration from behind it.

'Dangerous beast!' The detective strode down the hallway, one hand hooked into his mac, like a red-faced Napoleon.

Trotting behind him, Sergeant Littlewilly greeted JC like a long-lost friend.

JC wished both of them to hell. But not out loud. Out loud he said, 'Mother isn't here.'

'We're not interested in your Mother.' Detective Murtha's personality hadn't improved, but then neither had his veins. They still bulged grotesquely above his starched collar.

JC tried not to stare at them.

The detective walked uninvited into Mother's room. He began poking around, picking up Mother's little zodiac statuettes and putting them down again carelessly, way out of their rightful place.

'Don't touch them,' JC burst out as the huge hands reached towards Mother's precious candleholders.

Murtha grasped the heavy candleholder and swung around as if intending to strike JC with it.

The two men laughed when he instinctively ducked. Murtha patted JC's back with his free hand. 'Come on, son, it was just a joke.' He flashed his wide yellow toothed smile.

'Just a joke,' the faithful sergeant echoed.

Murtha carefully replaced the candleholder on the mantel. With his back to JC he asked, 'Your mother on holidays?'

'She's staying with a friend.'

'Ah yes! Miss Geraldine Stack, the revered medium!' Murtha swung around and leaned forward slightly, hands behind his back, eyebrows raised quizzically.

JC had the strangest feeling that Murtha was playing a part. It was as if he were on stage or TV. He was acting like someone in …? He suddenly realised who it was.

The detective thought he was Hercule Poirot! The busy walk. The frequent smile. Jesus, he was even growing a little moustache. All he would have to do now was lose about five stone in weight, drop his bog accent, and have a brain transplant. Jesus! It would be funny, if it weren't for the fact that Murtha's eyes were those of a deadly killer cobra.

'So ... your mother is staying with Madame Stack ... eh?' Murtha/Poirot shrugged his shoulders in what he clearly imagined was a gallic shrug.

JC tried not to giggle.

'Good, because I wanted to have a word with you, alone.' There, the French/Belgian accent was becoming even more pronounced.

JC decided to play along.

'I wanted to ask you about Mr Hugh Brophy.' Murtha/Poirot rubbed his chin.

'He's dead, *monsieur*.'

The gardaí looked at each other.

'Anything else, *monsieur*?'

'Don't you be so bloody cheeky.' Sergeant Littlewilly didn't look friendly any more. Clearly he wasn't in on the game.

Murtha/Poirot's brick-red face darkened. 'Don't play the fool with us, boy.' The French accent had disappeared. 'We want to know where you were at midnight, last Friday week,' he paused, 'sir'.

Jesus! Murtha/Poirot was now Fabian of the Yard.

Where had he been?

That was the night Hugh had died.

'Answer the question!' Fabian was becoming impatient.

'I ... I was here with Mother.'

'All night?' Poirot was back.

'No. I took my dog for a walk.'

'Ah!' Poirot's eyes narrowed with satisfaction, as if he had just out-manoeuvred a mass murderer. 'Where to?'

'I ... along the river bank, from the old mill to ... where they are building the new houses.'

'Quite near where Mr Brophy's flat is ... *was*.' Poirot almost twirled an invisible moustache.

'No. I didn't go anywhere near Hugh's flat. I ... we walked on the other side of the river.'

'We?'

'Me and Satan.'

Sergeant Littlewilly tittered.

But Poirot was moving in for the kill. 'So you were alone?'

'I suppose.'

'You suppose? Did anyone see you?'

'No.'

'Then you have no confirmed alibi for that night?'

'Do I need one?'

'Oh, you need one, boy, you need one.'

Poirot and Fabian were no longer in the game. Now JC was face to face with cold-eyed Detective Murtha. He wished Mother were here.

'What about this book that Mr Brophy was writing about you?'

'I ... er, he'd already written it.'

'Did you approve of the book?'

'I hated it.'

'You hated it?' Detective Murtha glanced at the sergeant, who was painstakingly writing in his notebook. 'Why did you hate the book?'

'Because it was ... I just didn't like it.'

'No, you said you hated it. Is that correct?' Murtha directed the question to the scribbling sergeant.

'I ... hated ... it,' Sergeant Littlewilly read out slowly in his proud high-infant fashion.

'Thank you, Sergeant.' Murtha smiled. 'Now the question is, did you hate it enough to burn down Mr Brophy's flat?' His veins bulged threateningly. 'We know that his publisher had just handed back his only copy of the manuscript for further editing. So we know that both copies were in Mr Brophy's possession. We also know that nothing escaped that fire. And before you answer, I should warn you that a neighbour of Mr Brophy's saw a youth skulking around the doorway of his flat shortly before the fire must have started.'

JC felt his head go numb.

'The neighbour thinks the youth might have had a dog with him.'

JC could hear Satan scratching at the closed kitchen door. He'd start howling at any second now.

'Mr Ryan?'

This wasn't a game any more, these men were serious. He wished he could think straight. He stared at the veins in Murtha's neck and tried to think.

'I didn't burn down anything. Why should I? I had no reason to, and anyway Hugh didn't have the only copies. There was one here.'

That took Murtha by surprise.

'I'd like to see that, please.'

Shit! JC knew he was in trouble.

'I'd like to see that copy please ... sir.' Fabian was back.

'I burned it.'

'You what?'

'I said, I burned the fuckin' book.' JC wished he was dead.

HE FULLY expected Fabian, Poirot, and Murtha to arrest him. They didn't. Instead, Littlewilly and Murtha took turns asking him dozens of questions. Questions that they clearly knew the answers to.

Somebody had been talking about him, and whoever they were, they didn't like him one little bit. Or Mother.

The gardaí were finally leaving. Littlewilly packed his red notebook away. He put the top back carefully on his new biro. Murtha started to smooth his already immaculate coat, then appeared to change his mind. He stared at JC for a second, then said, almost casually, 'Is it true that Hugh Brophy was your father?'

THE RINGING inside JC's head wouldn't stop. It kept on and on. Sergeant Littlewilly was holding a damp towel to his forehead. For such a big man, he was surprisingly gentle. His hands were as soft as a woman's.

The room had stopped spinning, but the ringing continued. JC pressed his fingers in his ears. The ringing eased a little but it didn't stop.

'Answer that.' Murtha stood a little distance away, as if he feared that fainting might be contagious. 'Answer it,' he snapped again at the sergeant who was on his knees beside JC.

The sergeant dropped the towel and obediently crossed to the door.

As soon as JC heard her voice, he knew he could relax. The ringing had stopped now. She pushed swiftly past the eighteen-stone sergeant.

'What have you done to him?' She bent over JC, feeling his wet forehead with her cool hand.

'It's just water, miss. I put a damp towel on his head.'

'Get out! Look at the state he's in. Don't you know that he's not too long out of a hospital bed? If you've harmed him, or put him in any danger, you'll answer for it.'

She confronted the two huge men, her slight figure dwarfed by both of them. But something about her, or perhaps her white uniform, made them step back respectfully.

But Murtha wasn't to be deprived of the last word. 'We'll talk to you again, Mr Ryan. Sir.'

THE ANGEL put him to bed. Then she pulled a chair close to it and sat by him. She stroked his hand where it lay on the quilt and sang softly to herself. It was all so strange. And comforting. He fell asleep listening to her sing.

He was in heaven. Mother was sitting opposite him, offering him tea and Battenberg. She was smiling. *I'll never let them have you*, she was saying. *It's just you and I, Jessie. That's all that matters.* He could hear the clients pounding on the door, ringing on the bell, but Mother ignored them. *Just you and I, Jessie*, she smiled. Then the drapes were flung open. This wasn't right. The drapes in Mother's room must never be opened.

He got up to close them, but they wouldn't close, no matter how hard he tried. He tugged with all his strength, but they wouldn't give. Then he saw what was holding them.

A tall figure, huge, was standing over him, grasping the cord that controlled the drapes. It was clearly a man, but he couldn't see the face. Just a massive towering figure, and big strong hands. Mother came to help him close the drapes. When she saw the figure holding them open, she screamed ... *Run, Jessie, run*. He began running, but the floor was moving. He wasn't gaining any ground. The faster he ran, the faster the floor moved. He turned to look at the tall figure. It was reaching out for him. *Run, Jessie*, Mother screamed ... but the figure was gaining on him, and his legs melted into the floor with fright as the big hands grasped his shoulders. *Help me, Mother, help me*. But the figure was turning him around, forcing his eyes open with his big strong hands. *No, no*. Hugh was smiling into his face. *It's me, son, don't you recognise me? I'm your father*. The skin on Hugh's face was burning, curling, becoming grey-black – it was falling off, leaving behind only a white gleaming skull, its fleshless mouth pleading, *I'm your father, JC, don't you recognise me? I'm your father.*

THE ANGEL shook him awake. 'You were dreaming, JC. It was just a dream. Everything will be all right. You'll see. You'll see.'

He looked into her pale calm face, into the wide green eyes that couldn't hold a lie. He looked at the soft mouth that could kiss away pain, and he knew. Other people might lie. Even dreams could lie, but not the angel. He clung to her.

That evening the phone rang. Mother was coming home. He had been right. The angel would never lie to him. Life was good again. Mother was coming home.

# CHAPTER 18

HE BARELY gave her time to drop her bag in the hall before he asked the question. It just burst out of his mouth. 'Was Hugh my father?'

He hadn't seen Mother laugh so heartily in years. Not even Hugh, with his droll way of putting things, had ever made Mother laugh like this. She stopped for a split second, open-mouthed, and held a hand to her chest, as if trying to regain control. Then the wild giggling broke out all over again.

Finally she wiped her hand across her streaming eyes. 'Oh, Jessie love, I'm sorry, but you really do me good. I needed a laugh, badly!' She struggled to control herself again. 'But what in the name of God made you ask me that?'

He shrugged, feeling foolish and stupid. She held out her arms to him. They hugged each other and giggled happily together. It was good to have her home. Only much later did he realise that she hadn't answered his question.

IT WAS like living with a completely different person. Oh, it was Mother's face that smiled at him across the table every morning. It was Mother's face that peeped happily around his bedroom door each night to wish him sweet dreams. It was Mother who stood in the kitchen asking him what he would like for dinner. And it was her eyes that watched him lovingly, whenever he played with Satan.

Yet she was different. It was as if one person had gone to stay with Geraldine and her other circle friends, and three weeks later, somebody altogether different had been sent to take her place at home.

This other person clearly had no memory of any of the bad things that had happened. The riot outside the hall, the death of the old man, and the girl, and certainly not Hugh's death and the terrible fire that had destroyed his building. She was lighthearted and happy. Joyous. She hummed, sang her way around the house. And burst into laughter at even his feeblest attempts at humour. Their days together flowed smoothly one into the other. And his nights were now unencumbered by dreams or desires. Mostly.

127

One morning he walked into the kitchen and caught her feeding Satan. It wasn't simply the fact of her feeding the dog that surprised him, although that was shock enough. It was what she was feeding him. She was holding up pieces of raw liver, and the dog was sitting in a begging posture, opening his dripping jaws wide to catch the offal that she dropped into his gaping mouth. The sight of the raw liver nauseated JC.

Except for when he shared JC's food, Satan had always been fed on dry, high-protein dog meal. He loved it, and it kept him healthy and happy. Now he stood licking Mother's hand where the liver had left traces of red-brown blood between the fingers. The dog's probing tongue looked unclean and bloody. JC's stomach lurched.

Mother turned and smiled happily at him. 'Look, we're making friends.'

Satan padded over to greet JC, and Mother began attending to the breakfast. She was humming.

JC pushed the dog away from him.


HE TRIED bringing up Hugh's name in conversation with her. Each time she quickly changed the topic to something totally unrelated. After a few feeble efforts he gave up.

He felt disloyal to Hugh. It was as if they were somehow reneging on him, on their friendship, by never, ever mentioning him.

But clearly Mother had her own way of coping with grief. She had been much closer to Hugh than he had, so her pain would go far deeper. He hadn't the right to ease his own hurt by forcing her to talk about something she wished to avoid.

The angel didn't call. Nobody did. Mother attended her circle meetings, which were becoming more and more frequent, but the other members didn't visit the house any more. They too were obviously allowing her to cope in her own way.

She sang and hummed her way through each day. She dusted off her appointment book, but she didn't make any appointments.

She baked mounds of bread, and then had to give most of it away to prevent it going to waste. She dusted and rearranged the furniture in every room in the house. Except his bedroom. She fed Satan, and she sang. It was as if she were marking time. Waiting for something important to happen. JC began to get used to the new atmosphere around the house. No demands, no outbursts, no raised voices, just a quiet calmness that permeated each and every new day. He felt that this could well be the portent for their future together.

It made him very happy.

And Mother appeared truly content.

Until the day Young Curate arrived back at their door.

# CHAPTER 19

OF ALL the people in Ballysheel it was, strangely enough, the celibate Young Curate who noticed the girls first. But then, enforced celibacy may well be the greatest sensitiser to such sights.

He was overseeing the training of the girls' hockey team when he first spotted it, or rather her.

Janis Meehan was tearing up the field, wielding her hockey stick like a deadly scimitar, her muscular legs propelling her at a rate of knots past her less able team-mates.

With her red-brown hair streaming out wildly behind her, she resembled a red-maned Grainuaile, desperately intent on conquering all before her. But it wasn't her new-found speed, or skill, that drew Young Curate's eyes. It was something even more startling.

Her previously benign-looking young breasts were heaving alarmingly as she ran. Pushing forcefully against the tightly buttoned white blouse, they threatened to spring from behind its restrictive cotton at any second. And a couple of inches below this awe-inspiring sight, crudely accentuated by the light sports skirt being blown back against it, was the most prominent, pregnant-looking stomach that Young Curate had ever laid eyes on.

No matter how hard he tried to avert them, his eyes were drawn back, again and again, to the massive bulge under the sports skirt.

God almighty, the girl couldn't be a day over seventeen. She was still in school! Studying for her Leaving Cert! Doing four honours!

And as far as he knew, there wasn't a boyfriend in sight, let alone the prospect of a husband. And surely to God no girl should be tearing around a hockey pitch like an unchurched pagan if she was carrying a child?

He watched her as she fearlessly tackled girls three times her weight, braved assaults that would prostrate a twenty-stone wrestler, and came up smiling and victorious each time. The girl was like a super-charged dynamo. She was tireless, radiant.

And very, very pregnant.

*

HE WAITED outside the changing room to speak to her. This wouldn't be easy. He knew the girl and her older sister well, but he was hardly on intimate terms with them. He had no idea how he was going to broach this subject. But he was their priest.

He had his duty. Was he not, after all, the girl's moral guardian, their spiritual adviser? He lowered his head and said a quiet little prayer that he might be given the grace to handle this situation with ... grace. For his sake as well as Janis's.

He wasn't getting on at all lately with Father Denny, and to be able to report a bit of discreet moral counselling back to his superior wouldn't harm his standing in any way. Not that this was his motive in deciding to approach the girl. Not at all. Her welfare, and that of her pregnancy, was all-important.

He prayed again that his gift of communication might not fail him when he needed it most.

Janis came out of the changing room arm in arm with another girl. They were both laughing. Heads thrown back, faces glowing, they both looked as if they didn't have a care in the world. Especially Janis.

Young Curate was just about to call her when he noticed that she was wearing a skin-tight pair of jeans. And no matter how hard he looked, he couldn't spot even a semblance of a bulge under the tight blue denim.

Her white cotton tee-shirt did nothing to disguise her breasts, which were as spectacularly prominent as they had been on the hockey pitch. But her pregnant-looking stomach had completely disappeared.

He broke into a cold sweat.

'Looking for something, Father?' Janis sounded amused.

From the sly, knowing grins on their faces he could tell that both girls had caught him staring at Janis's breasts. He found himself blushing, shifting from one foot to the other like a guilty schoolboy caught in a grubby, furtive act.

But why was he feeling guilty? He had no need to feel guilty. He hadn't been ogling the girl. He was simply here to offer advice! To counsel a young unfortunate who might be in trouble.

She stood in front of him, arm in arm with her friend, completely relaxed and at ease, while he stammered and shuffled, and finally blurted out some pathetic gibberish about rethinking their training schedules.

The girls glanced at each other, their amused faces feigning mock patience while he got caught up deeper and deeper in convoluted nonsense about hockey practice.

Janis finally interrupted him. 'Aw Father, sure it's just a game. Isn't it?'

Both girls broke into giggles at his embarrassment and walked away, deliberately swinging their hips like a pair of old-fashioned vamps in a B movie. He could hear them laughing all the way along the corridor.

The other girls coming out of the changing room stared curiously at him as they passed. To cover his embarrassment he began closely checking the discarded hockey sticks propped up against the wall.

*Five, six* ... oh God ... *seven* ... My God, why hast thou ... *eight* ... forsaken me?

THE FOLLOWING Thursday evening he was taking his usual choir practice. The church choir was his pride and joy. He jealously guarded his time with it, boasting to himself, and to anyone else who would listen, that not only did he guide every single note that passed their collective lips, but he chose their choral garb, decided on their stance, and frequently advised them on their diets before any strenuous choral performance. He even heard their confessions, and was not above giving them marital advice when they chose to discuss such weighty matters with him. In fact, as his second tenor once joked, he knew each and every one of them as intimately as the law and his vow of celibacy would allow.

But on this wet Thursday evening, at sixteen minutes past eight, he saw something that gave lie to this claim. His two prize sopranos, his two virginal, *belle voces* whose 'Ave Marias' made hard men weep, were both bulging formidably out of their choral gowns.

He watched in disbelief as they sang together, their voices soaring majestically up to the vaulted church ceilings and beyond, their hands folded piously in front of them. And directly underneath the pale nun-like hands, their swollen abdomens brazenly distorted the smooth lines of the celestial blue choral gowns.

He wondered if he could be hallucinating. After all, he had imagined Janis Meehan's condition, hadn't he? He had been under a lot of strain lately. What with Father Denny being difficult, and ... and his own personal problem. He used to think that having one testicle was traumatic. If only he had foreseen the problems that having two could bring.

He looked at the girls again. No! It wasn't his imagination. Their faces still held that sweet aura of the untouched. Their eyes shone with a rare purity, with that special inner light that radiates only from those who save themselves for the Lord. He knew with every fibre of his being that here stood virgins. Of that there could be absolutely no doubt.

But there could also be no doubt that they were both very definitely pregnant.

HE BEGAN watching young Mass-goers closely. He watched the young girls leaving the youth club. He even stood outside the gates of the two small secondary schools in the town and watched the girls file past him. This drew a lot of strange looks from the girls. But he stood fast. Until he saw the head-nun from the convent school approaching him. He moved away smartly then, and busied himself inspecting the big gnarled chestnuts that lined the wide avenue.

There had been a lot of talk about Dutch Elm disease lately.

The nun stood at the convent gate, hands on hips, eyes narrowed suspiciously, until he drove away. He hoped that she noted the 'Plant a Tree for the Future' sticker on the back of his Ford Capri.

After such a narrow escape from the wrath of the good nun, he resolved to be a little more circumspect in his investigations.

Prudence might serve him as well as, if not better, than enthusiasm in his search for the truth about this extraordinary thing that seemed to be happening in Ballysheel.

He had already reached one very definite conclusion: there was, without a shadow of a doubt, an epidemic of pregnancies among the most unlikely young girls in the town.

He had been aware, of course, that there was what Father Denny called, 'a loosening of morals values' about. It was after all, the nineteen-nineties. But what he had seen in the last couple of weeks was something beyond that. There was something strange about the girls. Something he couldn't quite name. But it was almost sinister – threatening.

Without exception they all had the same look about them.

They were shame-free, radiant. They carried their pregnancies proudly, almost like trophies, prizes! It wasn't natural.

And with so many young unmarried girls becoming pregnant, surely he should have heard from at least one concerned mother.

Perhaps a few discreet words with some of the more reliable mothers in the town would give him some clue. The first person who sprang to mind was a Mrs Gerber. She was one of the great stalwarts of the community. An arch conservative of the old school. Almost two years now since her husband had died, and she still proudly wore widow's weeds. She clung steadfastly to traditions that even Ballysheel had long since discarded.

She firmly believed that the current Pope was a far-out liberal, a man embarrassingly modern in his outlook. She also considered the Synod of Bishops to be dangerously close to free-thinking radicals. Closet revolutionaries all.

She did, however, have one small fault. She loved gossip.

'Have you, er – heard anything – any stories – about lax behaviour in the town?' Young Curate inquired of her.

She stared at him over her willow-pattern tea-cup. 'Lax behaviour? In Ballysheel? What on earth are you suggesting, Father?'

'I, I, er, couldn't help noticing as – as I went about my duties – there seem to be quite a few young unmarried girls who are,' he paused, embarrassed, 'well, not to put too fine a point on it – they appear to be – well, they seem to me ...'

Mrs Gerber stared wide-eyed at him. 'They seem to be what, Father?' Her pale pink neckscarf lent a warmth to her cheeks that he had never noticed before.

'They seem to be pregnant.' The words came out in a rush. He bent his head and scrutinised the tea-leaves in the bottom of his cup, awaiting the tirade against the youth of today that he knew she'd unleash.

There was silence.

He risked a look at her.

She was smiling pityingly at him.

'Now, now, Father, what would a young priest know about such things?' She tapped his knee with a pink-nailed finger. 'You look tired, you're obviously not getting enough sleep.'

She took his cup and placed it carefully on the table next to hers. 'You must be imagining things, Father. Father Denny is working you far too hard.' Again the pitying look. 'And sleep-lessness is a terrible curse. Pray to Saint Brigid. I do. She never fails me.'

Mrs Gerber was now smiling happily. It was a rare sight. 'Saint Brigid, Father.' She whispered the name close to his ear, as if she were afraid of being overheard.

She walked him to the door, holding him firmly by the elbow, guiding him as if he were simple, or blind. Or both.

He was opening his car door when her twin daughters walked past.

'Good evening, Father Bermingham,' they called out politely in unison.

They were both at least five months' pregnant.

# CHAPTER 20

WHOM COULD he discuss these extraordinary happenings with? Whom could he trust? Father Denny was out of the question. They were barely on speaking terms. The older man did manage to grunt 'Good morning' at him over his breakfast cereal, but that was about as communicative as they got these days.

They even opened the envelopes that contained the weekly parish subscriptions in silence now, and they no longer discussed, or even mentioned, how much they received for saying a Mass for the dead, or for a special intention.

No, Father Denny was not about to be sympathetic to his concerns, he was far too busy counting the meagre attendance at Mass. The numbers were rising slowly again each week, but Father Denny was obsessed now with speeding up the process, as if a person's eternal salvation depended solely on their quota of Mass attendances.

There could well be something happening in Ballysheel which might strike at the very core of Mother Church and her teachings, yet all Father Denny cared about was Mass attendance. Young Curate prayed for inspiration.

One of the lecturers from his seminary days was now living in Dublin. As a professor of speculative morals, he had always been prepared to listen to any seminarian whose conscience was troubling him. For two decades he had been revered as one of the most formidable intellects in the college.

Young Curate decided to visit him.

The lecturer had left the priesthood when it was discovered that he had spent one summer vacation in the company of his younger brother, who had successfully smuggled twenty pounds of Semtex and four boxes of Armalites into the country. The booty had been discovered in the back of an untaxed van which the brother was driving erratically while under the influence of weak Lebanese hashish and strong Scotch whisky.

The lecturer, who was with him at the time, had pleaded that he was merely under the influence of his brother. The legal authorities had believed him, and, in deference to his clerical collar, had let him off with a suspended sentence.

The Church authorities were not so forgiving, however, and rumour had it that he had not so much resigned as been defrocked, cashiered, from the army of the Lord.

The unfortunate brother had gotten twelve years. The lecturer had gotten a brand new set of friends and a trendy apartment, and was now a respected author and psychologist in Dublin.

THEY TALKED long into the night, Young Curate letting his hair down for the first time in years. He told his mentor all about his 'cure', all about his newly found testicle. He told him about Father Denny, how difficult and obtuse he could be. And finally he told him that he was seeing pregnant women everywhere he looked in Ballysheel.

His mentor sat in silence for some minutes. He closed his eyes wearily and drew in deep, even breaths. Then he stroked his fashionably unshaven chin.

'We are all victims of our culture,' he finally pronounced, 'all trapped within our given roles, unless we are brave enough, or foolhardy enough, to break free,' he smiled darkly, 'and take the consequences.'

He reached up and took a worn leather tobacco pouch from a bookshelf by the fireplace, retrieved a packet of cigarette papers from between the pages of *Psychoanalysis and Religion*, and drew a small silver-wrapped oblong from his breast pocket. He then proceeded, slowly and expertly, to roll a gigantic joint, and insisted that Young Curate smoke it with him.

The sound of Mahler's fifth symphony, rising to full volume, drowned out any hope of further conversation.

Next morning, over hot croissants and strong coffee, the ex-lecturer advised Young Curate to give up his celibacy, smoke more dope and join the real world. Then he drove off to his consulting rooms, his silver Mercedes gleaming in the morning sunlight.

For most of the long drive back to Ballysheel, Young Curate felt like throwing up. The road ahead of him shimmered hazily as if there were real heat in the mocking watery sun. He turned on the radio. It promised intermittent showers and cool breezes, and said that the Pope had told a group of women that every child, regardless of the circumstances of its conception, must be welcomed as a gift from God.

His head was aching and his eyes, when he glanced in the

driving mirror, resembled nothing more than twin lumps of polished coal. He had never felt so dispirited.

He was barely in sight of the town when his headache began to ease. Then the nausea faded. He didn't dare look in the driving mirror: two out of three was wonder enough. As the church spire hove into view, he felt his whole body relax. He was coming home.

This was where he belonged. He loved this place and its way of life. Dublin and its trendy followers of fashion were totally alien to him. He wanted no truck with them. Ballysheel, now, was God's own country. His place. Anything that threatened the way of life there was undoubtedly evil. Ungodly. He would take it upon himself to fight it.

First he would make a greater effort with Father Denny. Compared to the man in Dublin, Father Denny was a model of unswerving faith and devotion. Not for him the whims of passing fashion, the opting for what was more easily palatable instead of what was right.

Young Curate felt a tiny glow of affection begin to ignite somewhere deep inside him. As he pulled into the driveway of the parish house the glow became a flame. By the time he parked the car he was almost overwhelmed with feelings of love and admiration for the stalwart Father Denny. He couldn't wait to embrace him.

As if by some magical power of symbiosis, Father Denny appeared in the doorway of the house.

Dizzy with emotion, Young Curate leaped out of the car. His feet had barely touched the gravel when Father Denny tore into him. 'Where in the name of Christ were you? You should have been here ten minutes ago to start Mass. What sort of curate is late for morning Mass?'

Without waiting for an answer he bellowed even louder, What would happen if we were all late for Mass? Well? Well? I'll tell you what would happen. We'd be left with empty churches. Then where would we be? Well? Well? I'll tell you …'

And he did. Over and over. And over.

Young Curate trembled with the wonder of it all. This was surely a miracle. Father Denny was speaking to him again.

NEXT morning he called in to the obstetrics and gyne department of Ballysheel Hospital.

139

The attitude of the nurses left a lot to be desired, and he told them so in no uncertain terms. But they still refused to give him any information on their listed patients. They were decidedly unfriendly. Even rude.

'Only doing their job,' the sister in charge claimed when he complained. 'After all, we must protect the privacy of our patients.'

This in Ballysheel, where the mainstay of town life was the careful rehashing of every word, move and gesture of its inhabitants by other inhabitants.

He finally found a young doctor who would speak to him.

'Well, I'm the new boy here, but I can't say I've noticed any phenomenal rise in ... wait a minute.'

He flicked bony fingers over the computer keyboard in front of him, then peered at the screen.

'There is something unusual here, but it's not what you're looking for. Did you know that there were no recorded births here for over five years, not one single one?' His fingers were busy again. 'Of course the population is ... but not one single birth?'

'I want to know about teenage pregnancies. Tell me if ...'

A young nurse came into the room. 'You're needed in three, doctor.'

'Coming.' The doctor got to his feet, smiled apologetically at Young Curate, patted the nurse's behind, and left.

The nurse stood sullen-faced by the computer. 'Anything I can do for you, Father?' She sounded sarcastic.

'No, thank you,' Young Curate sighed in disappointment.


HIS DREAMS were full of pregnant women. They were floating, wafting all over the town, their huge pregnant stomachs billowing out in front of them. He could see the embryonic hearts beating under the thinly stretched flesh, but he couldn't make out any clear or distinct shape. He knew they couldn't be human, whatever they were. The women's faces all carried knowing smiles, as if they alone knew the secrets of the unborn. When he ran to the bishop to tell him of his concerns, the bishop laughed, lit up a huge joint, and said, 'We are all products of our culture, my son. Here, have a drag, and you'll feel a lot better.'

He tried to reach Father Denny, but in the dreams, Father

Denny was too busy preaching in the pulpit. He stood for long hours, days, weeks talking to an empty church, haranguing the empty pews for being late for Mass.

Outside in the church grounds, groups of women stood laughing, holding up their faces to the sun.

Each morning after such dreams, Young Curate woke up in a cold sweat. He began to dread the coming days.

HE WOULD have to approach Father Denny. Ask for his help.

Since the funerals of Thomas Nolan and young Ann O'Neill, the congregation had been filtering back to the church again. Not in huge numbers, but enough to obsess the old priest with filling the pews once more. It was all he spoke about. Yet Young Curate knew that if he could just once draw his attention, to the mystery pregnancies, he would make a powerful ally.

He knelt before the church altar to beg a special blessing on his endeavours.

He was just getting up from his aching knees when Father Denny walked in. This was clearly an omen for good, an indicator that the time was right. He would broach the subject now. Father Denny was bound to be receptive, standing here in front of his beloved high altar.

'What in the name of God are you talking about?' Father Denny didn't even bother to lower his voice.

The few people who were dotted about the church at that hour looked up, startled.

Young Curate indicated them with a worried incline of his head.

Father Denny ignored this. 'What are you bothering your head about expectant women for? What's that got to do with you?'

Even the most pious of the kneeling parishioners were now showing more interest in this priestly confrontation than in their religious devotions. Young Curate could practically see the antennae rising.

'Could we talk outside, Father?' Apart from the disrespect to the Blessed Host, Young Curate had no intention of being humiliated in front of these elderly parishioners.

'All right.' Father Denny gave a reluctant sigh, then bellowed at the top of his voice, 'Bring the whole family on Sunday, Mrs

Flood, including that layabout son of yours.'

The woman kneeling not two feet from him smiled. 'And God bless you too, Father.'

'Deaf as a post.' Father Denny hardly lowered his voice as he walked away.

THEY STROLLED around the old churchyard, the one spot in the parish, where ears were guaranteed not to flap.

The dates on some of the moss-covered tombstones went back several hundred years. Many of the words on them were now almost illegible, nature and poor workmanship having colluded to withhold their story. But Young Curate didn't doubt that Father Denny could quote chapter and verse on every soul who had ever been laid to rest in this small graveyard.

'Father, haven't you noticed the, er, proliferation of pregnant young women in the parish?'

Father Denny stopped walking, and kicked at a small pebble with his unpolished shoe. To Young Curate's surprise he actually managed to raise the pebble three or four feet in the air and, before it hit the ground again, kick it hard enough to send it flying above a row of green-hued tombstones.

'I used to play for the county. Did you know that?'

Young Curate didn't, but he also didn't really care.

'Three years in a row.' There was pride in Father Denny's voice.

'About this – these young girls, Father ...'

''Course we never won anything. But that wasn't the point. It was the honour of playing for one's county, representing your very own people. Showing the flag. The county flag.' The old priest kicked another stone upwards, this time missing it when it fell back to earth. 'It would have been nice to win though, just once. To carry the cup home in triumph. Just one time.'

'Father?'

'Yes, I know, you want to talk about pregnant women,' Father Denny sighed. 'Is that it?'

'We can't ignore it – them.'

'Maybe we should let their husbands worry about them.'

'That's just it, Father. There are no husbands.'

'I see. So that's what's really worrying you?'

'Father, we're not talking about one or two girls here. They are everywhere, everywhere I look.'

Father Denny peered closely at him. 'Are you sure about this?'

At last he had gotten a reaction. 'Of course I'm sure, Father, they're everywhere. I'm even dreaming about them.' The moment the words were out he knew he'd made a mistake. He tried to undo it. 'I don't mean …'

'I understand.'

Oh God, the man was actually being patient. He would have preferred it if he had bawled him out in his usual gruff way.

'What we'll do is arrange a little break for you. You're due some leave. I'll see what I can do.'

'No, Father, that isn't what I need. It's …'

'Everything passes, son, remember that. Look around you here if ever you need reminding. Everything passes.'

He walked away, nodding in agreement with himself.

Young Curate held on to a time-ravaged tombstone and cursed loudly for the first time since his boyhood.

# CHAPTER 21

BALLYSHEEL WENT about its daily business. The most absorbing topic among its menfolk was still what won the two-thirty at Newmarket. A variation on this theme was which jockey would ride the winner the next day. Only the truly radical refused flat out to discuss either horses or jockeys. They settled instead for backing greyhounds.

The pubs were as busy as ever.

The womenfolk mainly discussed the business of how their families were faring. And whether they could survive at all till next pay-day. Or, in some cases, survive without ever having another pay-day to look forward to.

Shopkeepers whinged about the opening of yet another new supermarket, and claimed that they'd all starve. At night they sank dark creamy pints in their local and bemoaned the fact that they themselves hadn't become publicans.

The children went to school, and came home again, heads brimming with facts, if not always enlightenment.

The truly elderly, of all ages, played bingo and gossiped. Not malicious gossip, for they tended not to be malicious people. Just the usual tittle-tattle of small towns everywhere, concerning births, marriages and deaths that had occurred in the wrong order.

Talk of the 'healer', and the tragedies that had surrounded him, had been put to rest. The boy was, after all, 'one of our own', and as such he merited the town's loyalty. Not so the visiting journalists, who, consensus had it, were most likely responsible for the whole ruckus anyway.

But they had departed now, heading out for more fertile fields, and Ballysheel could settle back to normal.

In the main street a new boutique selling maternity wear opened up.


YOUNG CURATE was driving along the main street when he saw the new shop. He almost ran down a young couple who were crossing the street towards it. But neither God's hand nor his newly lined brakes failed him when he needed them.

Without stopping to throw even a cursory glance at his trembling, pregnant companion, the young man in front of the car pounded furiously on its bonnet. Then he ran to the driver's door and tried to wrench it open.

Inside the locked car, Young Curate sat quaking. The man raged at him through the window. But he finally moved away, shrugging off his ashen-faced companions restraining arm.

Before disappearing down the street he turned to salute Young Curate with a stiffly raised middle finger.

Young Curate parked his car badly, and hurried into a small coffee shop across the street. He sat near the window, from where he had an unencumbered view of the new boutique.

The sign above the door said 'Motherware'. There was a large pink stork astride the word. Hanging from its beak was a gift-wrapped bundle, from which long streamers of multi-coloured ribbon fell. The whole edifice was garish and vulgar and totally out of sync with the other shops in the street.

A busy queue was forming outside. It consisted mostly of women, but there was an odd sheepish-looking man or two among them.

He spotted Janis Meehan in the crowd. Shopping for maternity clothes? And Claire O'Reilly? And the two young sopranos from the choir. And God almighty, there was Reena Scales, and her father not six months dead. That girl's mother arranged the altar flowers, the woman would die from the shame of it.

And there were the Gerber twins, brazen as ever. Mirroring each other. Flaunting their dual misshapen bodies. Showing them off, for all the world to see. Well, for all of Ballysheel to see. Shameless.

His breath caught in his chest. He could hear himself beginning to wheeze. His breathing was becoming painful.

'Can I help you, Father?' A young waitress stood by his table, her order book at the ready, her sharp eyes darting from him to the queue of pregnant women across the road.

'Er, yes, I ...' He caught his breath. 'I'd like a strong cup of coffee.' His breathing was becoming even more laboured.

'Is that all you'd like, now?' Her voice dripping with venom, she held her sharply pointed pencil as if it were a knife that she'd willingly plunge into his wheezing chest.

He looked up at her and was so taken aback by her expression that he got to his feet, startled.

'No ... cancel that order.' He pushed awkwardly past the small tables and out the door, but not before hearing her call loudly after him, 'Pervert!'

Safely outside, he glanced across the road at the girls, who were giggling and chattering in small groups. Apart from their pregnancies, they all shared that same strange look. It was definitely threatening. He didn't know why it was. Or why it should frighten him so much. But it did. It was the same look that the waitress in the coffee shop had.

That's what had startled him. Made him run.

That and the sight of the huge bump under her floral smock.

YOUNG CURATE hid out in the parish house for days. It meant ducking Father Denny. Missing out on meals. Spending hours in the bath. Pretending to be fast asleep at nine o'clock in the evening. Never answering the phone. And, most shameful of all, avoiding sick calls.

But he couldn't hide for ever. Neither his conscience nor Father Denny would allow that.

He had been invited to attend a local watercolour exhibition at the old manor house just outside the town. He steeled himself to attend. He should be safe enough there. The only people he was likely to encounter there were the county set. He had never found them to be threatening. And as a rule they were given neither to surprise pregnancies nor overtly virginal young women.

The exquisitely proportioned listed house was the pride of the Irish nation. Its owner was French. Her proportions were widely considered to be just as exquisite as her home's. She was definitely the most elegant woman in the county.

At thirty-three she had married a consultant cardiologist who was almost as rich as she was. They were rumoured to be extremely happy. Their only cross, in their five years of marital bliss, was her inability to conceive an heir for their excess of worldly goods.

She was standing in the long hallway when he arrived. Welcoming, gracious, beautiful – and pregnant!

HE TOLD himself over and over that it was pure coincidence. He told himself that she couldn't possibly be compared to all those young pregnant girls.

He told himself that nobody had more right to be having a baby. This woman had beauty, position, and a small fortune to bequeath to some lucky child. If she had a boy, he would even inherit her father's title which had bypassed her on account of her gender. All children should be so lucky.

Her husband was dancing attendance on her, proud as punch. His woman. His child. The man was besotted, and not at all ashamed to repeat the name of the person to whom they owed this little surprise.

'JC Ryan. Do you know him, Father ?'

AT WELL past midnight, when most of the other guests had left, the proud father-to-be drunkenly repeated the story for the umpteenth time, his clipped tones echoing around the big empty room.

'Had been everywhere. Consulted them all. The best in Europe. Best gyne men money could buy. No expense spared. Money no object. Blank cheque. What happened? Nothing! *Nada. Zilch.* Back to Ireland. Resigned. Give up. Hear about young fella in the town. On the QT.' He winked. 'Nicole says nothing to lose. Visits him. One time. Whammo! Up the spout before the week is out.'

He drunkenly poured another brandy into his glass. 'Credit where it's due, Father. The healer did the trick. No, no, Father,' he held up a protesting hand, 'realise that you are duty-bound to deny the blighter, but say what you will, the healer did the trick!'

He fell back against an antique chair, spilling brandy all over its damask seat.

'Credit where it's due. Young healer fella, changed our lives. All fine for celibates like yourself, but people like us who need heirs can't bugger about. Well, not forever.' He laughed and banged at a priceless antique table with his fist. 'Progeny! That's what we need, Father. Legitimate progeny!' He thumped the table again. 'And the man to see us right is the young healer. Credit where it's due.'

He collapsed into the brandy-soaked chair and began snoring drunkenly, the empty glass still clutched tightly in his hand.

*

HE HAD known about the Gerber twins; the whole town had known about that. The fits that had plagued both of them since birth had been cured by JC Ryan. He had heard some talk about Janis Meehan, and he had known about Reena Scales and her psoriasis – her awful, scarring psoriasis that had disappeared almost overnight. But he had never connected the healing with ...

And all the others? Had they all been cured by JC?

All of them?

His new testicle shrivelled in fear.

# CHAPTER 22

YOUNG CURATE was clearly off his head. He had either been quaffing the altar wine or sniffing the incense. Or both.

He was totally and utterly out of it, flying without a plane. Spinning without a top. The strange thing was that Mother didn't get at all angry with him. But then this was the new Mother. The old Mother would have torn strips off him, sent him away with a gigantic flea in his ear.

The new Mother stood calmly as Young Curate ranted and raved on. She didn't bat an eyelid at one word he said.

Not that the priest was actually accusing JC of anything. He was just rabbitting on about pregnant women. Pregnant girls! But the old Mother would have had him running down the street with his tail between his legs.

She'd have told him that they had enough to think about, what with the gardaí sniffing around again, talking all kinds of twaddle about 'suspicious circumstances', and the book publishers calling to ask if there was any possibility of resurrecting the book. What a word to use! Resurrecting! The new Mother had a good laugh at that word.

Now she stood patiently as the priest went on and on about pregnant girls. He didn't know how lucky he was that the old Mother wasn't here.

The priest was so excited that his words tumbled and crashed into each other as he rushed to get them out. He said there were dozens – hundreds – of pregnant girls all over the town. They were playing hockey, doing aerobics, singing in choirs, shopping and making obscene gestures – all at the one time, as far as JC could make out.

They were all under twenty, no, nineteen – well, perhaps not all. There was the heart specialist's wife, she was at least thirty-five, but then, she might not be like the others. Anyway ... oh, she was pregnant, no doubt about that, but she might be actually pregnant by her husband. Then again maybe not – although he certainly thought that it was by him, but then he wouldn't be the first, would he, to believe that? Cuckoos weren't the only known species to lay their eggs in another's nest.

Young Curate stopped to catch his breath.

But Mother had heard enough. She grasped him by the shoulders, turned him around and pushed him bodily away from the door. Then she slammed it closed so hard that the glass panel rattled dangerously.

'An out and out madman!' she pronounced.

JC went to the front window and watched Young Curate walking away. Hunched over like a dejected old man, he reminded JC of that first day he had called looking for his missing testicle. JC felt a sudden rush of pity for him. He opened the window to call out to him.

At first, he thought that Young Curate was praying aloud, chanting a litany of saints to himself. It was a litany all right but it wasn't a litany of saints. And he wasn't chanting.

He was methodically repeating a list of girls' names! Reena Scales. Janis Meehan. Claire O'Reilly. The Gerber twins. Alison...'

From the kitchen, Mother's voice rose sweetly as she sang one of her favourite old lullabies.

TRY AS he might, JC couldn't get to sleep that night. Long after he said goodnight to Mother and threw himself on to his bed, he was still tossing and turning. His brain was on overdrive, sending names running through his head, over and over, as if by some ticker-tape machine that he couldn't switch off.

Reena Scales *tic tic* Janis Meehan *tic tic* Claire O'Reilly *tic tic* the Gerber *tic* twins and ... Jesus!

And all the others. It couldn't be. Not all of them – it couldn't be. But why not? He hadn't taken any precautions. He thought girls always took care of that. Well, the truth was, it never entered his head that they might become ... He had only done it once with each one – hadn't he? Didn't that mean...? Oh God. Mother. How could he tell Mother?

Reena Scales *tic tic* Janis Meehan *tic tic* Claire O'Reilly *tic tic* ...

Mother always slept with her bedroom door open a little. The chink of soft light that escaped from her bedside lamp had always reassured him, made him feel safe.

It was there now, a pale narrow beacon, shining out across the dark landing. He pushed the door open fully.

Mother was lying on her back, her lipstick-free mouth relaxed in what was almost a smile. She was fast asleep. The floral-print pillow covers and matching sheets made her look as if she were sleeping in a bed of tulips. Even the wallpaper had tulips on it. And the curtains. But no earth-grown tulip had ever produced the unreal colours that this bedroom variety sprouted. They were a surreal mixture of deep purple, stark blood red, and an unnatural shade of boot-polish brown. The seed pack from hell.

Mother stirred slightly, but slept on.

JC coughed. No reaction. He cleared his throat as loudly as he could. She still didn't stir.

On his way out he made a last half-hearted attempt to waken her. He closed her door loudly and then opened it again quickly. He thought for a second that her happy expression faltered in her sleep. But no. She didn't stir. Only the overblown tulips rose up and down in response to her deep, even breathing.

He went back to his room and spent the rest of the night fretting. Satan kept him company.

Morning took eons to arrive.


HE HUNG around outside Reena's house till nearly midday. Although it was raining, quite hard, he got some shelter from the dense beeches that lined the quiet cul-de-sac. He got wetter when the rain stopped and a sneaky wind began whipping the beeches in every direction. He was about to step out from underneath them when he spotted Reena in her front porch. He waved to get her attention, but quickly moved back when her mother appeared behind her.

They were both smartly dressed. Chatting happily to each other. And laughing a lot, their heads nodding in unison.

Reena had never gotten along with her mother. It was her dead father who had demanded, and gotten, all her attention. That was when he had been alive, of course. But now the two women appeared thick as thieves.

He kept way back behind the trees as they passed. Even if he hadn't, he doubted that they would have noticed him, so engrossed were they in their conversation. Reena looked beautiful and relaxed, and was smiling widely at something her mother said to her.

But Father Testicle hadn't been lying. At least not about Reena. Even a blind man could see that she was well pregnant.

*

FINDING JANIS Meehan was more difficult. As always, she was involved in more weekend activities than any ten people could handle.

He finally tracked her down at a gym class in the town hall.

He stood on tiptoe to peer through the glass panel at the top of the swing doors. There were about a dozen girls inside, all doing some type of stretching exercise. They were dressed in almost identical black leotards, and black tights, all wearing their hair caught up in similar top knots. But Janis stood out from all the other girls. She was the hugely pregnant one.

HE RAN and ran until his breath failed him. Down the steps of the old hall, across the main street, ignoring the curious looks of the shoppers and traders alike. Past the new supermarket, and coffee bar, past the small group of women standing outside a garishly painted shop with a strange bird above it. He ran past the church and the empty school, almost knocking down a little girl who was rushing out the gate, laden with art equipment. He caught her arms to steady her. She smiled up apologetically into his face. Suddenly her eyes widened with recognition and she stared at him as if she were seeing an apparition. Her small freckled face lit up with delight. JC backed away from her. He began running again. Fast. After a few hundred yards he chanced a quick surreptitious look over his shoulder.

The child was standing, watching him. He ran faster. Just before he turned the corner to head for the river, he glanced back again.

She was still there. Still watching.

He had never seen her before in his life. Yet she clearly recognised him. Her smile had widened with delight, and – and what? What?

He felt panic rising in him again. Terror! At what?

He forced himself to take the next step. He had to know.

MRS GERBER opened the door to him. Her sour face broke into a broad smile of welcome. She greeted him as if he had come to tell her she was the single winner in the new state lottery.

'No, the girls aren't here, but do please come on in. Don't stand there on the doorstep. Come in, come in.' She didn't so much speak as gush at him, non-stop.

154

He kept waiting for the catch, for the axe to fall. But it didn't happen. She prattled on, gushing, offering him everything short of the family silver. He settled for a cup of tea.

Mrs Gerber was, clearly, very happy to see him.

'How are the twins?' he heard himself squeak.

'Haven't you heard?' Impossible as it seemed, her smile actually widened. 'They are both heading for Trinity.'

'Trinity?'

'Oh you haven't heard. Well, you must be the only one in the town who hasn't.' She was the cat that got the cream. If she had a paw she'd have washed her face with it.

The twins would both be setting out soon for Trinity College. That bastion of privilege and learning would soon reverberate to the dulcet tones of the clones that were the pride of the Gerber family.

Mrs Gerber had every reason to feel smug. From remedial classes to the halls of Academia – and all in less than one short year.

'Call again,' she kept repeating as he took his leave of her. And it may have been a trick of the light, but he could have sworn that Mrs Gerber, who was on record as saying that all young men were vermin, and should be medically castrated, winked conspiratorially at him.


ONCE OUTSIDE the house, he felt light-headed with relief. And not just to be safely beyond the reach of Mrs Gerber's hospitality. No, here was proof absolute that Father Testicle was way off his trolley. If the Gerber twins were heavily and obviously pregnant, would they be heading out to study law at Trinity College? Would their mother be smiling like a Cheshire cat with a grin which not only wouldn't fade, but which threatened to grow and grow until it engulfed all of humanity? The woman was only short of offering him bed and board. Would she make him so welcome if she had two pregnant daughters and even suspected that he might be – the culprit? Never!

There was still the matter of Reena and Janis, but if the priest was so wrong about the Gerber twins, then maybe, just maybe, he had jumped to the wrong conclusion about Reena and Janis. Maybe the fact that they both became pregnant at – at about – the time they were healed was sheer coincidence. Why not? Stranger things could happen!

They could! Walking along the narrow river pathway towards him were the Gerber twins. Holding hands as usual, they strolled along, their faces full of daydreams, their swollen stomachs full of the future.

They smiled at him, and passed on as if he were no more than a casual acquaintance.

JC began running.

# CHAPTER 23

HE KEPT going until darkness fell. For the last twenty minutes or so he had been climbing, unawares, almost unconsciously as the ground beneath him had begun to angle sharply upwards along a steep grassy slope. No roads here, not even a pathway, no houses, and certainly no people. Even the trees gave up after attempting the lower slope; all that remained growing here was some rough furze that every schoolboy knew was better avoided, as it indiscriminately tore at clothes and flesh without any regard for either. He plumped down exhausted on the grassy mound that was known as the Ballysheel Hill. The townspeople called it a fairy fort, but Father Denny told the pupils in school that it was the remains of a rampart that had once ringed an ancient settlement, that had long preceded their town and its history.

Some believed the priest. Others didn't. Knowledge of the fairy fort had long preceded Father Denny's time. Or any of his predecessors'.

JC looked down over the town where he'd been born. He watched as its night lights came on. The brightest of these were in the main street. There, the sharp street lighting blended with the fluorescence-washed shop windows and flickering electrical signs to cloak the whole area in mock daylight.

Further out, and behind the main street, small housing estates, and some single dwellings, formed their own minor light display, their bright squares and rectangles contrasting with frequent patches of darkness.

Further out still, the dark patches became bigger and blacker until they took over completely, except where invasive car headlights suddenly stabbed into them.

He could pick out where his own house was from here, but he couldn't see it. The church spire blocked his view. It was unlit.

The one building that was continuously lit, day and night, was the hospital. But from here it looked like an old Gothic mansion, its creeper-covered walls and turreted front windows giving no indication of the modern medicine that was practised behind its medieval-looking facade.

He wondered if the lights were on in his own house, if Mother were at home? Was she wondering where he was? He knew she wouldn't be angry if he were home late. These days, she was never angry; he could do no wrong in her eyes. Everything he did met with her approval. Everything.

But then he had never made a whole group of girls pregnant before. Even the new Mother might draw the line at that.

He lay back on the soft mound and tried to think calmly. He would have to tell her; this was Ballysheel after all, a difficult place to keep a secret in. The wonder was that nobody had already told her. Surely somebody else besides Father Testicle must have noticed the girls? Ballysheel was a town where people loved to talk. Especially the women.

In spite of knowing the hill, and his eyes becoming accustomed to the dark, on his way down he still got badly torn by the furze. It ripped at his clothes and stabbed viciously at his hands as he passed. Unlike the town, the hill had no tradition of hospitality.

He could see the lights of his house from the end of the street. Mother was home. He quickened his pace.

She fussed over his torn hands but she didn't question him. She searched out a bottle of disinfectant and a packet of cotton wool and began ministering to his cuts. She was full of chat about the circle. They were getting new members at an incredible rate. More applications than they could handle, in fact. One of them was that nice Mrs Scales from Beechview.

'Oh did that sting?' she fretted as he flinched. 'Never mind, I've almost finished.'

She chattered on about the circle and the new members, and how they would soon have to find a bigger place to meet.

'Mrs Scales has a huge house. She says it's far too big for just herself and Reena …' Her voice trailed off, as if she were thinking aloud. 'There, they won't become infected now.' She was brisk again, putting the stopper on the bottle and throwing the used cotton wool into the bin.

'Mother, there's something I want to …'

'Come on, talk to me while we eat.' She washed her hands and hummed her way to the table.

He did talk to her. About almost everything, and anything, and nothing and back to everything again. The only subject he strictly avoided was girls. And he even more strictly avoided the subject of pregnancy.

For her part, Mother went on and on about the new energy that was abounding at each circle meeting. 'Oh, and you won't believe who popped in the other night. Do you remember that lovely nurse …?'

JC almost choked on his fish.

'What was her name again, Jessie? You must remember, you met her once in Outpatients.'

JC started breathing again. 'The tall woman with the glasses? Yes, I remember. You discovered that you were both Geminis!'

'That's her.' Mother was like an excited child. 'Well, she's becoming a member.'

'That's great news, Mother. Great news.'

The fish on his plate stared at him with dead glassy eyes.

HE DID attempt to tell her a couple more times, but it was never the right time. Or Mother had something to tell him that wouldn't keep. Or she was on her way out. Usually to a circle meeting. The meetings were now stepped up to three and sometimes four a week. But who could begrudge Mother something that made her so happy – and kept her so busy?

The priest contacted him again about two weeks later. At least he tried to contact him. JC picked up the phone and when he heard the familiar stammering voice he pretended to be an answering machine.

'There is nobody home at the moment. Please leave your message when you hear the beep. Beep … beep.' He couldn't tell if the priest believed he was talking to a machine or not. Either way, he hung up and didn't phone again. Soon after that, Mother heard that Young Curate had been sent away on a holiday.

JC spent every day expecting one of the girls to contact him. Whenever the phone rang, which wasn't a lot, he almost jumped out of his skin. Even a ring on the doorbell was enough to set him quaking.

He took to wearing the kaftan in bed. It guaranteed him a good night's sleep. He had always felt invincible when wearing the kaftan. But then it was this very feeling that had gotten him into trouble in the first place.

When Mother saw him in the kaftan she smiled, just long enough to stop humming. She never mentioned healing now. She just smiled and hummed, both of which were beginning to get on his nerves. But then everything was getting on his nerves now. Why didn't one of the girls contact him? Did nobody care about the paternity of all these children?

# CHAPTER 24

HE WAS half-woken by the phone ringing. He shook his head, trying to free it from the clouds of sleep that clung to it. The ringing stopped, but he was wide awake now. Almost. The clock said three-thirty.

He could hear Mother's voice. He couldn't make out what she was saying, but her voice was rising with excitement. He got out of bed and went to peer over the landing.

Her head was nodding in double quick time. 'Yes, yes, yes – of course. We'll be there. Yes, both of us.' She smiled up at JC as he stood shivering in the kaftan. 'We'll be there.'

She put the phone down. 'Get your shoes on, we're going to the hospital.'

JC stared blankly at her.

'Do as you're told. And wear the kaftan.' The old Mother was back. She picked up the phone and began dialling. 'Go on, get ready.'

He was coming down the stairs when he heard her making another call. 'Yes, now. I know it's early, but not much. They say everything is going well. Yes, I'll see you then. No, I can't believe it either.' Her voice became thin, squeaky with suppressed excitement. 'Yes, yes.'

JC put his mac on over the kaftan. 'I'm ready, Mother.'

A CAR appeared at the door. It was driven by a certifiable lunatic. JC realised this as soon as it left the kerb. They reached the hospital in minutes, mainly because the woman drove like a bat out of hell. The fact that they got there in one piece was attributable, JC felt, to the goodwill of some higher power.

His stomach was still lurching as he followed Mother into the hospital. The lunatic followed close behind.

Inside the hospital, Mother seemed to know exactly where she was going. She ran up a short flight of stairs, with JC and the lunatic trailing behind her. A small group of women stood on the tiled landing. Their excitement was palpable. Two nurses came hurrying to join them.

'This is Jessie.' Mother waved an arm in his direction.

Every eye in the place turned to stare at him – for a full second.

Then they huddled excitedly together again. He recognised some of the faces from Mother's circle group. Signora Goretti was there, elegant as ever, even at four in the morning. Geraldine stood looking as if she had just leaped out of bed, but then Geraldine always looked as if she had just leaped out of bed. But her startled-looking face and hair made JC suspect that he knew who had driven her here. The others were complete strangers to him.

Then a familiar face and body arrived. It was the angel.

The group parted and allowed her into their centre. They made a tight circle around her, eager to hear what she had to say. All except the lunatic, who chattered so loudly to JC that he couldn't hear a word the angel was saying.

As the angel stopped speaking, so did the lunatic, closing her twittering mouth at the exact same time.

A door swung open silently and a masked figure in green came out.

'Is this …?' The figure indicated JC.

Mother pushed forward. 'Yes, this is Jessie.'

'You'll have to wear a gown, and a mask.'

JC opened his mac to indicate the kaftan. 'But I thought –'

The masked figure hooted with laughter. 'Don't be ridiculous.'

'Mother, I don't understand.' JC looked pleadingly at Mother. 'You said …'

The whole group smiled indulgently, even Mother.

'It's all right, Jessie.' Her voice was calming, soothing – the voice that grown-ups use when talking to a child.

He was pushed through a doorway, a gown and mask were expertly tied on him, and then he was led, gently this time, into a brightly lit room.

It was an operating theatre. There were unfamiliar machines, huge arc lights, strange canisters, and a high table surrounded by people in green masks and gowns. He was led to the front of the table. Green-garbed figures stood back to let him through.

Lying back against a mound of pillows was Reena. She was draped in hospital linen, with only her head and arms showing, apart from … oh Jesus. The room began to tilt. Jesus. No way … oh please …

162

'Catch him, he's going to faint.' It was Reena's voice. But why didn't she sound like those women he had seen on TV who were about to give birth?

Where was the gasping, the panting, the begging for it to be all over? Why wasn't she crying out in agony, with beads of sweat dripping from greasy lank hair that looked as if it belonged to an old crone?

Why did Reena sound as if she were at a party, having a wonderful 'wish you were here' time? She was stretched out – exposed – with all this paraphernalia surrounding her. All these medical people. She shouldn't be enjoying this.

'You can't faint here. If you feel like fainting, tell me, I'll sort you out.' It was the lunatic again. Even under the cover of the mask and long gown, he couldn't fail to recognise her.

'Leave him alone.' Reena actually giggled. 'Come here, JC, stand at this end.'

The green-garbed figures made room for him once more.

Reena reached out and caught his hand. This end of her was as beautiful as he remembered. Her dark hair was like wild silk against the pillows, and even the harsh theatre lights couldn't fade her honey-coloured skin.

He felt his knees begin to give way again. He held on to her hand to keep himself upright.

'Any pain?' The doctor's voice was crisp.

'No, I just feel weak.'

There were a few smothered titters from behind him.

'Reena! Any pain?'

'No pain, I feel wonderful.'

'None at all?' There was disbelief in the questioner's voice.

'None!' Reena shook her head.

'There it goes, look, that's the contraction.'

Everybody turned to watch some wriggling lines on a monitor. Everybody except JC. He watched Reena's face.

'Anything?' It was the doctor's voice again.

'Well, maybe something.' Reena frowned. 'Like a feather being drawn across my stomach. Yes! Like a feather.'

There were fists raised in clenched salute around the theatre, and low whoops of delight.

'That's enough of that,' the doctor frowned, 'we're all professionals here, not soccer hooligans. And we have a long way to go yet.'

'Not for this delivery,' the gowned figure sitting at the end of the table said. 'Here we gooo.'

There was a sudden flurry of activity around Reena's rear end.

'Easy …'

'That's it, Reena, bear down a little.'

'Hold it, hold it … now … that's it … that's it. Here she comes!'

'Your beautiful, beautiful daughter. Look, Reena.'

The gloved hands held up the tiny black-haired creature for all to see. A subdued cheer went up. Then the tears started.

'Here we go. Cord cut. Here you are … mother.'

The baby was placed in Reena's arms. She was a mini replica of her mother. She was also the only female in the theatre who wasn't weeping.

JC realised that he was the only male in the theatre. But he cried his eyes out anyway.

Reena's daughter stared at him, her inky blue eyes wide with mystification.

Her mother said, 'Thank you, JC.'

Every eye in the theatre was turned on him. He suddenly felt terribly alone. And his throat hurt.

When they finally arrived back at the house they could hardly get in, it was so crowded. There were champagne corks popping in every room.

The women congratulated each other, as if they themselves had just given birth. They were slapping each other on the back, kissing cheeks, toasting the mother and child.

Nobody congratulated him. He didn't really mind. Not really, it was Reena's baby after all.

And they did fill his glass every time he emptied it.

And he was the only man privileged to be there.

He was privileged, wasn't he?

# CHAPTER 25

THE FOLLOWING morning he woke up late. The first thing he noticed was that Mother, or somebody, had opened his blinds. The second thing was that somebody else was using a pneumatic drill inside his head. He crossed the floor inch by painful inch and closed the blinds. The sound of their swishing almost blew the top off his head. There was a phone ringing somewhere, at a million decibels above the human pain threshold.

Two identical Mothers came into the room. They were both fuzzy around the edges. They asked in unison if they could get him something.

He refused both of them. The only thing which could put an end to his agony was decapitation, he pleaded. Both Mothers smiled and said that wasn't an option.

The Mothers disappeared. He had barely closed his eyes when they were back. At least one of them was. She asked if he felt any better.

SHE GAVE him some herbal tea and aspirin. He felt a lot worse after that.

He tried to go back to sleep but the drilling in his head wouldn't allow it. Satan padded into the room. He was wearing hobnailed boots.

His headache wasn't confined to his head. It was all over his body. Even his nails ached. Yet somewhere deep down inside him there was a happy memory trying to emerge. Only he couldn't remember what it was. Then he did. Reena had had her baby! A small black-haired infant who was already smart enough to view the world with suspicion.

Reena had had her baby! And he was lying here feeling sorry for himself, just because he was in unbearable agony. He dragged himself down the stairs and rang the hospital. Sorry! They had no patient called Scales here. No, there hadn't been one. Ever! Not of that name, sir. He described Reena; perhaps she had used another name. No, sir. He described the birth, as best he could. The voice on the other end giggled. I don't think so, sir. Perhaps somebody has been playing a joke? A trick?

165

He put the phone down. Mother was in the kitchen humming. He crept up behind her.

'Where is Reena?'

'What?'

'Reena and the baby? Where are they?'

'Baby?' Mother looked mystified.

He sat down quickly. 'You brought me to the hospital. Last night. You and all the women, remember? Reena had her baby.'

She put her hand on his forehead. 'You haven't left your bed for two days. You've been feverish. That aspirin we've been using hasn't worked at all. You go straight back to bed and I'll call Dr Mary.'

Why was she pretending not to remember?

'Mother, the house here was full of people, women – drinking champagne, singing.'

She looked at him pityingly. 'Of course it was. Of course they were. Back to bed with you now. Come on, I'll make you a herb drink, we have to get that temperature down.'

'I haven't got a temperature. I have a hangover from drinking too much champagne.'

She put her hand across her mouth. At first he thought he had upset her, but then he realised that she was trying not to giggle. She was laughing at him.

He held his head, and tried not to yell. 'Mother, I have a hangover.'

'All right, Jessie. All right. But let's just see if you have a temperature as well.' She took a thermometer from the kitchen drawer.

'I ...'

'We'll just pop this into your mouth.'

Before he could protest, the thermometer was stuck into his open mouth. He had no choice but to stand there, silently fuming.

Mother hummed happily. She checked her watch, her mouth still twitching.

He pulled the thermometer from his mouth. It read 103.

She brought a herb drink to his bedroom. He sulked and refused to drink it.

'Call me if you need anything.' She actually laughed out loud. 'Not champagne, I'm afraid I can't run to that. And you'll have to look elsewhere for your dancing girls.'

He could hear her laughing as she went downstairs.

HE DREAMT of Reena and a little black-haired baby. The baby was calling him Dada, until a doctor wearing a balaclava snatched it from his arms. Reena's eyes were full of tears. 'I'm sorry, JC,' she kept repeating, over and over.

Mother stood in the dream doorway. 'Bide your time, Jessie. We did.' She giggled behind her hand, like a little girl.

He stroked Reena's silken hair. She gave happy little grunts and snorts of pleasure.

He woke up to find himself patting Satan's massive head.

Every bone in his body was aching. When he tried putting his feet to the floor, his legs refused to hold his weight. He dropped back on to the sweat-drenched bed.

He knew he was dying.

THE MEDICAL prognosis was that JC would live a long and healthy life.

'A bad dose of flu,' was how Dr Mary summarised the hellish two weeks of soaring temperatures, hallucinations and agonising pains that had wracked every muscle and bone in his body. But that's all behind you now.' She snapped her medical bag shut.

JC lay back on his overplumped pillows and waited for death.

Mother tried tempting him to eat with the widest variety of foodstuffs he had ever laid eyes on, from his favourite corned beef and cabbage to saffron-coloured rice dishes that looked as if they should be gracing the colour pages of an exotic Eastern cook book. He gave them all to Satan, who developed a flatulence problem and a thorough dislike of kidney beans.

Mother held off on her prognosis, but insisted that fresh air and exercise were what JC needed most now that he appeared to be eating all before him again.

Satan farted loudly.

When JC flatly refused to leave his bed for the third week running, Mother became concerned. She showed this by yelling at him for the first time since she had become the new Mother. She accused him of being self-pitying, lazy and obstructive.

JC didn't answer. He turned his face to the wall and went to sleep.

Next morning, the angel appeared at the end of his bed.

Mother said, 'I'll leave you two alone,' and went downstairs to prepare another gigantic meal.

Satan padded after her.

But JC couldn't respond to the Angel. Nothing she did or said affected him. He lay on the bed disinterested and uncaring.

He heard her sharp intake of breath when she realised just how thin he had become, how clearly visible and even remarkable were the bones and blue veins under his grey-tinged skin. He saw her eyes fill with tears. But it didn't matter. Nothing mattered. He had never been a healer. He had never helped anyone in pain. He had never contributed anything at all to anyone's well-being. Jesus, he had even given the dog wind. What kind of healer would do that? It had all been a fantasy, one big hallucination. Or a trick? And that was even worse. He had tricked the girls into... into what? He couldn't even be sure any more what was real. Were any of the girls even pregnant? Had that been a fantasy too? He thought about Reena, but he had to stop. It hurt too much …

'JC?' The angel touched his face.

He turned away.


'NURSE SAYS you're not eating?'

Mother bustled into the room, carrying a tray. She appeared puzzled. 'She says I'm to feed you soup. Now!' Her voice was determined. 'No, don't turn away, Jessie, you'll eat this, or you'll be taken into hospital and force fed.' Her eyes widened in fear. 'Where will we be then?'

She fed him spoonful after careful spoonful, wiping his chin with a soft napkin even when there was no need. She sat wordlessly, alternatively dabbing at his chin and raising the spoon to his lips, and all the while big salt tears flowed non-stop down her face.

The hot soup seared his aching throat, but he swallowed it dutifully. He couldn't add to her distress.

'Try to finish it, Jessie.' Her voice was gentle, pleading.

When he finally shook his head, she set the tray aside and smoothed his burning forehead with her cool hand.

Satan crept into the room and lapped up the discarded soup.

Mother rounded on him like a fury. She hit him with the large soup spoon, slapped him with her free hand and yelled at him like a fishwife.

A startled Satan barked back defensively.

The noise was more than JC could bear.

# CHAPTER 26

YOUNG CURATE felt wonderful. One hundred per cent better. A week's retreat at the Mother House was just what he'd needed.

Praying, walking, even sleeping among other young celibates had had a rejuvenating effect on him. He felt cleansed, energised, and fully prepared to attend to his duties again. Father Denny had been right all along. Seven days of prayer, peace and meditation were indeed balm to the soul.

Not to mention the body.

His confessor had helped too. In a quiet, authoritative voice, he had reminded Young Curate that sometimes our own little weaknesses have a tendency to distort our view of other people. This in itself was not a sin, he had emphasised.

'Temptation can never be considered a sin,' he continued. 'Wasn't our Lord Himself tempted? It's the indulging in the temptation that becomes the sin. My advice is to keep yourself busy. Active. Don't let your eye linger where it might encounter temptation. And if it should do so, never underestimate the value of a cold shower.'

No more than Father Denny did he take seriously Young Curate's insistence that there were shoals of strangely pregnant young girls in Ballysheel. Girls that were threatening, frightening.

Instead he told him to concentrate on the positive aspects of celibacy, to use the extra energy it afforded young priests – energy that came from God, and could be used in many, many ways as a salutation to Him. 'Concentrate, my son,' he said.

And Young Curate did.

At choir practice, he concentrated on the glorious notes that rose in a musical hymn of praise to the Lord. At the girls' playing fields he concentrated on the actual games. When he was asked to bless the new extension to the old town hall, he concentrated on the building, hardly glancing at the girls from the aerobics class who formed a leotard-clad guard of honour for the visiting dignitaries.

When he had to walk through the town centre, he made

171

sure to walk on the opposite side of the street from the awful boutique with the dreadful pink stork above it.

The first time he did this, he averted his eyes by looking straight into the little coffee shop. But standing close to the window, order pad in hand, was the waitress he had encountered when he was going through his neurotic phase. He nodded to her to indicate that what was past was past. She smiled back widely at him and then slowly and obscenely raised two fingers high into the air.

After that he took care to keep looking directly ahead. And concentrating. He was amazed at how simple it was.

How had he ever considered life to be complicated?


IN THE following weeks, the church choir won three major choral competitions. They came last in a smaller one, but that one didn't count as it was held in northern Ireland. The whole choir was ecstatic. Their successes were widely reported in the national papers. With photographs. At a grand celebration dinner, they presented Young Curate with a large glossy reproduction of the biggest and best press photo. In it, the two pregnant sopranos stood proudly at either side of him as he held a large leaded crystal ball in his hands.

The girl's hockey team lambasted their opponents in a preseason friendly. Nobody was surprised. Everything Young Curate touched was turning to gold.

Even the American tea party which he organised with the Young Wives' club was a rip-roaring success. It made three hundred pounds, and a lot of young husbands extremely happy.

A delighted Father Denny asked Young Curate if he would like to give the homily on the next Family Sunday.

'My cup runneth over,' was his reply.

He worked late into the night and for most of the following day on the sermon. He wrote, changed, and rearranged until he was satisfied with the message he wanted to convey. Having been so well served by his fellow priests, he could in turn do no less for the good people of this small parish. He would use his own experiences and observations of life, as a foundation for his sermon. But his message would be couched in simple metaphors. He would touch their hearts as Christ had, by using the simple language of the people.

The church was almost full. Family Sunday could always

guarantee a good turnout, and besides, the local football team was playing at home this afternoon.

He waited for the ritualised clearing of throats to end. Then, after a quick glance at Father Denny, who nodded encouragingly, he began.

'There was once a group of choristers who were, individually, all fine singers. But as a choir, they failed abysmally. Try as they might, their choral successes fell far short of their aspirations. Again and again they tried – to no avail.' He paused. 'Then suddenly, they began winning all before them. They beat choirs that had been feted for decades as the best in the country. Unbeatable.

'And what had brought about this metamorphosis? What had wrought this great change in this little choir? Had their voices improved beyond measure? Had they begun to practise more? Had they changed their repertoire?' Looking down at the blank faces below him, he slowly shook his head.

'No.' He almost whispered the word.

'They had simply learned to perform as a unit! A cohesive unit!'

In the front pew a man stifled a yawn.

'And what is a family if not a unit? But what kind of unit is your family? Is it a group of people all following their own selfish paths,' he held up his hand, fingers splayed wide, 'or is it a cohesive unit bound steadfastly together with one main purpose?' His hand became a clenched fist. 'You can judge for yourselves which would make the most invincible force.'

Down below him, Father Denny coughed loudly.

'Whether it's a choir …' He looked directly into his prized soprano's face. She leaned back so that her pregnant stomach jutted forward aggressively.

'Whether it's a – a choir, a hockey team, or …'

Janis Meehan was sitting in the third pew. She smirked brazenly at his discomfort, her swollen stomach clearly visible even from the tall pulpit.

'Or …'

The Gerber twins and their mother sat near the centre aisle.

'Only by supporting each other, by –'

Claire O'Reilly was sitting below him, head tilted to one side, listening intently. Her mother, sitting beside her, had a hand cupped protectively around Claire's pregnant stomach.

173

She looked directly into Young Curate's eyes. He felt the sweat break out on his forehead. Jesus. Two other girls, not more than seventeen, sat side by side, relaxed, contented and hugely pregnant. The rest of their pew was taken up by nuns from the nearby convent school. One of the nuns glanced sideways at the girls – just a quick glance, but it was enough for Young Curate to catch the look of almost maternal pride on the nun's face as she turned and – Oh sweet Jesus, that was it. How could he not have seen it before? It was so clear now. Even the young waitress in the coffee shop, the girl in the newsagents – Oh dear God, Mrs Spencer in the manor house – They were all in on it, all the women together – a cohesive unit, all supporting each other … He sank to his knees, trembling. The devil's children … The demon is among us … He is in our midst, taking on human form, taking bodies as well as souls – and they were all in it together. The women. All the women … Oh Jesus, Jesus … He heard a voice screaming, wailing …

Father Denny got to him first. He tried to pull him up from his knees. But Young Curate clung to the lower pulpit, sweat running down his ashen face. The new local GP took the pulpit steps two at a time, but when Young Curate saw her he screamed even louder than before. She couldn't placate him. Whenever she opened her mouth he screamed. In deference to her condition, Father Denny drew her away, then turned back to deal with Young Curate.

The church was in an uproar. Nobody knew for sure exactly what had happened.

Had the priest had a turn? A fit? A fit in the pulpit? In God's house? Somebody mentioned the IRA. Oh God, was there a bomb planted? Word spread along the pews. There was a bomb in the pulpit! Young Curate had spotted it. There was a surge towards the doors. People began screaming. Everybody wanted out. They were pushing each other, being knocked down, crushed against statues. An old woman who was being buffeted back and forth by the wave of panicking people gave up any attempt at escape. She clung to a blue-robed statue of the Virgin with one arm, raised her other arm in supplication and sang. 'Hail Qu-e-e-n of Heaven, The O-o-cean Star, Guide of …'

From the pulpit Father Denny called for calm. The terrified

congregation ignored him. He finally bellowed at the top of his voice, 'Remember where you are. This is the house of God! Show some respect.'

It was a measure of the esteem in which the people held either Father Denny or God that they did begin to vacate the church, in which they believed a bomb was about to explode, in a fairly orderly manner.

And the old woman continued singing, 'We cl-a-im, thy care. Save us from p-e-ril and from woe. M-o-ther of Chr-i-st. Star of the sea. Pr-a-y for the s-i-n-ner. Pr-a-y for me.'

THE town was abuzz with gossip. It hadn't been an IRA bomb after all.

It was the UVF. They had heard about the healer. And now, with statues of the Virgin Mary beginning to move all over the place, they were afraid that a wave of fervent Catholicism would spread, and sweep across the country taking the border with it, pushing Protestantism into the Irish sea.

In turn they would bomb every Catholic pulpit in the country.

Several other likely theories regarding Young Curate's inexplicable behaviour abounded.

The one person who could explain it, who could perhaps categorically deny the presence of a bomb, was incommunicado. He was 'resting' in the hospital.

On his behalf, Father Denny did deny the bomb story. But not too emphatically. Some bombs were easier to deal with than others.

In his meeting with the bishop, it was agreed that a little discretion was never a bad thing. Celibate priests and their attitude to women were always a thorny subject, never more so than in recent times. It wouldn't do for the press to get hold of the notion that a serving priest was claiming that every woman in the town of Ballysheel was in league with the Devil.

YOUNG CURATE refused flat out to speak to a psychiatrist. He was feeling perfectly all right now, he insisted. And no matter what anyone said, he knew he had merely had a blackout.

They ran in his family, he explained. From his grandfather down, every single male member of his family had suffered from blackouts. It was normal for them, almost a family tradition in the male line, a rite of passage. As soon as they hit thirty, they had blackouts. Nothing major. Nothing dangerous. Just simple blackouts. Surely the medical profession had heard of them?

He had no objection to medical tests, he informed them. They could test him to their heart's content. Physically. But no psychiatrist! Under no circumstances! Did he look like a madman? Did he look disturbed? Well then, why would he need a psychiatrist?

They left him alone to think about it. And he did. He thought about it day and night, for almost a week. He didn't sleep, but then he didn't need sleep. God almighty, he was lying in bed all day long, wasn't he? What would he need sleep for?

He had to admit that he didn't have much energy. But his brain was careering ahead non-stop, sending fleeting images of women flashing through his mind. All sorts of women. Women who were tall, thin, short, fat, dark, fair, obese, sensual, tempting, dewy-eyed and beckoning. But they were all, without exception, pregnant. Hugely pregnant. And they all carried that strange air of triumph about them. The look that he recognised. The mark of the demon. That sly knowing look that set them apart from what all decent modest women should look like.

He realised that they must be aware that he was on to them. Otherwise why would they have tried to destroy him in the pulpit?

He would have to destroy them. Not just for his own sake, but to prevent the demon from taking over the world. But they were too many. They were legion. They were even here in Ballysheel Hospital. Well disguised, of course, but he could spot them. He knew their mark. One of them had pretended to be a psychiatrist but luckily her white coat had fallen open and he had spotted her giveaway swollen stomach.

He would have to be careful. He must remain clear-headed. And pray. That way he could hope to defeat them.

One thing was certain, all roads led back to the healer. He was clearly Satan's instrument on earth. He had, after all, merely to touch his body for a second testicle to appear without warning. That was without a doubt a demonic act. For what just God would ever direct that a missing testicle be delivered to an anointed celibate?

He had been touched by the demon. He was now unclean in the sight of the Lord. There was only one clear route to salvation. He would have to kill JC Ryan. And the girls. All of them.

# CHAPTER 27

AFTER THE hullabaloo over the soup, Satan was strictly barred from the sickroom. But Mother did see to it that JC was never left alone. Not even for a single moment.

Whenever she had reason to leave the room, someone else always stood watch. Sometimes it was Geraldine. She stood beside his bed looking as perplexed as ever, as if she wasn't quite certain why she was there. Her frizzy hennaed hair formed its usual startled halo around her pale face, but the deep worried furrows on her forehead were new. Every now and again she would gently touch his wrist, with the distracted air of someone who was concerned, without quite knowing why.

Sometimes it was Signora Goretti who sat with him. Her olive-skinned hands were constantly taken up with some intricate piece of needlework, but her shrewd eyes never left his face. She didn't speak at all. She simply watched.

There were others. He would waken up to find some strange woman, bending over him, checking his temperature or gently wiping his sweat-drenched forehead. They were all so different from each other. They appeared not to have anything at all in common. They were of all ages, types and creeds. Or so it seemed. One sat hunched over the Koran. Rather, that's what she claimed it was when he asked her. He couldn't even make out the strange lettering on its mouldy cover.

The one who replaced her was glancing through a tabloid that Mother normally wouldn't allow into the house. The youngest and best looking one rambled on about her Persian cat and the great difficulties it had in shifting hairballs. After a whole morning of hairballs, he found himself wishing for the return of the black-moustached but monosyllabic Koran reader.

Mother fed him four meals a day. The food was light but he still found it hard to stomach.

But she sat and cut, and forked small dainty quantities into his protesting mouth, until his plate was cleared each time.

Pleading nausea or an overly full stomach gained no sympathy from her. She stubbornly held out each forkful until he gave in and opened his mouth like an obedient child.

His gaunt reflection in the bathroom mirror gave no indication of all this feeding. He was still skin and bone, his eyes underscored by deep black circles. And now even the trips to the bathroom were draining what was left of his energy.

The women were clearly becoming more and more concerned about him. They took to whispering together when they thought he was sleeping. He knew he was the subject of their conversations, by the anxious glances that were thrown in his direction every couple of seconds.

HE WOKE up late one night to find the angel and four of Mother's circle friends standing by his bed.

The angel bent over him. 'Don't worry, JC, everything will be all right. You go back to sleep now.'

He tried, but every bone in his body was aching. And the drill had started up inside his head again. But the low murmuring of the women's voices, became soothing and comforting.

He fell asleep, listening to the rhythmic flow.

HE WAS alone in the room when he woke. It might have been the following morning. The sun squinted weakly through the slatted blinds. There was a siren wailing somewhere in the town. But it didn't hurt his head. He sat up in surprise.

His head was clear. He stretched out his arms, then his legs. They felt almost normal, pain-free. For the first time in weeks there was no pain, anywhere.

'Mother?'

He didn't wait for her to come to him. The stairs were easy, they didn't jar his bones any more.

'Mother?'

She was sitting at the kitchen table, her back towards him. He knew before she turned that something was wrong. The room was too quiet. There was no humming, no clattering of dishes. No sound of the kettle whistling and – and Satan was nowhere to be seen. No snuffling, or whining to be walked, no happy little yelps of greeting.

It was written all over Mother's tightly drawn face. Exactly what, he couldn't have said, but it was something bad, and he knew it had to do with Satan. There had been a time, when he was much younger, when he was convinced that he could read Mother's thoughts. Standing now in the silent kitchen, he had that same eerie feeling all over again.

She stood up and embraced him, pressing her tear stained face into his pyjama top.

She didn't have to say it. He knew.

'How did it happen?' She sniffled into his chest.

'It's all right, Mother. It's all right.'

He didn't know why he said that. It wasn't all right. It was fuckin' terrible. Fuckin' fuckin' fuckin' terrible.

'He ran straight out into the road. He never did that before. Even in all the years Mr Dunne had him, he never did anything like that. He was always such an obedient dog. Everyone said so.' She wept on his shoulder.

'The gardaí are saying terrible things. Well, they would, wouldn't they. It's not that I don't feel dreadful about the detective, of course I do, but they carried on as if poor Satan deliberately caused the accident. A poor dumb animal! Just because he was a detective!' Her indignation stopped her tears.

'Mother?' He held her at arms length, to look into her face.

She held a hand to her head as if to help her recall. 'Detective Murtha was on his way here, to … to talk to you. He was probably driving too fast … you know the way they do … if anyone else dared they'd …'

'What happened, Mother?'

'He … he was driving too fast and when Satan - when the dog … I don't know how he got out. I hadn't even missed him … Someone must have left the back door open … How could I keep watch? So much to do, so many people in and out, in and out …' She drew a deep breath. 'The dog ran straight across the road. The car hit him and then it crashed into one of those big old oaks on … by the river. The whole thing went up in flames … he didn't stand a chance. They say he was unrecognisable …' She shuddered.

JC saw it as clearly as if it were happening in front of his eyes. The car headlights picking out the big dog, too late. Murtha's huge neck veins swelling even larger in that moment of blind panic when he hit the brake, knowing before it happened that the car would veer across the narrow road out of control. Seeing the massive oak tree standing in wait. He could hear the crunch of buckling metal as it struck two hundred years of solid Irish oak. He heard Murtha's screams as the car hit and then his howls of agony as the flames engulfed him, welding him to the crushed metal. He could see the open mouth still forming a scream even after the flames had washed the flesh from the skull.

Mother was still talking. 'At least that was a blessing, because normally they travelled together. But the sergeant was down with the flu yesterday, didn't report for duty. Of course Detective Murtha has no family. He never married.'

She made it sound like a dereliction of duty.

'But still, it's a terrible tragedy.'

JC had loved Satan, but the image of Murtha trapped in a burning car was so horrific that it obliterated all thoughts of the dog's death. He hadn't even liked Murtha, but nobody would wish a death like that on him. On anybody.

To feel your flesh burn, while you were still breathing. To have it blacken and encrust before your eyes. For your final earthly sensation to be one of searing agony ... It was too horrible to contemplate.

When he was about thirteen, JC had become fascinated by stories of the druids of ancient Ireland. The vivid tales recounted about them had so stirred his imagination that he began to fantasise about them, making up his own fables and embellishing them grandly with druidic lore about their gifts of healing and magic, their affinity with all forms of life, and nature. Then he discovered that they burned men alive in sacrifice.

Their preferred victims were the deviants and lawbreakers of the time, but failing the availability of any of these, they weren't above using a total innocent for their important rituals. Finding this out had upset him so much that he had had nightmares about it for weeks afterwards.

Only Mother's soothing lullaby could calm him, and banish the terrible pictures of burning flesh from his dreams.

She lamented now against his chest. 'The poor, poor creature. May God have mercy on his soul.'

She was talking about the detective, of course. Wasn't she?

# CHAPTER 28

THE WHOLE town turned out for Detective Murtha's funeral. Most of the people there couldn't stand the man when he was alive, but that wasn't the point. In death people could acquire the stature and dignity that they aspired to in life. That was the way things were. Besides, somewhere deep down, there was the shared feeling that a failure to witness his funeral rites might somehow be a punishable offence.

So people gathered together and prayed. Some of them even gossiped.

Familiar faces smiled at JC outside the church. People came up to him and shook his hand and said they were happy to see him well again. They said they were sorry about his dog. They said he was a fine dog, if he had been a greyhound he'd have won the Master McGrath trophy, no bother. People said, shame he wasn't a greyhound, if he had been he would have been worth breeding from. Wasn't he the dog that attacked that English reporter last year? Good dog that. Shame he wasn't a greyhound.

JC didn't know who to approach to offer condolences on Detective Murtha's passing. He spotted Sergeant Littlewilly and was heading in his direction when he lost his nerve. But the Sergeant had already seen him and was walking towards him, both brawny hands extended.

JC tried not to wince as his right hand was almost fractured by the crushing grip.

'How are you, son? Terrible tragedy altogether.' Littlewilly pumped JC's hand as if he were the bereaved.

JC couldn't think of anything to say. He nodded and tried to free his hand, but Littlewilly kept pumping.

'He was coming to see you, you know.' Littlewilly's eyes were filling up. 'A heart of gold that man had. That hour of the night, and he was coming to give you the good news.'

He saw the surprise on JC's face.

'Nobody told you?' Littlewilly shook his big head in disbelief. 'The coroner's verdict on your journalist friend? No foul play at all! The man fell asleep with a cigarette in his mouth. In a room full of paper!' His little squinty eyes attempted to roll heavenwards in judgement at the sheer stupidity of mankind.

He finally released JC's bloodless hand and turned to join his gardaí friends.

Then, as if he had just remembered, he called back, 'And the man's heart was sound. Sound. It was the fire that got him.'

For a split second JC thought he was referring to Detective Murtha. Then realisation dawned.

INSIDE THE graveyard everybody responded enthusiastically as Father Denny gave out the rosary. The soft accents of men and women, young and old, blended the familiar words into each other so they rose and fell like some ancient unbroken mantra. They called on the mother of God to 'Prayforuss-innersnow-andathehourofourdeathamen,' over and over, hardly stopping to draw breath.

From where he was standing JC could see the tip of the Ballysheel Hill. It was surrounded by low grey cloud, a sure portent of rain that coming night.

But he was wrong about the rain. It didn't wait until night. Father Denny had barely finished giving his final blessing to the departed when the deluge began. It pounded down on to the ornate coffin, threatening to swamp it before the gravediggers could decently cover it with the dark rich earth. It lashed on to the bare heads of the men as they shovelled in clay that was washed from the gleaming coffin almost as soon as it touched it. They did finally succeed in covering it, but it was perhaps unfortunate that in front of the whole town Detective Murtha was finally laid to rest, not so much in his beloved native soil as in its runny mucky sludge.

The crowd began running. They held newspapers and prayer books above their heads in vain attempts at keeping dry. The funeral cortège that had approached the graveyard as a slow dignified procession left it at the gallop, for all the world like an unruly, bedraggled mob. And the relentless rain beat down regardless, drenching saint and sinner alike. Nobody could escape it. Except the one in the coffin.

THE HOUSE was empty when JC got home. He wasn't surprised; Mother had a circle meeting that morning. That's why she hadn't attended the funeral. But she had specifically requested that JC be there. It wouldn't do for both of them to miss the funeral. That would cause talk.

And there had been more than enough talk already, she'd added darkly.

He changed out of his drenched clothes. The house felt cold, and damp. He put extra turf into the kitchen stove, and tried to rake it into life. It belched dense black smoke at him. Coughing, he opened Mother's brandy and took a mouthful. It ran down his throat like liquid fire, making him gasp. So he drank some more.

The stove finally stopped smoking and began to give out some heat. He pulled a low chair towards it and sank back into it's worn cushions.

He couldn't count the times he had come down to this kitchen as a sleepless small boy to find Mother sitting in this exact spot. She invariably held a delicate teacup in her hand. Sometimes the only light in the room came from the tall, pale candles that he would always associate with her. He remembered watching her from the doorway and thinking that he had the most beautiful and perfect mother in the whole wide world.

He must have been ten or eleven before he realised that it wasn't tea that she constantly sipped from the delicate china cup. Still, she never over-did it. He had never once seen her the worse for wear.

And today of all days he could certainly understand the solace people found in drink. He'd go through the whole damn bottle if it would help him blank out this morning. Help to wipe out the vision of Detective Murtha's sludge-covered coffin rocking perilously from side to side in the water-logged grave. Each time a shovelful of runny muck had hit the coffin, he had been convinced it was about to tip over and disgorge its charred contents for everyone to gape at.

He'd had enough of funerals, and coffins – and death. He didn't need any more reminders of Hugh. Or even Murtha. Or Satan.

He tried to recall the face of the little baby in his dream. Reena's baby. He smiled to himself and drank another mouthful of brandy. It still made him gasp, but the taste was improving.

He thought about the tiny baby and how it had looked directly into his eyes.

His face broke into a smile again.

He slammed the brandy bottle down on the table. He had to know. The dream, if that's what it was, had been so real. He had smelled that peculiar mix of antiseptic and talc that lingers only in hospital corridors. He'd felt the heat from the battery of lights above the delivery table, and he had smelled Reena's perfume. He had smelled her perfume, for Christ's sake! Could you dream the smell of violets? And above all, could you dream of something that had never before entered your consciousness – the enigmatic look in the wide-open eyes of the newborn?

He strode into the hallway. It was cold there after the warmth of the kitchen, but Mother's brandy made the perfect insulator.

He grabbed the phone.

He had to re-dial twice before he got it right. Then the number rang for so long he was convinced there was nobody there. Suddenly there was a voice at the other end.

'Reena? Reena, it's JC.'

He could hear soft breathing. His heart began to pound. Then the phone went dead.

He dialled again, very carefully. This time the phone was picked up quickly. And just as quickly slammed down again. Next time he dialled he got the engaged tone.

It took him some time to find a number for Janis. He checked the local directory. Her parents were dead and she lived with a married sister in a tiny council cottage just outside the town.

He racked his brains to remember the sister's married name. It began with a C, that much he was sure of. Or was it a K? Kershaw. There it was. John Kershaw, Rosevale Cottage. He remembered Janis laughing at them calling it Rosevale when, according to her, there was neither a rose nor a vale within sight of it.

A posh woman's voice answered.

'Hell-o.'

'Could ... could I speak to Janis please?'

'Janis ... phone!' The yelling voice dropped its over-refined vowels.

'Hello.' It was Janis.

'Janis, I ... I ...'

'Who is this?'

'It's JC. JC Ryan.'

The phone went dead.

He dialled again.

This time there was no pretence at refinement. 'Who is it?'

'It's JC Ryan, I'd like to speak to Janis please.'

'Well, she doesn't want to speak to you, so feck off.' The line went dead.

# CHAPTER 29

HE HAD gotten as far as the hospital steps when his resolve began to waver. Maybe he should have waited for Mother to come home, and asked her again. Surely she'd tell him the truth, if he really insisted. If he explained how important it was to him.

But he knew she wouldn't. She'd just convince him all over again that his imagination was running riot. Especially when she found half her brandy missing. It was the brandy that had fuelled his courage this far, given him the idea of approaching Young Curate.

The fact that Young Curate was in the very hospital where Reena's baby might have been born was even more encouraging. What wasn't encouraging was that Young Curate was apparently suffering from a nervous breakdown.

Stress-related, the hospital said.

Sex-related, the town said.

But it also said that Young Curate had warned the ambulance driver to watch out for dangerously pregnant girls. And for women who were witches. It said that he had then announced that he possessed an extra testicle, and had stripped off naked in the ambulance to prove it. Despite claiming to have laughed till they cried, both the ambulance driver and his assistant had clearly stopped laughing long enough to check, because the whole town now knew that Young Curate had only the same number of balls as any other man.

JC had to talk to him.

At the hospital reception, the bad-tempered porter said that Young Curate wasn't allowed visitors. Then his surly face disappeared back behind the heavy glass partition.

JC tapped apologetically on it again.

'Could you just ring through to his room? Please. It's …'

There was a hand on his shoulder. 'Remember me?'

She was dressed in the carefully starched nurse's uniform, but its tiny white cap was perched jauntily on her head, its short blue cloak draped loosely around her shoulders. Her face radiated goodwill.

189

'I showed you a picture of my mother? She was very ill with cancer? Do you remember?'

He did. But could this possibly be the sad-faced little nurse who could hardly speak for crying?

It was. She smiled.

'So your mother was cured?'

'Oh no! She died! But I have been born again. It changed my whole life.' She exuded happiness. 'Have you met Jesus?'

JC managed to convince her that he would be happy enough to meet Young Curate and progress from there.

She walked ahead of him up the three short flights of stairs. It deprived him of the pleasure of watching her smiling face. He had to be content with the back view of her white starched uniform and her black-stockinged legs.

Outside the door of Room Six, she smiled and told him Jesus loved him.

JC smiled back at her. 'Oh, I hope so.'


YOUNG Curate was propped up in bed, gazing in adoration at the ceiling. He looked fitter than most of the people JC had passed in the street, and he didn't appear at all surprised to find JC's face peering around his door.

'Is ... is it all right if I come in?' Even the brandy couldn't prevent his voice cracking a little.

'Come in, brother, come in.' Young Curate held his arms out wide.

JC's wavering courage collapsed. 'I can come back another time,' he hesitated hopefully.

'This is the time, brother.' Young Curate threw another adoring look at the ceiling. 'Do you believe in Jesus?'

'I – I've just been told that he loves me.'

'Praise God! Come here.'

JC tiptoed nervously towards the bed.

He found himself grasped in a fierce bear hug. It was Littlewilly in the cemetery all over again, except that this time he was also being fervently kissed on both cheeks.

'Praise God that you are saved, brother. I prayed for you. Did you know that?'

'I, er ...'

'I admit that at first, when I realised that you were being used, I wished you ill. I'm ashamed of that now.' Young Curate looked ashamed. 'But now that I see how remorseful and penitent you are ... You are remorseful, aren't you?'

'Oh, oh yes. Extremely!' Jesus Christ, this man was sick.

'Are they still out there?' Young Curate's voice was a confidential whisper.

'Em ... I'm not sure. Should they be?' This man belonged in a rubber room.

'Bend down.'

Oh Jesus.

'I want to whisper.'

JC leaned cautiously towards him.

'I've written to Rome. I've explained everything. They'll be sending on an emissary any day now. Don't tell Father Denny, he may be in their power. I warned him many, many times but he dismissed it out of hand.' Young Curate's voice dropped dramatically. 'Even when they burned the second man!'

JC frowned in puzzlement.

Young Curate winked slyly. 'Ah! You didn't think I'd hear about that in here. Ha! I have my ways. That was their big mistake, burning the second man so soon. When I find out what they needed that sacrifice for, I'll have all the proof I need.' He caught JC's arm. 'Perhaps you could find out for me?'

'I have to go, Mother is expecting me,' JC lied.

The grip on his arm tightened. 'Just try to find out if any of them were going into battle? That's what they need a live sacrifice for. It protects them in battle.'

Wild giggles were starting up in JC's throat. How could he ever have considered believing anything this poor lunatic might say?

He tried to keep a straight face. 'Of course I'll find out if any of them were going into battle. Did you have any particular battle in mind? Hastings? The Somme?'

But Young Curate had lost interest. He lay back and began adoring the ceiling again.

JC was halfway out the door when the priest suddenly called after him, 'Find out if anyone was extremely ill.' His voice was strong and clear now, it was no longer the voice of a madman. 'Find out if any one of them was very sick. Or someone very close to them. And if they had a sudden, unexpected recovery. An inexplicable recovery!'

JC's stomach lurched. The brandy began repeating on him.

# CHAPTER 30

MOTHER WAS planning a special dinner party. It was to be a celebratory meal, she said. She had invited all of the women who had helped nurse JC back to health.

He wondered what kind of reaction he'd get if he suddenly announced to the women, in the middle of dinner, that the jig was up, they were sussed, he knew they drank hemlock and danced naked beneath the moon – oh, and burned men alive in their spare time. He wondered what they'd say if he told them, that a priest had warned him to watch out for 'the women'. They'd probably laugh and say that he wouldn't be the first priest who thought that women were the root of all evil. He wouldn't even be the first man. Hadn't Ballysheel parish church a marker above the door that was a permanent monument to misogyny, as Mother called it?

It was a piece of granite stone set high into the ornamental archway above the main entrance. It was placed there to disguise where a stone sheela-na-gig had been crudely chipped away, over seventy years before. Everyone knew the story, or at least a version of it.

One of Father Denny's predecessors, a new broom at the time, had insisted that the vile image be removed from the house of God. Some of the townspeople had protested that to remove the sheela would be unlucky. In no time at all they had the whole town on their side, even the handful of Protestants who lived there, although half the people admitted that they weren't quite sure what the sheela was, or so the story went. But whatever it was, it had been there since the original church wall had been built.

From its lofty pinnacle it had looked down on generations entering and leaving the church. And every newly christened baby, every blushing bride and groom, even the coffins of the dead had solemnly passed beneath the grinning sheela for as long as anyone could remember. To remove it would be like a sacrilege. It was part of Ballysheel's heritage, and shouldn't be disturbed. Ballysheel didn't like things to be disturbed.

The priest was adamant. The archway was church property,

and the sheela had to go. A town meeting was convened, a show of hands called for. The people decided. The sheela would stay.

Next morning the attendants at early Mass were greeted by a bald chipped stone where the sheela used proudly to display her stone genitals.

Nobody ever claimed responsibility for her removal. A stonemason from a nearby village was called and he fitted a piece of suitable granite over the defaced stone.

There was a flurry of wild talk and a few veiled threats, but there was a civil war raging in the country at the time and the stone sheela and her saga were poor competition for stories about red-blooded fighting men and their brave exploits.

The sheela was consigned to history.

MOTHER HAD dressed the table lavishly, using her best glass-ware and silver. Every single piece had been tirelessly polished until it dazzled the eye. Fresh flowers and tall ivory candles, lined the centre of the extended table. It looked like the setting for a regal banquet. She had gone to town on the wines, spending way over their normal budget. She had even replaced the missing brandy without a word.

JC hardly recognised the women when they arrived. They had all done remarkable things to their hair and faces. Some of them looked years younger than they had while sitting with him. And without their baggy sweaters and shapeless skirts, they had bodies like … well, they had bodies! Even Geraldine, in a short black velvet dress, looked … interesting.

But without a doubt, it was Signora Goretti who was the belle of the ball. She wore a long tight dress made from some kind of shiny material that enhanced every curve of her body. JC couldn't keep his eyes off her and she knew it.

She deliberately leaned forward until her full breasts threatened to fall right out of the barely concealing dress. She stretched, and reached, and bent over at every little pretext in what seemed like a determined effort to release her wondrous breasts from their restricting support.

He could see that the other women were fully aware of these sensual gymnastics, but their only reaction was an indulgent smile or a dismissive shrug of well-dressed shoulders.

Even Mother, whom he recalled becoming almost apoplectic

when the Signora once made moves on him, just laughed. She even seated the Signora next to herself at the table.

Each carefully prepared course was greeted with oohs and ahhs of delight, then consumed with great relish and enthusiasm. The wines received equal treatment. Mother had always enjoyed serving good food, but tonight she had excelled herself. Throughout the meal the women constantly sang her praises, and frequently raised their glasses in spontaneous toasts to her.

JC caught her eye several times and she smiled jubilantly at him, her face becoming pinker and pinker as the night wore on.

They were just finishing their luscious dessert when she stood up.

'Ladies ... and Jessie,' she added to a little giggle of appreciation. 'I would like to thank all of you for ... coming here this evening, and ... and ...' She swayed.

Jesus, she was drunk. JC felt an embarrassed flush begin to creep up his face, then he thought, why not?

Why couldn't this woman, who had worked her heart out all day over this sensational meal, be a little bit tiddly – nothing to be ashamed of, she was entitled to it. That's what part of him said. The other part wanted to crawl underneath the table, because Mother wasn't just tiddly. She was pie-eyed, rip-roaring, pissed.

His mother! 'Ladies, ladies.' She tapped her wine glass with her dessert fork for attention. As the dessert fork was still laden with chocolate mousse and cream, she got it. All eyes were drawn to the large blobs of brown mousse and white cream, which splattered the sparkling glass and then began sliding down its long slender stem. Mother stared at the mess as if she had no idea how it had gotten there. She swiped at it drunkenly with her napkin and succeeded in knocking the glass, complete with its accompanying decor of cream and chocolate, straight on to Signora Goretti's over-exposed chest.

The women broke into good-natured laughter. And, after her first startled squeak, so did the Signora. She then calmly removed the intact glass from her lap, scooped up the mixture of cream, chocolate mousse and white wine from between her breasts, licked the spoon clean and solemnly adjudicated: 'The mousse and whipped cream ... *perfetto!* But white wine at body temperature? Tsk tsk ... never!' She waved a reprimanding finger at Mother.

The women hooted with laughter and burst into applause. The Signora stood to receive her acclaim and then indicated Mother, in the manner of a prima donna acknowledging her accompanist.

Nobody was at all embarrassed by the flying-cream incident, except for JC who felt thoroughly ashamed. Ashamed that he had ever considered, even for one second, that there might be something sinister about these wonderful, good-humoured women.

After dinner they played Strauss waltzes and danced tirelessly with each other and JC until he begged for mercy. The women danced on until the small hours, their energy seemingly endless. When they'd had enough of Mother's records they played JC's and jived wildly together to even the loudest rock music.

Their capacity to hold their liquor was also a revelation to him. After three glasses of wine and as many dances he was fit only for bed. He felt like the oldest person in the room.

After her little performance at the dinner table, Mother had given up on any attempt at a speech, but her inebriated condition appeared only to improve her ability to dance. She whirled around the floor like a dervish, as graceful and fleetfooted as any trained ballerina. Her hair fell loose and for once she made no attempt to restrain it. Tonight she didn't look like anybody's mother. She might have been a teenager out for a night of fun at a disco.

He realised that he hadn't the faintest idea how old she was. When he was very young it hadn't mattered. And as he had gotten older he had assumed that it was some kind of vanity that prevented her revealing her age. But looking at her tonight he wondered.

He needed some coffee.

He was drinking it black and strong when Signora Goretti appeared beside him in the kitchen. She still had traces of dried chocolate on her breasts, and on the pale fabric of her dress.

From Mother's room the sound of heavy rock suddenly shuddered to a halt, to be replaced by the more melodic strains of a Viennese waltz.

'Dance with me, JC.' The signora opened her arms.

They began dancing in the tiny kitchen, moving together carefully in time to the music. But JC was no dancer; he felt awkward and ungainly, clumsily matched with the graceful woman he was holding. He almost ran both of them into the stove.

The Signora laughed and swung them away just in time.

She was suddenly serious. 'Are you happy, JC?'

The question took him by surprise.

Her brown eyes were full of secrets. 'Are you happy?'

'I – I suppose so.' He let go of her.

'Good.' Her eyes gave nothing away. 'We want you to be happy, JC. All of us.'

Mother came into the kitchen. 'Fresh coffee, I think, for everyone.' She waltzed over to the press.

JC moved away from the Signora, but she caught hold of his arm with a surprisingly strong grip. 'JC says he's happy. Do you believe him?' She turned to Mother.

Mother was standing on tiptoe, intent on reaching for the large percolator which was kept on the highest shelf.

JC reached over and handed it down.

'Thank you, Jessie,' she smiled.

'I asked you if you believe that he's happy?'

Mother carefully began to arrange a coffee filter. She frowned in concentration.

The Signora swiped the paper filter from the percolator and threw it across the room.

Mother and JC stared open-mouthed at her.

'Look at him! Does he look happy to you?'

Mother didn't answer.

'He's not a child any more. You have to let go. You promised!' The Signora retrieved her shawl from a chair and swept it dramatically around her bare shoulders.

The last notes of the waltz were sounding as the front door slammed behind her.

'I'll make the coffee, Mother.' JC took the percolator from her trembling hands.

She went back to join the other women.

JC made the coffee for twelve. He knew the Signora wouldn't be back.

# CHAPTER 31

THE OLD churchyard lay directly behind the parish church. But no doorway opened on to it. The only entrance was through a narrow outside gateway, the latch of which had badly rusted through disuse. But in spite of long neglect, or perhaps because of it, the churchyard had developed an eye-catching beauty that was all its own.

Encouraged now by the bright September sunshine, the tawny russets and red browns of early autumn were beginning to enliven the tired leaves of the old trees that overhung the cemetery boundaries. And the Boston ivy that had cloaked its crumbling walls in dull green all spring and summer was now boasting a fiery red glow. Even the wild grasses that grew between the tombstones were taking on an exotic sun-baked look, waving their newly plumed heads in a last frenzied dance before the first frosts arrived to cut them back into the earth again.

The whole place gave JC the creeps.

What purported to be nature at its most flamboyant was, he knew, no more than the beginning of the death throes of living things that had served their purpose. This was a place where death masqueraded as beauty.

But it was also the place where Signora Goretti had insisted they meet. She claimed it to be the one spot in Ballysheel where they wouldn't be interrupted.

JC didn't like it. It made him nervous. It forced ugly pictures into his head. Pictures of things he didn't want to think about. Vivid images of what might be lying beneath the tilting gravestones. Beneath the weeping stone angels with resigned faces and crumbling hands. Beneath the prettily waving grasses.

He didn't want to think about blackened rotted flesh, decomposed beyond redemption, entombed in mouldy crumbling coffins, but the pictures kept coming.

Where the hell was the Signora? She'd said eleven o'clock, and he had arrived promptly at barely five past, but she wasn't here. There was nobody here – at least above the ground – except him and the whole place was nerve-wrackingly silent except for a soft, intermittent creaking sound, for all the world like a hand forcing old, protesting wood. He hoped it was coming from the trees. Jesus, there it was again. It had better be coming from the trees.

He began walking quickly towards the gate. It was much further back than he had realised. He lengthened his stride, moving as quickly as he could, without actually running.

Why the hell hadn't she come? It must be at least half-past by now. There was the same creak again. Only it was much louder this time. Closer. Oh Jesus.

He ran as fast as he could, reaching the gate in seconds. He raced through it at breakneck speed and crashed straight into a black-clad figure hurrying towards it from the other side.

Jesus Christ! His pounding heart almost stopped with fright.

The Signora caught his arm.

'Were you leaving?' she asked indignantly.

With her free hand she pushed back her fur-lined hood. Despite the sunny morning, her hands were encased in black leather gloves.

'Well?' She waited.

'I, er, it's ...' JC stammered, indicating his watch.

'It's what?' She smiled, and touched his upper lip with a black gloved-finger.

It was fifteen minutes past eleven. But it didn't matter any more. It wouldn't have mattered if it were fifteen minutes past twelve, past one – it wouldn't have mattered if it were fifteen minutes to. She was smiling up at him, her huge dark eyes making promises that he knew she wouldn't keep. But it didn't matter. To be here with her was enough – to watch her full red mouth drawing back to reveal her slightly overlapping front teeth and the tip of her pointed little tongue. He had never noticed before how arousing overlapping teeth could be. He wondered how it would feel to –

She kissed him warmly on either cheek, then linked her arm through his, brushing his bare hand with her black-gloved one. He found the black leather caress almost as arousing as the gleaming little teeth.

They walked back through the gate together, the Signora tilting her face upwards to catch the sun.

But the sun was everywhere now. It reflected back from the overgrown, gravelled pathways, from the grey tombstones, from the raised heads of the tirelessly praying angels.

The Signora was unusually quiet. She kept pace with him but her thoughts were clearly elsewhere.

He tried not to stare down at her mouth and the tiny overlapping white teeth.

'You said we should meet here?'

She blinked up at him, frowning slightly as if she had forgotten his existence.

'Oh. Yes of course.'

They walked in silence again.

Was this it? A silent walk in a graveyard? He had hardly slept last night, his head had been so busy spinning fantasies about what might be revealed here today. The possibility that it could be some dark, ancient secret had both excited and terrified him.

When she had phoned and insisted that they meet alone, he had instinctively known that she was about to divulge things that nobody else would dare tell him. When she had chosen this place to meet, he hadn't been at all surprised. It had somehow seemed appropriate.

Now he wasn't so sure.

Who in their right mind would choose to meet here?

There was a sudden crash behind them. They both swung round, startled.

A dead branch had broken away from one of the overhanging trees and landed midway across a grave. It had knocked over a stone urn that once might have held flowers, but now clearly housed a myriad of spiders and other insects that scattered and ran in all directions from its shattered pieces.

'Oh poor things.' The Signora knelt by the grave, and for a second JC thought she was about to pick up and embrace the scurrying creatures.

'Oh the poor dears, see how frightened they are.'

She was so clearly upset that he was terrified she was going to insist that he pick up the crawling things.

She looked up pleadingly.

Oh Jesus! Don't ask me that, not those squirming, crawling –

'JC, do you want to see Reena and the baby?'

Maybe he hadn't heard her properly. Maybe he wanted to hear those words so badly that his mind had conjured them up.

'JC?'

The inscription on the tombstone behind her stood out in sharp focus.

SARA RUYANE
BELOVED WIFE.
JAN. 16, 1868 —- FEB. 14, 1885
RIP

Reena did have a baby. It wasn't a dream. Lower down on the tombstone it said:

SARA VICTORIA RUYANE
DEAREST DAUGHTER.
FEB. 14, 1885 — FEB. 14, 1885.
RIP

The words began to swim before his eyes.

Signora Goretti stood up. 'Are they tears, *caro*?' She touched his face.

He swallowed hard and indicated the tombstone.

'She didn't even get to be one day old.'

The Signora read both inscriptions carefully. 'Perhaps baby Sara was one of the lucky ones.'

'What...?'

'They were bad times for women, even worse than now. See, her mother was barely seventeen. Childbirth for her would have been excruciating – long, long hours of unrelieved pain, distress.' Emotion made her accent even stronger, almost indecipherable.

She sniffed, and pulled herself together. 'But then one blessing,' she said brightly, 'she remained seventeen forever. Destined never to grow old, but to remain young and beautiful for ever.'

JC thought of what they might find if they dug up this grave now. He shuddered.

'Don't be afraid of death, JC. It's merely a doorway.' Again her accent was becoming stronger.

'Oh yeah? Well, it's one doorway I'm not anxious to rush through.'

'Not even to gain immortality?'

He couldn't tell if she were serious or just teasing him, but she made him uneasy. He drummed his heels nervously on the pathway. They made pathetic little squishing sounds.

'You are cold? We should walk.'

'No!' He made up his mind. 'No more walking. I want to know about Reena and the baby.'

She was suddenly all smiles again, her expression almost smug, as if it were her special secret that she might or might not share with him. She began walking.

He caught her roughly by the shoulders, forcing her to stand still. 'Tell me about them. Now.'

Her face froze in distaste.

Ashamed, he quickly let go of her. 'I'm sorry. I'm sorry. But it's been driving me crazy. They told me there was no baby. I saw it being born. I saw it. Yet they tried to convince me there was no baby!'

He felt the big stupid tears beginning to well up again. He didn't know if they were for himself, or for Reena and the baby. Or even for the long-dead Sara Ruyane, now well rotted beside her poor dead infant.

He found himself caught against the Signora's warm body. She wiped at his wet eyes with her black gloved-fingers. Then she stood on tiptoe to kiss his eyes, his cheeks and finally his mouth. She kissed him like a mother comforting a favourite child. Except for the kiss on his mouth. That was a full-blooded overlapping-teeth kiss.

He instinctively kissed her back. She tasted unbearably inviting, sweet and salty all at once. The long hungry kiss might have gone on even longer, or even turned into something more, if the fallen branch behind them hadn't suddenly shifted in the wind.

It prodded eerily at his legs like stiff, blackened fingers.

'Aaah!' He jumped out of its reach.

The Signora gave a regretful little sigh. Then she took his hand and led him back towards the gate.

Outside the graveyard, they both had difficulty looking at each other. The Signora smoothed his ruffled shirt-front.

'You can see Reena and the baby any time, JC. Nobody will stand in your way.'

She made it sound as if a momentous decision had just been made. Some kind of giant step taken, instead of a simple walk in a graveyard.

In spite of the warm sun, he began shivering.

'I must go, JC. I'm already late.'

For the first time ever, she didn't kiss him goodbye, just pulled up her hood and strode off in the direction of the main street. She walked purposefully, intent on wherever she was going. He stood watching her. She had almost reached the corner of the main street when two of the sisters from the nearby convent appeared from the opposite direction. She stopped and spoke briefly to them; then to his amazement, she turned and retraced her steps, walking with them back up the hill towards the old convent.

As they passed the front gates of the church, all three lowered their heads and crossed themselves respectfully. From where he was standing, they looked like three pious nuns hurrying back to the shelter of their convent.

# CHAPTER 32

'I'M GLAD it's all out in the open, at last.'

Mother sounded glad. She even walked like a person who was glad as she tripped happily along beside him for the half-mile or so journey to Reena's house.

'After all, in this day and age why be secretive about it? That's what I say.' She didn't say why she had been the one who was the most secretive.

She didn't say why she had tried so hard to convinced him that Reena's baby didn't exist.

When he challenged her about this, she appeared shocked by his lack of understanding. 'I had to protect you from being hurt!'

He tried to keep his voice even. 'But I was already hurting.'

'You don't know what hurt is,' she replied flatly, and stopped to select a bunch of flowers from a wrought-iron stand outside the newsagent's.

'Would she like these, do you think?' She held up a bunch of pale yellow chrysanthemums.

JC realised that he had absolutely no idea what Reena might like, or dislike. In fact, he knew very little at all about her. He knew that her father was dead. He knew that she had become closer to her mother since his death. And he knew that she had given birth to a baby girl. And, of course, he also knew that he had impregnated her, when she had only come to see his birth-day gift. But apart from that, he didn't really know her at all.

Mother didn't wait for his opinion on the flowers. Instead, she chose three large bunches of mixed bronze and yellow chrysanthemums.

Three?

'Don't want to appear mean.' She smiled at the mystified shopkeeper. 'Wrap them all together.'

Reena's mother was expecting them, if not the gargantuan floral display. She put the flowers aside for Reena, and served JC and Mother tea and homemade scones in front of a blazing log fire.

JC was so nervous he barely sipped at the scalding hot tea.

The fire didn't help, causing him to perspire freely in the three-piece suit he had worn to make a good impression.

Reena's mother was an attentive hostess, asking him several times if he were too warm.

'No, I'm perfectly comfortable,' he lied as his best shirt stuck to his back with sweat.

Mrs Scales turned her attention to Mother. She carefully explained the importance of keeping a house well heated when there was a new baby in residence.

'I couldn't agree with you more!'

Mother emphasised her agreement by nodding her head continuously like the small furry animals stuck to the back windows of cars.

She said 'Oh I agree' frequently, sometimes before Mrs Scales could finish saying whatever it was Mother wanted to agree with.

Then the two women tried to outdo each other in the humility stakes by telling long meandering tales of all the silly mistakes they had made as young mothers. Both their heads were nodding now.

JC felt dizzy just watching them. He began counting the roses on the elegant wallpaper. He had reached nine hundred, when he decided that both women were playing some clever game. He had counted over a thousand pink roses when he realised what it was. They were playing for time.

But no matter how many roses he counted, he couldn't come up with a reason why.

Or maybe he could?

'Is – is the baby –' he attempted.

The two heads stopped nodding.

'The bathroom. Could I?'

Mrs Scales directed him to a toilet just off the hallway.

He spent his time in there listening for giveaway sounds from upstairs, but all he could hear, above the drip of the filling cistern, was the low buzz of the women's voices in the living room. There were roses on the bathroom wallpaper but he decided against counting them.

He was walking back into the sweltering living room when he heard a door slam upstairs. It seemed to be the signal Mrs Scales was waiting for.

She stood up.

'Well, I think we've gotten to know each other well enough, haven't we?' She smiled at JC, who was listening for further sounds from upstairs.

Mother was doing her nodding-dog impression again.

Mrs Scales rubbed her hands together briskly, as if she could hardly contain herself.

'Let's go, shall we?' Her excited voice implied that they were about to circumnavigate the globe.

JC nervously counted the bannister supports as they walked up the stairs. There were thirteen. Unlucky thirteen.

'Reena?' Mrs Scales called out.

There was no answer.

'Reena, are you there?'

Reena wasn't there. Or anywhere that JC could see.

Undaunted, Mrs Scales led them to a room at the end of the narrow landing. A wave of heat hit them as soon as the door opened, but neither Mother nor Mrs Scales appeared to be at all aware of it.

The room was large and sunlit. It was at least twice the size of JC's bedroom, with wide uncurtained windows that were edged with strips of heavy white lace. The pale walls were decorated with colourful animal motifs, and there was hardly a shelf space or window ledge that didn't hold a collection of stuffed toys or rigidly smiling dolls.

Hanging from the centre of the ceiling was a delicate mobile made of slim silver chimes that perpetually turned and tinkled musically, even without the benefit of wind.

Directly underneath the chimes was a tall bassinet. It was smothered in layers of pink and white frills.

'This is the baby's room!' Mrs Scales announced.

The three of them tiptoed over to the bassinet. But peer as he might into the depths of the thing, all JC could make out was yet another pile of frills under the hood.

'Isn't she beautiful?' Mrs Scales trilled.

To JC's utter amazement Mother nodded, and made clucking noises towards the heap of frills.

Mrs Scales joined in.

JC glanced in disbelief from one to the other before checking the pile of frills again. There was definitely nothing there.

'Who does she resemble?' Mother asked with a straight face, staring directly at the frills.

'Oh well, now.' Mrs Scales's white skin flushed with what could have been feigned modesty or embarrassment or the stifling heat, but whatever the cause, her colour definitely rose.

JC decided that, in fact, there really was no baby at all. The whole thing was a cruel charade, a trick, being played on him.

He turned away.

The door suddenly burst open and Reena ran in, panting.

'Sorry. My apologies! I meant to be here. I stopped off to collect the new quilt.' She dropped a large cellophane-covered box on the floor. It had a picture of a padded quilt on the lid.

Another fancy cover for the non-existent baby.

'Did she waken at all?' Reena was playing the game to the hilt.

She leaned into the crib and picked up the bundle of frills. Watched closely by the two women, she slowly peeled back the layers of pink frills to expose the tiniest, most perfect human being that JC had ever seen.

His doubting heart did a full somersault.

He heard himself say, 'Ahhhhh ... look.'

The three women turned to look at him. They were laughing but he didn't care. He was face to face with the most beautiful creature he could ever have envisaged. But she was more than beautiful, she was bewitching, entrancing.

He watched in awe as she slowly opened her eyes. They were the same deep indigo that he remembered from the hospital.

They looked directly at him, steadily holding his gaze.

And in that split second, he knew. He looked into the baby's eyes and he knew. He knew.

'I understand,' he whispered.

The baby farted loudly. Her small face puffed up until her remarkable eyes almost disappeared into her flesh, which was turning a dangerous shade of vermilion. Then, just as quickly, her face relaxed, and became a healthy pink again.

She closed her eyes.

A vile smell wafted through the room.

'Will you change her, mother, or shall I?' There was a distinctly pleading tone in Reena's voice.

JC WAITED downstairs while the baby was changed and fed. He wanted to talk to Reena. There was so much he had to say. So much to discuss. So many questions.

But Reena was uncontactable. She had entered some mysterious world that he couldn't gain access to. No matter how hard he tried to communicate, he couldn't reach her. Oh, she smiled at him, she had even kissed him when she came downstairs. She had touched his face tenderly when she had seen how moved he was at the sight of the baby. But they never really made contact.

He couldn't even understand the language she was using now. Mother understood it, so did Mrs Scales, but it was an alien tongue to him.

They spoke of lactation, and fontanelles, and other strange stuff that sounded like disbanded Seventies pop groups.

He couldn't get through the impenetrable wall that surrounded Reena and the two women.

Before leaving he kissed her, and the baby, who was now blissfully ensconced in her arms in the baking-hot living room.

Reena smiled distractedly at him. The baby belched loudly.

FOUR DAYS later Janis's sister phoned.

'She wants you here. You better get here bleedin' quick, if you want to make it in time.'

He made it.

Janis's baby was every inch as beautiful and mysterious as Reena's. The birth had gone as painlessly, and the baby looked as if she had just woken up from a long peaceful sleep. Her skin was smooth and pink, her small body covered with soft downy hairs like those on a sun-ripened peach.

The two midwives, and Janis's waspish sister, cooed in adoration over the tiny newborn.

Janis turned over and went to sleep.

When she woke she was offered the baby to feed.

'I said bottle,' she grinned good-humouredly.

'Please, Janis,' the younger midwife pleaded, looking far more exhausted from the birth than the grinning Janis did.

'Bottle.' Janis reached into a bedside drawer and took out a pack of cigarettes.

'Put them away!' The second midwife's voice was sharp.

'Sorry,' a contrite Janis did as she was told, 'but it's been nine long months. I'm gumming for a ciggy.'

'Here!' The baby was placed ceremoniously in her arms.

'Howaya baby?' She made a funny face, then looked across the downy head towards JC. 'What do you think?'

'She's beautiful.' He had been sitting quietly in a shadowy corner of the small bedroom, trying to keep out of everyone's way.

'You hold her.' Janis held the baby out to him.

The baby gave a little meowing sound as he took her. Then she opened her eyes and looked up at him. His throat constricted.

She was abruptly lifted out of his arms.

'I'll feed her.' Janis's sister disappeared out the door with her.

The two midwives charged after her, protesting loudly.

'Shut the door,' Janis whispered. She pulled the cigarette pack from the drawer again and lit up brazenly.

JC watched the door nervously.

'Ah, don't mind those old biddies,' Janis dismissed the midwives, one of whom could only have been a year or two older than herself. 'She is beautiful, isn't she?' She blew out a long train of smoke.

'Beautiful? Oh, the baby,' he laughed.

'Well, you're certainly happy.'

'It's seeing the baby, she's so ...'

'I was afraid she'd look like me. Ugly as sin.'

He was so taken aback he didn't reply.

Janis gave a loud hoot of laughter. 'You're supposed to say, "Oh no you're not, you're beautiful".'

'You're not. I mean you are beautiful.'

'Too late. It doesn't count when you have to be forced to say it.'

'Oh no, Janis, I really mean it, you're ...'

The door opened and her sister carried the baby back in.

'Jan, you should see how she ...' Her face changed. 'Are you smoking?'

'No, just holding this for JC.' Janis's face was a picture of innocence as she held out the cigarette to him.

'Put that out!' The sister glared at him. 'What sort of pig are you, smoking in a room where a new-born infant has to breathe?'

'He's not a pig.' Janis winked at JC. 'He's been telling me how beautiful I am.'

'Really? Well, we all know about his silver tongue, don't we? Look baby, he's the famous Ballysheel healer. Not much to look at, is he, without his long shining robe?'

'That's what you think!' Janis laughed suggestively. 'If you ever saw him without his robe you'd –'

'You should be ashamed of yourself, Janis Meehan, and you only given birth.' But in spite of herself the sister giggled. 'Here, you take care of your child, that'll keep your mind off impure thoughts.'

The sisters laughed together as they transferred the baby between them. For a second JC could have sworn he heard the baby chuckle.

Janis's sister began to straighten the bedclothes and tidy up the cluttered room. No matter which way JC moved he appeared to be in her way. She exhaled like a steam train in exasperation.

He glanced towards Janis, but her eyes were starting to close sleepily, her head nodding in the overpowering heat. The baby was already fast asleep against her breast.

He mumbled goodbyes and began to leave. Nobody appeared to notice. Before closing the front gate behind him, he looked back at the little cottage. The two midwives stood watching him from the curved front window. They were drinking tea from large brown mugs, but the leaded glass window panes blurred their movements. They distorted the appealing outlines of the younger pretty one, making her appear old and haggard, while the other one hardly resembled anything female at all.

He latched the gate securely, and then glanced up again. Now everything was reversed. Both women were now slender pretty young girls. Almost childlike. They appeared to be raising their arms in a salute to him. He waved back.

Walking towards the town he felt close to euphoric.

Instead of the expected outrage at the births of the babies, all he had encountered was goodwill. Including Janis's bad-tempered sister, everyone connected with the girls had seen the births as a reason to celebrate.

He had come across Mrs Gerber several times in the town lately, and although the twins were now living in Dublin, Mrs Gerber appeared to be permanently shopping for baby clothes. And permanently smiling. Each time their paths crossed she greeted him like a long-lost relative, the one with a gold mine. It was a good feeling, to be saluted and smiled at all over town.

The sun was warm on his back as he walked. In the distance

across the fields a combine harvester grumbled as it gathered in a late crop. He hoped the weather held for it. Heavy rain now, or a sudden sharp frost, could be devastating. He looked up at the clear blue sky and wished that the weather would remain fine.

# CHAPTER 33

IT WAS the most unseasonal December in living memory. Or so people claimed. With temperatures climbing towards the mid sixties, it was certainly unusual weather.

'July was colder. And wetter!' became the common complaint.

This December, the sun shone every single day. And it wasn't the usual muted winter sun, but a dazzling yellow orb whose relentless heat forced daffodils, crocuses, and even small hibernating animals, out of their winter sleep.

The people of Ballysheel were uneasy with this strange turn of events. It didn't bode well for the coming spring. A good spring needed a crisp cold winter to precede it, if it were to produce its rightful bounty. All things had their season. And winter was the season for sharp cold days, leading into freezing, or sometimes rain lashed nights, that threatened to last for ever. That was how things were. All this warm sunshine couldn't be healthy.

It was for some. The batch of new babies that had been born during the autumn were basking now in the late Indian summer.

Chubby little arms and legs were becoming sun-kissed and golden. Unremarkable downy hair was being transformed into strong, sunbleached, almost flaxen curls as day followed glorious day. The babies happily soaked up every available ray of sunshine, and consequently blossomed like exotic hot-house flowers.

Their mothers regularly exhibited their little princesses for all to see, and admire. They dressed them for this purpose in an ever-changing array of colourful babywear, and only a heart of stone could fail to be moved by the sight of such eye-catching little creatures gurgling contentedly in the warm sunshine.

Besotted grandmothers fought for the privilege of wheeling their prams around the town. Curious children stood on tiptoe to peer in at the beautiful babies. And older children wished they were even older, so they too could have babies just like these. Old and young alike broke away from whatever activities they were engaged in when the babies passed. Even the canniest of shopkeepers kept valued customers waiting as they bent over the prams of the newborn.

People might whine and bemoan the terrible heat, yet no one could begrudge the sunshine to these hale and hearty little beings. That would be tantamount to flying in God's face.

UP AT the Manor House, the summer-like temperatures didn't at all impede preparations for the annual Christmas party. This year it would be a double celebration. This year the Spencers were also celebrating the birth of their first child.

In honour of this great event Mrs Spencer had decided to invite all the children of Ballysheel. To everyone's surprise, her husband had agreed. But what appeared to be a huge about-face for Mr Spencer, who was not renowned for his love of children in general, was not perhaps such a great act of generosity, because if there was one thing Ballysheel didn't possess, it was a glut of children. In keeping with the times its birth rate had been falling slowly, almost imperceptibly, for quite a few years. And in the previous six not one single birth had been recorded.

This year's sudden bonus of babies was unlikely to inflict any damage on Mr Spencer's property, seeing as they were still babes in arms. Besides, he had come up with a masterly stroke to keep the invited children at bay. His wife had been prepared to facilitate all the guests in the long gallery, but he had insisted on outdoor amusements.

'Let's make the most of this God-given sunshine,' he cajoled, omitting to mention that he had hired the amusements at a vast discount long before he had any notion of what the December weather might hold. When the good weather held up, even improved, he felt that God was indeed on his side. And why not? He wasn't an unreasonable man; he simply didn't want every Tom and tinker's child running amok in his exquisitely decorated house.

He stood now admiring the timeless picture his wife made as she sat feeding their baby daughter in the nursery. Her white cotton dress was unbuttoned, the bodice folded back modestly to expose only one rounded breast, and even that was partially covered by the baby's downy head. The expression on his wife's face was that of a contented madonna as she gazed down at her feeding infant. Even the angry blue veins that traced their way across her pale breast couldn't detract from her almost virginal perfection, he felt.

She leaned slightly forward now so she could see out of the

tall velvet-draped window.

'Oh look, *cheri*, all those lovely, lovely toys for you, all for your party.'

She stared down into the sun-drenched garden, where groups of young men were erecting old-fashioned carousels. The strenuous physical work, combined with the hot temperatures had caused most of the men to strip down. To brief shorts in some cases. She gazed down as glistening sweat ran down their muscular backs and heavily knotted thighs.

Rocking her feeding daughter gently, she crooned, 'All those lovely, lovely playthings!'

Mr Spencer was indescribably moved. He was a gruff man, not given to sentiment, but the sight of his beautiful wife whispering promises into his tiny daughter's ear provoked an uncharacteristic display of affection from him.

He patted his wife's head.

THE STRANGE weather was affecting the whole town. Even the dogs in the street fought and snarled at each other. Patience was in short supply, everywhere. Neighbours who had lived in harmony for years began little sniping matches, over the most trivial of matters. Blood feuds were begun over such minute irritations as long-borrowed garden tools, bickering children, and barking dogs.

In the pubs, after race meetings, vulgar and coarse threats were overheard. These were directed mainly against sluggish race horses! Slothful jockeys! Slapdash trainers! Wild fanciful notions about bloody and illegal geldings were bandied about. Some punters even went so far as to say that they should be inflicted on the horses. The mildest of tempers were beginning to fray.

Shopkeepers were accused of short-changing customers. And previously well-trusted barmen were scrutinised closely as they measured out the shorts in bars. People stood in the hot streets and reminisced about freezing December days when they'd had to huddle around roaring fires to keep warm. The fuel merchant by the river fed the ducks all day, and checked the skies hopefully at night.

In an effort to stimulate business, the bookie gave even odds on which would break first, the weather or the fuel merchant. The smart money was on the weather.

But as the heat kept rising it began to feel as if Ballysheel itself might explode first.

Directly behind the main street, in God's house, Young Curate knelt before the high altar. The stifling heat was even beginning to invade the tiled, lofty church. Young Curate felt weak and faint. But he was here to give thanks for finally being released from the stultifying hospital. He was at long last free to go about the Lord's work.

His groin might ache from the pressure of the too-tight underpants that he had taken to wearing as a recompense to the Almighty for sinfully coveting a second testicle. And underneath his immaculate cassock, his body might be covered in a painful, red-raw heat rash, but he was content. He had finally completed all his arrangements. Everything was in place. All he had to do now, was wait and pray.

And suffer.


JC STOOD under the freezing cold shower and tried to think clearly.

Was it his imagination or was Mother avoiding him?

Whenever he walked into the room she found something urgent to do elsewhere. She served his meals quickly and silently, and moved on. When she did sit at the table with him, she ate wordlessly, her eyes looking everywhere but at him.

But she did give him second helpings of everything. Then she was gone again, before he could protest that he couldn't possibly eat spicy beef stews, or steaming hot custard pudding, in this weather.

Maybe the unreal heat was finally getting to her. It was daily becoming more oppressive, cloying. Nothing at all like the dry pleasant heat that Signora Goretti constantly boasted was the lot of her beloved homeland.

This heat was moisture-laden, and sticky. It clung to him, giving him a permanent headache. He woke up each morning feeling as if his sinuses had been blocked overnight with rancid putty.

Breathing became a chore. Living became a chore. He flopped around the house like a misplaced sea creature forced to live on dry land. Standing under the cold shower was his only release.

Mother watched him guardedly from under her lashes. He couldn't interpret the look, but whenever she was caught in the act, she hurried off about her business. Whatever that was, nowadays.

He passed his time lying on his bed, listening to rock music and sniffing at a ineffectual nasal inhaler. And standing in the cold shower.

He didn't think about the girls much, any more. Or even the babies. He had thought for one blinding second when he looked at Reena's baby that he finally understood what it was all about. But even that had passed. Everything passed except this stupid weather. It made nonsense of any order or design.

There seemed to be no rules anymore.

Even Ballysheel itself was becoming hostile.

Its people were changing.

The old nightmares returned to plague him.

As often as he woke up and escaped from one, there was another lying in wait to trap him the moment he dropped off again.

There was no escape.

THE DAY of the big party arrived and the weather still hadn't broken. The town hadn't seen rain for almost three months.

By two o'clock in the afternoon there was a trail of gaily dressed women and children walking out the sunlit road towards the manor house.

The youths in charge of the amusements had already set tapes playing through loudspeakers which were judiciously placed around the overly manicured gardens, and the repetitious strains of 'Favourite Nursery Rhymes For All Ages', could be heard as far back as the town.

A screeching party of house guests, their cut-glass accents rivalling their brimming wine glasses for precision, strolled down the curved stone steps of the big house. They began a gushing chorus of admiration for the brightly painted merry-go-rounds, exclaiming loudly over one parti-cularly colourful one which wasn't yet in motion.

Two of the men, who had clearly wined too well, broke away from the group. To the delight of their friends they drunkenly attempted to clamber on to hobby horses that would barely accommodate a six-year-old. After failing several times, the more rotund of the two finally managed to mount successfully. He sat triumphantly astride a miniature piebald, his gigantic buttocks dwarfing the more petit rear end of the horse.

Holding up his now half-empty glass, he acknowledged the applause of his friends, then in a slurred voice ordered the youth in charge to start up the roundabout.

The boy glowered sullenly at him.

'Start it up, I said.' The man kicked out half-heartedly at the boy, his suede boot missing the tousled head by inches.

The boy flushed angrily, but held his ground.

The would-be horse rider let loose a torrent of abuse. He accused the boy of being a witless gipsy, a travelling tinker.

The boy ignored him.

Enraged with frustration, the man threw the contents of his wine glass into the boy's face.

A woman's voice cried out in protest. But the boy recovered quickly and, with wine still trickling down his cheeks reached over to pull a switch. The roundabout suddenly jerked into motion. Too suddenly for the precariously perched rider. He was thrown headfirst a full five or six feet on to the hard dry ground. Thick dark blood spurted from his nose, and ran past his mouth and double chin like a foaming red tide before soaking into his white shirt-front.

His friends rushed to his assistance, pushing past the stubborn-faced boy.

Just as the man was being helped to his feet, the Spencers arrived on the scene. The bruised nose was diagnosed by Mr Spencer as non-terminal, and as there was no further damage, barring that to the man's pride and the shattered wine glass, he was given consoling sips of fifty-year-old brandy that had mellowed with age, as all things should.

The boy was given a severe telling-off.

But he stood unrepentant, his head held defiantly high. If anyone had stopped to listen they might have heard him mumble, 'Think youse own the fuckin' world so youse do! Youse will get your fuckin' comeuppance so youse will!' But the roundabout was in full swing now, with speckled horses and smiling unicorns all creaking their way up and down and round and round on the gaily painted carousel. And the loudspeakers were calling on everybody to 'Ride a cock horse to Banbury cross'. So nobody heard the boy.

Apart from this minor incident, nothing occurred to interrupt the happy carnival atmosphere that permeated the vast grounds and gardens of the manor house and overspilled all the way back to Ballysheel's sun-baked main street.

The town was prised out of its gloom. Shopkeepers dropped their shutters and closed up early for the day. What business would they do anyway, with most of the women occupied elsewhere? Elderly people opened their windows and doors to listen to the sounds of gaiety.

Uninvited teenagers crept up and over the high manor walls to join squealing children bouncing on a giant inflatable castle. They stole frozen ice lollies that were intended for the children, and warm dry sherries that were intended for their elders and betters. Then they hid behind wilting shrubberies to press their lolly-stained lips against other lolly-stained lips before moving on to explore the illicit pleasures of sherry-tasting tongues.

As the day wore on the music became louder and the laughter more raucous. Chilled beer and cheap wine helped make the heat bearable. Everyone appeared to be having a wonderful time.

The only dissenting voice was that of the old man who chalked up the board in the bookies. He mopped his perspiring brow and stood in the street to listen to the sounds of distant revelry.

'Mark my words, it will all end in tears, so it will,' he predicted as he searched the sky for signs of rain that might soften the going for the next day's list of runners. Then he watched covetously as two giggling young girls in light summer dresses skipped along the road towards the manor house.

# CHAPTER 34

JC COULD hear the music clearly from his bedroom window. He had propped it wide open, hoping to encourage some cool air into the suffocating room.

Instead the words of an old nursery rhyme floated in.

'Humpty Dumpty sat on the wall. Humpty Dumpty had a great fall. All the King's horses and all the King's men couldn't put Humpty together again!'

There was a brief pause, then the sound of happy childish laughter rang out. Then the song started up all over again.

He wasn't sure why he put on the kaftan. Maybe it was the heat. Maybe it was because anything else was just too much bother. Maybe it was just for devilment.

It felt cool and fresh as it slid along his body, in the stuffy room. Nothing else that he wore, ever felt as much a part of him as the kaftan now did. It was like being enveloped by a safe protective cocoon. Even its strong smell was comforting today. It wafted around him, wending its way effortlessly through his blocked sinuses, and down into his lungs. He began to breathe more easily.

Mother was standing in her room when he came down the stairs. The heavy window drapes were drawn, as usual, behind her. She had made no concessions at all to the extraordinary heat. It didn't seem to be troubling her. But something was.

Her face was in the shadows, but he knew she was wearing her tight distant expression.

'Are you sure you won't come with me?' he ventured, knowing full well what her answer would be.

But she didn't answer. Instead she walked guardedly into the sunlit hallway and hugged him fiercely. He had forgotten how strong she was.

'Mother?' he began nervously.

But she had stepped back into her room, back into the shadows.

He was closing the front door when he thought he heard her call him. He listened out for a second, but the only sounds were those coming from the distant party.

One of the kids saw him first. She was ahead of him on the road a few hundred yards out of the town, skipping along happily with a friend. He slowed down a little, suddenly self-consciously aware of the long flowing kaftan.

He half-expected the girl to laugh at the sight of him striding along in it. But instead she stood, and watched silently. The other child stopped skipping and joined her.

They were no more than ten-years-old, solemn little girls with wide eyes that hardly blinked, even when he looked directly into them.

He nodded in greeting and walked on past, quickening his pace again.

The little girls fell into step behind him.

They were within sight of the manor when another two joined them. By the time they entered the gates there were five or six children trailing along in his wake.

The Spencers were standing at the top of the long driveway, chatting among a group of their smart friends. They stood slightly apart from the main body of people thronging the amusements. Even if they hadn't, their sophisticated clothes and affected mannerisms would still have declared them to be a separate breed.

But as JC drew nearer, he noticed that the elegant shirt-front of one of the city men was covered in dried blood, and his grossly swollen nose looked as if a huge fist had collided painfully with it. Yet the man was laughing, gesturing theatrically as he acted out a story for his friends.

He spotted JC and stopped his storytelling, turning instead to bellow loudly, 'Good God! Look at the state of that! Is it male or female? Or both?'

Even amid the noisy carnival sounds, his autocratic voice carried. Every head in the vicinity turned as JC and the small band of children walked up the gravel driveway.

Mrs Spencer was at JC's side in seconds. She greeted him matter-of-factly, behaving as if tall men in full-length glittering kaftans, complete with an entourage of small children, were an everyday sight on her immaculate country driveway. Then, puckering her lips, she completed her gallic ritual of kissing him soundly on both cheeks before turning to introduce him to her friends.

The children watched silently.

Mr Spencer gave a nervous laugh and shook JC's hand just a little bit too enthusiastically. The other men nodded, or grunted. Some did both, and shook his hand at the same time.

But the one in the bloodstained shirt remained aloof.

'Mandrake the Magician, I presume?' He sniggered, causing a bubble of blood to float free of his swollen nostril and sail away into the air.

There was a quick flurry of introductions to the women in the group, not one of whose names JC managed to catch.

The women stared curiously at him, until they were led away by their men.

JC was turning towards the children when he spotted Young Curate.

He was standing near the house, his hand nervously tugging at his crotch, his white face glistening with sweat. Beside him, rocking a large old-fashioned pram, was a uniformed nurse.

'Bring my precious over here,' Mrs Spencer called out.

The nurse wheeled the pram towards them.

'You take her, JC.'

He took the warm lace-wrapped bundle from the nurse.

'Isn't she just too, too wonderful for words?'

'Mmm,' he smiled down into the tiny puckered face.

As if in recognition, the baby cooed happily back at him.

'She likes you.' Mr Spencer was bursting with paternal pride.

The young mothers from the town began to gather around JC with their babies, holding them out for him to touch. In their billowing summery dresses, with the bright sun shining behind them, they were like floating clouds of butterflies. Moving as effortlessly as weightless creatures, they wafted in and out of his line of vision, sometimes appearing to defy gravity as they brushed against him from all angles, light as thistledown, floating, whispering, smiling their secret smiles.

He felt an overwhelming surge of love for each and every one of them. He wanted to embrace all of them at once, hold them close to him for ever, shield them from any dark shadow that might threaten their happy existence. He wanted – suddenly Reena was in front of him, smiling, holding out her baby. He reached out to her ...

'Come, there are others I want you to meet.' Mrs Spencer was pulling at his arm, drawing him away.

Somebody took the baby from him. When he looked back Reena was gone. The other mothers were also moving away. They were leaving him, rejoining the laughing throng moving about the gardens.

And all around the shimmering sunlit gardens, children were being lifted on and off carousels. They were being hugged, given drinks, having their noses wiped, their scuffed knees kissed, their questions answered. There were laces being tied, hair ribbons being straightened. Cardigans were being buttoned now that the sun was going down. Hands were touching and comforting. Reassuring. Embracing. Loving. All around the gardens mothers were doing what they always did.

But he couldn't see any of the small babies any more, no matter how hard he tried. They were lost in the crowd.

The bigger children were everywhere. He hadn't realised there were so many. But the babies had disappeared from sight. They were nowhere to be seen.

He felt the pain start up in his head. This scene was so familiar. This was the land of his dreaded nightmares. This was how it always began – with spinning carousels and nursery rhymes, roustabouts calling out and the milling, laughing crowd. This was how it began. The pain in his head tightened. He knew what would happen next.

He turned to warn Mrs Spencer but she was gone. He was surrounded by strangers. Who would listen if he were to call out that he knew something terrible was about to happen? He had seen it so many times. The laughter and gaiety turning to horror. He had seen it. He had seen the flames.

He began running towards the amusements, peering anxiously into the thinning crowd. Searching for one recognisable face. People stared back curiously at him. Strangers. All strangers with staring eyes.

The fear was choking him now, slowing him down, exactly as it did in his nightmares. Soon he wouldn't be able to move at all. He wouldn't be able to stop the horror. His only escape had always been in wakening, but this time he was already awake.

Suddenly he saw the girls, and the babies.

There was no mistaking them. Even from a distance. Even with the laughing crowd and spinning carousels blocking them from view every couple of seconds.

In their flimsy gossamer dresses, with their flaxen-haired

babies held high in their arms, they looked almost ghostly, wraith-like – as if his nightmare had already happened and all that was left were the spirits of what they had once been.

They were moving towards the house, walking one behind the other up the wide stone steps. And at their head, like a black-clad Pied Piper, strode Young Curate, his ankle-length cassock billowing out behind him as he walked. But he was no ghost.

JC watched as the girls disappeared one by one through the carved double doors.

He felt weak with relief. So much for his nightmare as a pre-monition. Inside the gloomy, badly lit house, the girls couldn't be further removed from the picture he carried of them standing before a backdrop of flashy spinning carousels and gaudy coloured lights. He'd seen the flames leaping before them in the garden. It never varied. In his nightmare he was always looking down into the garden as the flames shot up between them like a solid wall of fire.

Relief surged through him again. He knew now that his nightmares had been just that. Nightmares. And everybody had nightmares, didn't they? And he was no different to anybody else. Except for his imagination. But he was learning to control that. No more fantasies. No more seeing things that didn't exist. He might even get rid of the kaftan. In the nightmare he was always wearing it.

'It's a special blessing!' The young roustabout standing behind him suddenly spoke.

'What?'

'The priest arranged a special blessing for the girls and the babies.' He gave an ironic little laugh. 'If you ask me it's that other lot he should be dousing with holy water.'

'What do you mean?'

'That lot staying at the house. The fur coat and no knickers brigade. They're the ones who need to be sprinkled with holy water. Drenched in it more like.'

'Drenched in ...?'

'Well that's what one of the lads said will happen. And he's the one who showed the priest how to work the system.' He nodded at the perplexed look on JC's face. 'Aw, he's a mad fucker all right. But what priest isn't?'

He lifted two little six-year-olds on to brightly painted unicorns, and started the carousel moving.

'What are you talking about?' JC had to shout to be heard above the music now.

'Above in the house,' the roustabout bellowed. 'Soon as the girls hold up the lighted candles the new sprinkler system will douse them with holy water.' He became convulsed with giggles. 'Jasus, I ask you!'

He turned to attend to his small charges.

The pain was back in JC's head now. Why would Young Curate go to the trouble of filling a sprinkler system with holy water to bless the babies? All he needed was one of the holy water dispensers from the church. Why mess with the sprinkler system?

'You think that's crazy?' The boy was talking again. 'Yesterday one of the lads caught him messin' with a can of petrol! Said it's for cleaning statues. Statues? In there?' He looked towards the house. 'Mad fucker!' The boy shook his head in disbelief.

Petrol? No, it couldn't be! No sane mind could hatch such a plan. It was too wicked even to contemplate. Wasn't it? No sane ...

He started running. The boy called after him but there was no time.

He ran past the startled faces in the hallway, up the gleaming staircase. If he were right, he knew which room they'd be in. Mr Spencer had boasted about having priceless wallhangings restored there, but then complained about the strong acrid smell of some of the chemicals being used by the restorers. There was only one room in the house where the smell of petrol wouldn't be easily detected.

He could hear the final line of an old hymn being sung as he raced towards the door of the gallery.

He didn't even pause for breath as he threw it open.

'Out! Out! Everybody out!' he yelled.

Startled faces turned towards him. The girl's singing petered out, but Young Curate continued singing loudly, apparently oblivious to the sudden interruption. He jauntily placed slim lighted tapers in the hands of the front row of girls.

'No! Put them out!' JC grabbed as many as he could and stamped them into the polished floor.

Young Curate frowned at him as if he were trying to recollect who he was. Then he turned back to the girls and calmly lit more tapers.

'I said put them out!' JC yelled louder this time and a startled baby began to cry. 'And get out of here, all of you.'

Unsure now, some of the girls refused to accept the tapers and began nervously to inch away from Young Curate. Babies started to wail as he pushed lighted tapers into their mothers' unwilling hands.

'Let us continue with our blessing,' he intoned piously.

'Get out of here now, run!' JC began pushing girls towards the door. As he grabbed an already lighted candle from one girl, it spilled hot wax on to her dress and down the front of his kaftan.

'Oh dear ...' She reached out apologetically.

'Get out!' JC brushed her hand aside impatiently.

'No! You mustn't leave!' Young Curate's voice was soft, pleading. 'Not until we complete the blessing. It's for the babies.' His tone was becoming fatherly now.

JC could sense the uncertainty in the girls.

He knew what he had to do. He realised that he had always known it would come to this. Even while denying it to himself he had known. And it wasn't at all difficult. He wasn't at all frightened.

He began to rise up from the floor inch by inch until he was looking down at the upturned faces below.

'Oh sweet Jesu!' Young Curate's voice crackled with disbelief.

JC ignored him.

He looked instead at the faces of the girls. They stared wide-eyed, back at him. But even as they did their features were changing, reshaping, until he recognised people who couldn't possibly be there. Signora Goretti was staring up at him, her face tender and concerned. And Mother, her face tear-stained and sad. And there was the angel, and Geraldine, focused for once. Even the Koran reader and the Persian-cat owner. All the women.

A baby cried sharply, startling the others, who set up a chorus of wails. Now the room was full of frightened young mothers again, all comforting their babies at once.

*'Go now! All of you!'* JC raised his hand.

And they did, all the young mothers clutching their babies, unlit candles discarded, trodden underfoot into a floor that was already littered with blackened tapers.

Not one of them looked back.

Young Curate turned on JC in fury. 'Damn you! Damn you!'

JC floated slowly down towards him, but Young Curate was already leaping upwards. Six inches above the floor they collided, Young Curate still grasping a fist full of lighted tapers.

'Damn you!' he spat.

JC smiled.

Then the world exploded in flames.

DOWN IN the garden the crowd of mostly women and children stood transfixed with horror as they watched the whole frontage of the manor become engulfed by fire. Behind them some of the untended carousels still turned, their coloured lights brightening up the December twilight. The women had already watched in disbelief as a wall of flame had suddenly surrounded the two men framed in the window above.

Some of the young roustabouts had made several attempts to get inside the house, but everyone knew they were mere gestures; nothing and nobody could get in or out of that inferno.

Even the firefighters from the town, when they arrived, could do little. After that first unearthly flash, the house had gone up like a tinderbox, its old wood panelling and newly restored paintings and wallhangings providing perfect fuel for the voracious blaze. The brand-new sprinkler system clearly hadn't worked at all. The young mothers who had been in the gallery seconds before it all began wept bitterly. Some of them called JC's name. Then they held their babies close and thanked God for sparing them.

When his mother arrived she wept openly. As did her whole circle. Yet they carried a strange air of resignation about them. And they were the only ones who could give comfort to the young mothers.

Nothing would remain of the house or its contents. But the women stood watch until it was all over. Even the babies were quiet now, no more tears as the flames reflected in their big staring eyes.

The rain came at midnight. But nothing was left by then except smouldering ashes. The women finally went home.

# EPILOGUE

PEOPLE CAME from all over for the funeral. Some said there were even Americans there.

The main road into Ballysheel was jammed with cars backed up as far as the eye could see. There were even special cars laid on for the hundreds of floral tributes that had poured into the town.

Father Denny gave the homily of his life. It was inspired. It made people cry for days. Even the man who chalked up the board in the bookies sobbed into his dusty hanky. Nobody could remember when the town had last cried so much.

Father Denny said that for one so young to touch the hearts of so many, God had to have a hand in it somewhere. The congregation nodded and a whole new wave of sobbing broke out.

They even shed a few tears when Father Denny turned to the second coffin. He said that for a young troubled priest to be found in death, tightly embracing the young man with the gift of healing, was indeed a symbol of the everlasting brotherhood of man.

The women of Ballysheel said nothing.

Father Denny said that brave firefighters had wept at the scene. He didn't mention that none of them could tell which charred bones belonged to whom, so they had simply divided them evenly between the two coffins. So when the pilgrims eventually began to arrive in Ballysheel to touch the young healer's grave and claim cures from it, they were also touching the last resting place of at least half of the earthly remains of Young Curate.

But that was all in the future.

For now the the women of Ballysheel sat in silence. The young mothers among them held their babies close, and the babies' large wondering eyes looked around them at this strange world that they would change beyond recognition.

But that was also in the future.

For the present the women of Ballysheel managed as they always had. There was still a long hard winter to get through before spring would arrive.

# MORE EXCITING NEW FICTION FROM
# BASEMENT PRESS

## *Singles*

## Elizabeth O'Hara

A true seventies woman, Nuala Byrne has everything going for her: beauty, buckets of energy and plenty of qualifications under her belt. But all she can think about is marriage. Will Eric, her dashing Danish lover, oblige? Or Robin Allwood, English lecturer? In the meantime a girl must survive, and to everyone's suprise, including her own, Nuala ends up with a job in the Department of the Environment. It's not a marriage but it keeps her out of trouble...

Seldom have the intoxicating delights of the civil service and the bohemian city life of the seventies been so hilariously portrayed.

£5.99

# THE GRAINNE JOURNALS

*Collins's Lover - Dev's Assassin*

## Robert C. Coyle

### Dublin, 1994

Peace negotiations are beginning. There is talk of a ceasefire. But for the bullying, unkind Frank and his unhappy wife Theresa, the war begins when they discover the tattered bundle of copybooks containing the astounding - and dangerous - Gráinne Journals.

### Dublin, 1919

Molly is a young Protestant girl, working in Dublin and in love for the first time. But then the Irish War of Independence catastrophically changes her life. Almost against her will, Molly is drawn deeper and deeper into the struggle by the 'Big Fellow', the charismatic General Michael Collins, who transforms her into Gráinne, the most feared killer of the IRA.

Their affair, her capture and torture lead inevitably, tragically, to one of the greatest mysteries of Irish history - the assassination of Collins on a lonely road at Béal na Bláth.

£5.99

# THE WAY OF THE BEES

## An Ovarian Yarn

## A.P. Clarke

1996 and Mother Nature is in crisis. Her multinational company is having trouble imposing its newly developed regimen on the island colony of Ascourt, whose rebellious inhabitants have done away with males altogether, striving to create a scientific breakthrough that will allow woman-to-woman reproduction.

*And* her lover, Saint Gubnet of Ballyvourney, has upped and left her...

A brilliantly witty and imaginative combination of fantasy, detective story and affectionate satire, *The Way of The Bees* hurtles through many worlds: high finance in New York; low sex in London; *haute cuisine* in Zurich; the Celtic underworld and the Department of Agriculture; the stormy coast of West Cork and, finally, the sunshine of Florida. The whole book is also a riddle only the most astute readers will solve.

It is a completely original work from a hot new talent.

£5.99

April 1995

# *DROWNING THE HULLABALOO BLUES*

## Michael O'Dwyer

Alex was three and a bit when he killed his parents. He didn't mean to.

If he'd known that he would end up being adopted by his father's ex-mistress he'd have dpone things differently. If he'd known that his adopted family included a temperamental artist, a strange Albert Strange, a pair of silent twins, a drug-addicted butler called Mister Goodley and the monolithic and incompetent nurse McMurphy, then he definitely would have done things differently. And if he'd known that his adopted brother would turn out to be a serial killer, he wouldn't have gone near the Wave Monster at the end of the world.

Alex has the Hullabaloo Blues and wants his mum and dad back. All he has to remind him of them is a trunk full of old photographs and Jasper God Walker.

Jasper's a stuffed dog on wheels.

You can't have anything.

*Drowning the Hullabaloo Blues* is a blackly funny and hilariously dark novel from one of Ireland's most exciting young writers.

£5.99

August 1995